John Harris was born in 1916.
Sea Shall Not Have Them and
Mark Hebden and Max Henne
journalist, travel courier, cartoon
the Second World War he served   ..wo
navies. After turning to full-t   ..g, Harris wrote
adventure stories and created a sequence of crime novels
around the quirky fictional character Chief Inspector Pel. A
master of war and crime fiction, his enduring fictions are
versatile and entertaining.

JOHN HARRIS

GETAWAY

HOUSE OF STRATUS

This edition published in 2001 by House of Stratus, an imprint of
Stratus Holdings plc, 24c Old Burlington Street, London, W1X 1RL, UK.

www.houseofstratus.com

Typeset, printed and bound by House of Stratus.

A catalogue record for this book is available from the British Library.

ISBN 0-7551-02212-5

FOR MY WIFE

PART ONE

o n e

Joe Salomio sat on a box on the deck of his boat, the *Tina S*, poking at the peeling paint of the cabin hatch with a clasp knife and gazing across the water of Woolloomooloo Bay towards Bradley's Head and the teeming north side of Sydney Harbour.

"Money," he said thoughtfully, with an accent in which the Australian was strongly overlaid with his native Genoese, "is a cow. A fair cow."

Morosely, he eyed the cloud of gulls that mewed and laughed over a patch of floating rubbish, their wings etching patterns in the sky, only half-aware of the cla-clank of cranes behind him and the smell of decaying potatoes that wafted across to him from the warehouses like the bad breath of the city.

"Yeah," he repeated. "Money is a fair cow."

His wife looked up at his remark. "Nothing wrong with money," she said calmly. "It's not having it that's no good. Especially when you got to pay a mortgage."

Joe stood up and flung his arms heavenwards in a gesture that had no roots in Sydney but came untrammelled all the way from the Italy he had left behind him forty years before. "Morgitches! Morgitches! Morgitches!" He spat into the water at his side. "I don' unnerstand-a morgitches."

"Don't alter the fact we've got to pay 'em. Robert Rossi's gettin' awful troublesome about his money."

3

With an air of desperation, Joe lit a scorched fag-end which he unearthed from the thick grey hair round his ear. He rose, hitched up the faded blue trousers which seemed in imminent danger of dropping round his ankles, and sat down again. Pushing to the back of his head the old straw hat he wore, the tear in it mended with sticking plaster cadged from the dockside first-aid man, he stared dispiritedly at the flat-sided cubes of the business quarter beyond the 'Loo, then he stuck his knife into the planking and stood up once more, restless, his fists in his pockets, the greasy patches on either side of his behind, where he always wiped his hands after a job or before a meal, gazing backwards like two smudged dark eyes.

His wife watched him with a cautious affection on her face that was tempered by the faint, contemptuous knowledge that so long as he was within reach of the shore he was *always* restless and in danger of disappearing. His predilection for the bars along the waterfront had left its mark in the potbelly that marred his short square frame. Where he had once been broad-backed and strong, he was now as round as a toby jug and beginning to stoop with age.

She studied his deeply lined features calmly, and the shock of crisp hair that had thinned to a tonsure round his head, then she put down the last of the potatoes she was peeling and walked heavily across the deck to throw the dirty water overboard, in a deliberate effort-saving movement that indicated she had performed it hundreds of times before, shuffling in the bedroom slippers she wore to ease her bunions. She swept her greying hair back and returned to her seat, Joe following her every inch of the way with his eyes.

"How long-a we got, Rosa?" he asked.

"End of the week," his wife said slowly.

"What happen then?" Joe was slumped against the cabin top, his shoulders hunched up round his eyes, his whole frame listless.

Rosa turned on him. "You got any ideas?" she asked.

Joe gave an embarrassed shuffle on his box.

"I thought you hadn't." Rosa provided her own answer.

Joe stared sadly at her, reflecting bitterly that the habit of speaking respectfully to him had long since died out in his family. No one ever indulged in it – not Rosa, nor Francesca, his youngest child, nor Florentina, his eldest. Even his son, dead these fourteen years, hadn't had much respect for him.

"You sit on your behind," Rosa was saying, "happy as Larry, asking what we're going to do next, and that's all. If you'd saved some of the money you've wasted, we might still have the boat next week."

"These-a city bums," Joe said weightily, trying to direct his wife's anger from himself to the cause of their worry. "They too smart for a coupla old Italians like us."

He watched his wife slap-slap to the cabin hatch and ease her bulk below-deck, then he sat staring heavily in front of him, conscious of the perspiration that stood out on his face. He fanned the hot air about him with his hand, feeling a spasm of relief and pleasure as his senses told him a southerly buster was due, gathering itself among the waves of the Tasman, whirling itself into a ball, ready with its cool breath to burst out of the horizon over the sweltering city, rattling up the harbour and whistling through the bridge, stirring the wave-tops to white and flinging the birds in ragged flocks from among the chimneys.

Sydney waited for it in a breathless stillness, the sun glaring from the golden bowl of the sky, stretching the shadows like sooty squares across the streets and up the sides of the buildings opposite; while the smoke stood straight up into the air, in wavering lines, all the way along the water's edge from Watson's Bay and Vaucluse to Darling Harbour and the old Pyrmont Bridge.

Down in the 'Loo, the tall buildings that rose beyond the wharfside in towering sierras, range upon range of them, reflected the heat in shimmering waves, and that part of the wharf where the *Tina S* lay, being the oldest and most disreputable, was the hottest of all.

To one side of the little boat were other craft, motor fishing vessels most of them, squat ships with hut-like wheelhouses and single masts; and on the other, soiled by the gulls and the dockside sparrows, the water-logged dinghies, the weather-blackened dumb barges with their weed-festooned ropes, and the worn-out tugs with their old tyres and burst fenders, all the junk of the harbour; so that the *Tina S* seemed to be the point where the living became the dead.

Joe stared irritatedly at the coils of old rope on the wharfside and the heaps of stacked coal where a knife-backed cat moved, its yellow eyes steady on the sparrows that twittered and hopped among the debris of the dock like so many puff-balls of wool, its fur electric with its tension. He was well aware of the *Tina*'s incongruity among the trawlers that surrounded her, well aware of her drabness against their bright colours and italienate flourishes of the paint brush.

Sentimentally called after his first-born, a dark-haired Italian flower of a child who had long since broadened into the parent of five strapping boys fathered by a Brisbane greengrocer, the *Tina* was shaped like Joe, more for strength than speed. Her untidy decks were of solid teak and though she had the tall mast and booms of a fore-and-aft rig, she had not worn her patched canvas since the Blessing of the Fishing Fleet the previous year when Joe had been too broke to buy fuel for her ancient engine and his wife had been too steadfast in her religion to let him miss the occasion. With her old tyres and peeling paint, she sprawled like a fat old charlady, blowzy with lack of care, against the green weeds and orange fungoid growths that speckled the piles of the wharf.

Joe threw away his cigarette end angrily and climbed down to the cabin where Rosa was clustering pans round an enamel coffee pot that was spotted with chips like a leopard. About her, pinned to the bulkhead, a splash of colour behind her dark hair, were the familiar brightly coloured pictures of scenes from the Bible – the Last Supper, the Parable of the Loaves and Fishes, the Foolish Virgins.

Joe sighed noisily and from the spare bunk his youngest daughter, Francesca, looked up from the film magazine she was devouring, her knees hunched under her chin, her untidy dark hair hanging round her eyes.

"Howsit, Pop?" she said casually.

"How long you been back, Frankie?" Joe demanded.

"Ten minutes." She brushed her hair aside and grinned. "You were right. The storeman said 'nuts'. No money, no paint. He said you were an old bum."

She turned to the magazine again, and, wriggling further down on the bunk, promptly forgot him.

Her father studied his daughter's heart-shaped face affectionately. She was a slender underdeveloped child who had arrived long after Joe and Rosa had ceased to expect children. Her great dark eyes were forever smudged to shadows by long black lashes that unmanned Joe a dozen times a day as he looked at them, making him form promises about working for her and giving her a good education which he never remembered for more than a few minutes. As he watched her, she sniffed at the smell of food and, putting the magazine down again, pushed her slender body from the bunk and stood up, clad in dirty jeans and a T-shirt.

Joe stared round the cabin for a while as he sat down, then he lifted his eyes again to look at his wife.

"Mama," he said. "What-a we going to do?"

Rosa thrust a chubby hand into the fold of her dress and with it lifted the coffee pot to the table and banged it down with an air of determination. Frankie promptly banged down a tin mug alongside, and, pouring coffee into it, took it back to the bunk and retired once more behind the magazine.

Rosa was staring thoughtfully at the table. "If they think they're going to get the *Tina* they're mistaken," she observed and there was something in her tones which made you feel she might be right in what she said. She was a big woman, olive-skinned and sloe-eyed like her husband, but confident with a certainty of authority that Joe had never possessed. For all her Italian features, her accent was all Australian, for she had been born in the ebullient city of Sydney among the southside fisherfolk and only in her emotions and her features was there any trace of her ancestry.

Joe shuffled on his box against the iron bed that was jammed into the end of the cabin, ugly but curiously enough not incongruous on the old boat which often wore Joe's vests and Rosa's drawers for bunting. They had had to remove two bunks and the cabin top to get it in but Rosa had insisted on its comfort when they had first decided to live aboard to save money.

Joe sighed again, rubbing the palms of his hands along his thick thighs uneasily. "So," he said, shrugging in a graphic gesture of despair. "Here we go again. You say-a that for weeks. Mama, we don' get nowhere."

Rosa turned on him. "This ship belongs to us," she said stoutly. "It would have belonged to Georgie by this time – only – only – " she halted, her eyes on the gaudy, coloured photograph of a young man in sailor's uniform that was screwed to the bulkhead, and as she became silent her calm face was brushed with the uneasy memory of pain.

Frankie looked up quickly over the magazine, her eyes anxious. "Steady on, Mama, don't go over that again," she said.

"The war's over and done now," Joe put in. "We don' got Georgie no more."

Rosa straightened up, thrusting the past behind her so that her heavy face was smooth again, and Frankie returned satisfied to her magazine, absorbed in the glowing activities of the stars.

"All right," Rosa said, shrugging away Joe's hand. "I've finished now. Well, like I said, she would have been Georgie's if he'd come back. Well, he didn't, so its going to belong to Georgie's son as soon as he's grown up. Florentina's OK. Her children don't need no boat. They got the shop."

"What about me, Mama?" Frankie put down her magazine again. "Don't I get a look-in?"

"You'll get married and change your name like Florentina. Then you'll be some other family's responsibility."

Frankie snorted. "Nuts! Nobody need be responsible for me. I can look after meself."

"Maybe you can," Rosa agreed. "But Tommy's different. He's got nothing. Not even a father. He'll be old enough to leave school soon."

Joe snorted and shrugged hugely. "The strength is more important than the brains in fishing. Giuseppe Salomio don't need no schooling to get around."

Rosa listened to him with indifference as she had been doing for years, hardly hearing. "Yes, you get around," she said, "from bar to bar, from bottle to bottle."

Joe looked sulky. "Well, why don't Tommy come and take over now, Mama? He's growing. Why don't he leave school already? Frankie's left school. She's got a good job."

Frankie gave a sarcastic grunt from behind the magazine.

"Georgie married a girl with more sense than we had," Rosa said. "Lucia's getting Tommy to learn a few things first and when he's learned 'em, he'll be a better business man for it. He'll be buying up other boats before he's thirty, like Angelo Carpaccio does."

"He'll finish up by being a clerk at the fish-manure factory or something, he'll be so clever," Frankie said. "Especially if we ain't got the *Tina* no more."

Rosa rounded on her. "No, he won't. Fishin's in his blood and they won't take the *Tina* off us. We'll hide her first."

"Hide her?" Frankie flung the magazine aside and sat up sharply, her long thin legs hanging over the side of the bunk.

"Yes." Rosa had not really meant anything in particular when she had suggested defiance but now, as an idea occurred to her, her face lightened suddenly. "Yes, that's it. We'll hide her!"

"Where'll we hide her? Under a tree in the Botanical Gardens?"

"No." Rosa's face lit up with enthusiasm as her idea grew in her mind and she chuckled. "No. There's a better place to hide her than that."

"Tell me, Mama!" Joe affected a studied patience that indicated his very impatience. He hung his hands by his side, his head tilted, a monument of attentiveness. "See," he said. "I wait."

"Joe!" Rosa's face was glowing now. "There's islands. Dozens of 'em. Hundreds of 'em. Thousands of 'em."

"Millions of 'em, Mama, you like it that way. Go on."

"Straight off this coast. Straight out. You can go on for ever. Right out into the Pacific."

What she was getting at began at last to penetrate Joe's slower brain and he jumped off his soap box, his dark eyes bulging, his jaw dropped open.

"The islands, Joe," Rosa went on. "The islands in the Pacific! We can hide her for months among the islands. We can hide her for years if necessary. Other boats go from here to the islands."

Frankie jumped down from the bunk and stared at her mother, her hands flat on the table, her dark eyes bright in her gamin face, her harum-scarum soul uplifted by the prospect of adventure. "Dinkum, Mama? You mean that?"

Joe was silent, busy with a momentary mental picture of the *Tina S* trudging away from a Pacific blow like a stout old lady running in vain to catch a moving bus. His voice dropped as he answered and his tones became a theatrical whisper.

"Mama, those-a boats are big ships, not little pudding-a-basins like the *Tina*."

Frankie whirled to face him. "Come on, Pop," she begged. "Don't go all jelled-up on us."

Rosa wasn't looking at them. Her dark eyes were staring unseeingly in front of her, blissfully oblivious of her husband's sarcasm, his agitation, everything except the magnificent glow her idea threw across her brain.

"Big ships. Little ships," she said. "That don't matter. If *they* can go, so can we."

Joe stamped his foot dramatically and pointed to the deck. "Mama, not this old barrel! She don't get built for these waters. She sink." He whirled his hand and executed a flourishing spiral to indicate the *Tina* disappearing to the bottom of the sea.

Frankie clutched his hand excitedly. "Pop, break down and give yourself a treat! Let's have a bang at it. It's a beaut' idea."

"No." Joe flourished his fingers again, then, as his hand dropped, he eyed his wife, seeing himself caught between the known thunder of her temper and the unknown thunder of the Pacific. "Mama," he begged. "We sell her and pay off the debt, eh?" He smiled nervously. "That's what we do. And I'll go outback on a sheep-a-farm. Away from the booze, Mama. I send you money regular."

Before he finished speaking, the temper he had feared burst out of Rosa as she saw his pleas as an attempt to deprive her of the idea that was the first warm thing in her life for weeks.

"Let's sell her," she snorted. "Who'd buy her? Let's lie down and die! That's all you ever think of. Giving up. You've got no backbone. You couldn't keep a job a week. You know you couldn't."

"Go it, Mama," Frankie was yelling excitedly. "Give him what-for! You know the islands, Pop. You worked 'em for years when the slump was on. You told me often."

"You worked the ships out there in the winter," Rosa broke in, "when the fishin' was bad and the boats laid up. You know 'em like the back of your hand."

"Mama, that was years ago. I forget."

" 'Course you don't. It's like swimmin'. You never forget."

Joe's voice cracked with the earnestness of his plea. "Mama, OK. So I don't forget. But what we live on? We got-a no money. What we going to buy fuel with?"

Rosa was standing by the table still, majestic in her subdued excitement, one hand on the coffee pot, her feet splayed comfortably for the ease of her bunions, her eyes staring at the greasy boards of the bulkhead unseeingly. Frankie stood watching her, her eyes glowing with fascination.

"Fuel?" Rosa spoke over her shoulder without turning her head. "That bag of old iron in the engine room hasn't gone for months. We'll use sails."

"Now, Mama – " Joe waved his arms in entreaty, his voice rising, his hair standing on end with his anxiety " – the sails get old. They all-a right round here. But, Mama, I don't trust 'em a long way from home."

"We'll make 'em do."

"Sure we will," Frankie chimed in. "I'll help fix 'em."

Joe glared at the two of them, the everlasting man baffled by the unreasonableness of woman. "OK. You are so clever, the two of you." His voice rose rapidly as he waved his arms again, despairing and using his despair as an argument. "So we got sails. But what we eat?" He made a gesture of scratching round on an empty plate with a knife and fork and looked up at his wife with goggling brown eyes. "You don't tell me that yet, Mama."

"There's plenty to eat out there," Rosa snorted. "You've said so yourself. We can eat coconuts."

"I don' like coconuts," Joe said plaintively. "They give me indigestion."

"We can eat fish. You know how to fish, don't you?"

"There's pigs and wild goats and birds," Frankie yelled. "I've read about 'em. Things grow. They grow like mad."

"Now, Mama – " Joe backed away and put out his hands as though he were warding off a physical attack " – I think you sick. I talk but it is like water off-a the duck's back. You're crook. You don' feel well."

"I've never felt better in my life!"

Joe sighed noisily and tried a new angle. "Mama, we're too old to work this boat. That's why we have to borrow money from Robert Rossi. This boat need three strong men. That's why we stay here all-a time. We don't afford to pay a coupla hands."

"I can help."

"So can I, Pop."

Joe was almost in tears now. "That's three of us, OK," he said bitterly. "One ol' man, one ol' woman, and one little girl."

"I'm not a little girl," Frankie exploded. "I'm sixteen. Practically seventeen," she added. "Cripes, Pop – " she ducked as Rosa's hand swung instinctively at the expletive " – I'm nearly a woman."

"Excuses – that's all it is." Rosa's temper flared up again at Joe. "We can find someone willing to work their way from one place to the next."

"And if we don't, we kill ourselves."

"*I'm* willing to kill myself so long as I take long enough over it for young Tommy to grow up into a man."

"So'm I, Mama."

Joe stared at his daughter, jigging from one foot to the other in her excitement, then he turned again to Rosa. "What about Frankie's job at the factory?" he asked.

"That dump," Frankie said indignantly. "I been waiting to get out of it some time. It's enough to stiffen the crows."

"You earn good money."

"Good money!" Frankie snorted her contempt.

Rosa silenced her protests with a gesture. "You want to go, Frankie?" she asked.

"Aw, Mama, what a question!"

Rosa smiled at Joe. "She can pull on a rope as well as you and me. She'll be useful."

"I can cook, Pop," Frankie pointed out. "I can handle the boat. I'll wash dishes," she ended in a burst of self-sacrifice.

Joe's voice was low again now and he mouthed his words deliberately, his eyes rolling, the sweat standing out on his dark skin. "You ever been in a storm, Mama?" he asked fiercely. "A bad one – out there, I mean."

"You give me a pain in the neck," Rosa snorted furiously. "You're only thinking of excuses. There's islands, aren't there? Millions of 'em."

"The map looks like it is fly-blown."

"Well, we can shelter when a storm comes up."

Joe's voice was a wail as he answered. "Mama, some of them islands don' got the shelter for a rowing-a-boat. You don' ever hear of reefs?" In his ears was already the roar of the surf on the coral and in his eyes the glittering spindrift that the combers flung high into the air. He had seen fine ships – far finer ships than the *Tina S* – smashed to matchwood on the fangs of rock and flung in splintered planks across the sun-bright sand. He licked his dry lips nervously. "We ain't-a got no charts, Mama. We got nothing to tell us where to go."

"We don't need no charts," Frankie said. "I'll go to Lucia's and borrow Tommy's atlas. It's a good one. A big one. Lotsa maps in it. I'll go now. She'll be in."

She ducked under the rusting hurricane lamp that had smudged a smoky circle on the boards of the deckhead in the period since their lighting had failed, and almost fell up the ladder in her haste. They heard her feet clatter on the deck, then a distant "Hi, Charlie" as she sped past the watchman's hut.

Joe stared at the sky through the cabin hatch where she had disappeared, then he turned again to Rosa.

"Rosie – " he interlaced his fingers and spoke in an attitude of entreaty " – maps ain't charts. They don' make-a no reefs in maps."

"We got a lead line."

"Lead line!" Joe beat furiously at his forehead with the flat of his hand. "Mother of God, all she say is 'lead line'. Like that. Lead line. Like it navigate-a the boat." His voice rose to a shout. "Mama, you don't got the time to use a lead line in the dark when you're running before the wind. Bic boc! The boat is high and dry and we are all swimming. Like fishes," he added, trying a few feeble strokes with his arms.

"Listen," Rosa said patiently. "We've got to find two hundred and fifty pounds by the weekend or we're living in some rotten little shack ashore with no future – "

Joe shrugged. "I'm too old to have a future."

" – And no future for Frankie. And no future for Tommy. He's got to grow up, hasn't he? He's got to earn his living and it won't be long now. He needs this boat. We can take on a few stores here – "

"What we use for money? Old-a rope?"

"Joe – " Rosa beamed at her husband and immediately Joe backed away, suspicious " – you can't tell me you couldn't scrounge a few potatoes and tins of meat and things."

"They don't let me have any no more," Joe said sulkily. "They all-a know me."

Rosa's smile faded at once. "Then try somebody who don't. Go to Mrs Potniak's. She's too old and stupid to notice who you are. Go to Mama Gisorsky. Go to O'Hara's up in King's Cross. Anywhere."

"Mama – " Joe shook his head wearily " – they *all-a* know me."

"Then borrow a handcart and go to the other side of the city where they don't." Rosa stared unseeingly in front of her. "How far is it to Brisbane, Joe?"

"Brisbane?" Joe's eyes opened until they looked ready to drop out at his feet. "Mama, I can't walk to Brisbane."

"No, you old fool." Rosa snapped back to the present. "How far is it to *sail* to Brisbane?"

Joe shrugged. "Four hundred mile. Five hundred mile. I don' know."

"We could sail that with our eyes shut. How far outwards to the first of the islands?"

"Three hundred. Four hundred. Mama, I don' like-a this."

"We'll take on more stores at Brisbane and head east."

"And how we pay for 'em at Brisbane?"

"Same way. Never – never."

"Mama, that ain't honest."

Rosa laughed contemptuously. "How much do you owe round the city for booze? How many times you scrounged tobacco? How much money you lost on the horses and never paid back? How much you swiped from me when I wasn't looking?"

"Now, Mama – " Joe was beginning to look uncomfortable again.

Tomorrow, you borrow a handcart. Put your best suit on and a collar and tie."

"Collar and tie! I don' wear a collar and tie for years."

"Well, you'll wear one tomorrow. It looks more respectable and people'll trust you more. You still got that old celluloid one. We'll leave on the afternoon tide. We'll get Angelo Carpaccio to tow us out to the Heads. We can cast off there and put up the sail. It's a beautiful sail," she exulted as the soaring Italian enthusiasm in her triumphed over the Australian phlegm. "I helped to make it myself."

"Mama!" Joe was shouting again now and waving his arms. "This is not a deep-a-sea boat. She is not even good for fishing. She is a crayfish boat. She is built in Cape-a-Town many years ago."

"She sailed here from Java in the war when the Nips came," Rosa pointed out. "She got from Cape Town to there some-damn'-how. She didn't sink."

"All-a-same, she didn't float so good. Mama – " Joe made a last desperate effort " – you don't-a just sail away like that. Not into the Pacific. We need books. *Pacific Islands Pilots.* We want instruments. Parallel rules. Dividers."

Rosa looked at him. "Ah, you old fathead. When something's wanted you use it as an excuse. I'll borrow the instruments. I'll get Tommy's geometry set. That's got dividers in it. What else do you want?"

Joe gave up the unequal struggle. His knowledge was no match for Rosa's enthusiasm. Where he could see danger, her excitement overrode it. "Mama," he said sadly. "You'd need a compass – not this old bit of magnet we got. It don't been swung for years. You need a chronometer – a sextant – "

Rosa swept his objections aside. "I'll get everything we want. We'll make a list. I'll borrow 'em from Mr MacGillicuddy. He was mate of a ship till he started drinking too much. He's got 'em all. He'll lend 'em to me. I've done his washing many a time. I'll tell him I want 'em for Tommy."

She paused, struggling with her conscience over the lie, for she was a religious woman to whom lies did not come easily. "I do really," she said. "You'd better go this afternoon for the stores. I'll have everything ready by the time you come back. There's a southerly buster coming and we won't get out while that's blowing."

t w o

The sun was slipping down towards the uneven skyline of roofs when Joe returned but, though his brown face was drawn with exhaustion, his heart lifted as he saw the water broaden out before him from the wharfside to where the great steel bridge stretched like a shining spider web that glowed bright gold in the sunshine. Out on the sparkling waters were the hurrying ferries from the quay to Kirribilli and Cremorne.

Slogging back to the *Tina* with his cartload of stores, Joe's grizzled hair had become slicked with sweat and his shirt stuck to his back like a cold poultice. Prayers and imprecations stood together on his lips, each the background music for the other, for Joe was often tempted to short-circuit the priests who ministered the Gospel, and take on the Lord on his own.

He felt as though he had tramped every one of the straight streets that stretched away from the waterside in rectangular blocks to King's Cross and Surry Hills, funnelling chasms either for the wind or for people as they streamed from work, a mass of turn-of-the-century tenements with cast-iron balconies and shabby frontages.

Mrs Potniak had not been too old and stupid to recognize him, and Mama Gisorsky and O'Hara's in King's Cross had been too smart, and he had had to retire beaten to the other end of Bourke Street. His only satisfaction had been that the shopkeeper who had finally succumbed to his velvet words and pleading eyes had been big and noisy and threatening, and Joe always got pleasure from besting men like that. It soothed some of the resentment he bore in his breast that there were wealthier men than he, cleverer men, even men who had the energy to work harder. Joe was always downcast when he thought of his poverty and his complete inability to do anything about it. But warm sun was made for sitting in, he always believed, not working in, sweating in, pushing handcarts in – the length of Bourke Street, he thought savagely, down the length of the airless gutter while the kids cat-called him and the lorry drivers told him to get the hell out of it.

As he trundled to the wharfside, he noticed with alarm that Rosa was on deck studying a school atlas that Frankie held for her, crouching on her knees before her on the cabin top. He realized she had obviously not changed her mind and that filled him with even greater alarm. Pushing a handcart was bad enough, but sailing into the wide Pacific – the biggest and fiercest ocean in the world – in the *Tina S* was worse. Joe approached his wife with trepidation.

Frankie's smile cheered him for a moment, then his shoulders drooped again as Rosa looked up, her expression still full of enthusiasm. Her idea was burning its mark on her brain, for in it she saw the means of defeating all the forces that were ranged against them in their trouble, the harshness of the wealthy, the grasping greed of Robert Rossi, the intractability of the police, and the craftiness of the lawyers who baffled them with long phrases. Always she had fought against such people – from the days when she had romped in the crowded alleys of King's Cross; in her adolescence against people who had called her a Wop as she went to work in a sweet factory underneath the great spans of Sydney Bridge, fighting with a vocabulary she had culled from three generations of docksiders. She had married Joe thirty-five years before when he had been square and straight and strong as an ox, expecting to find things easier, but she had found he was lazy and irresponsible and over-generous to the wrong people and she had had to go on fighting, and now that he was old and lazier than ever she was still fighting – harder now than at any time before.

But in this idea of hers she saw the opportunity to square things up a little. The niceties of detail didn't enter her head. To people like Rosa, fishing people to whom the sea was a living, the only important thing was to keep their boat – above all, above storm and tragedy and wreck, above meanness and stupidness and debt.

The warmth of her idea made her smile as she looked at Joe. "Look what we got," she said.

She indicated an ancient sextant and a hand-bearing compass both in mouldering cases green with mildew.

"Mr MacGillicuddy didn't offer any objection," she said. "He was drunk. We got this too: Lucia's alarm clock. That's as good as any chronometer. Never loses a minute."

Frankie's grin was encouraging and Joe picked up the books. "*Pacific Islands Pilot, Volume 1,*" he read. "*Admiralty Sailing Directions, 1916.*" He pawed among the yellowing charts, dog-eared with age. "Mama," he said sadly, by this time resigned to the adventure, "you see-a the date on these? 1907. And this one is only half a chart. He use the other half some time to light his pipe, I suppose."

Rosa's smile died, then it sprang to her face again as Frankie jumped up and dug under the debris. "Look, Pop," she said. "I got these too."

She handed Joe a bundle of brightly coloured folders containing glowing descriptions of the Great Barrier Reef holiday islands, Tahiti, and the various other places that attracted tourists.

"I went round all the steamship companies," she boasted. "They've all got maps in 'em. They wanted to know why I wanted so many. I said I was thinking of taking a cruise. Y'oughta seen the look on their faces."

Joe raised his eyes to the sky. "Mother of Mercy, holiday guides!"

Rosa suddenly looked at the alarm clock she had brought and the pleasure in her face died.

"You're late," she said.

Joe jumped as she turned on him. "Mama," he excused himself indicating the cart, "I grow too old to push-a that lot about. All-a way down Bourke Street. You know how long is Bourke Street."

Rosa's heart was touched with compassion as she noticed his drawn face, and she took pity on him at once.

"Was it hard work, Joe?" she asked gently.

"I feel I am like Samson," Joe said heavily. "Only I ain't so strong."

Rosa moved to let him sit down, then she smelt his breath and her pity disappeared at once. "You've been drinking." She made it a statement rather than a question, and Frankie looked up from the charts with interest.

"Beer, Mama," Joe pointed out with a shrug. "Thin beer."

"Pity you didn't save your breath to get more stores."

"I can carry beer," Joe said sulkily. "I gotta to *shove* stores."

He climbed across the deck back to the wharfside and sat down on a bollard. The knife-backed cat which was still there waiting for sparrows, eyed him hostilely, the last inch of its ginger string-thin tail twitching angrily.

"Thank the Lord Jesus for that," Joe said fervently as he settled his broad bottom. "My feet is pumping up and down like the pistons on a Manly ferry at rush hour."

Chivvying Frankie before her, Rosa collected the charts and instruments and disappeared below. A moment later, they returned to the deck and, climbing to the wharfside, began to unload the cart. Rosa had unfastened the neck of her dress and rolled her sleeves higher. She turned to Joe, a box of corned beef in her arms.

"Well," she said, "you tired or something?"

Joe looked up at her, startled. "Mama, I only just sit down." He pointed fiercely to the bollard.

"Ain't no time to sit down."

Without bothering to wait for his reply, Rosa swung the box of corned beef into his arms and, picking up a carton of tinned milk, lifted it to the deck of the *Tina*. Joe sat nursing the corned beef, watching her as she reached for another carton, then he sighed, swore softly to himself and followed her, the box on one hip.

"You want-a to sell me," he said loudly, waving a handful of waggling fingers at her. "And buy-a the donkey!"

It was as Rosa turned to reply to him that she noticed the young man sitting on a crate a few yards away, feverishly smoking a fag-end and watching them intently.

As she stared, he caught her looking at him and returned her stare with a calculated defiance. He was only a young man – indeed he was hardly more than a boy – and he was clearly uneasy and on the look-out for something, his eyes constantly covering the wharfside in nervous sweeps.

Rosa paused in unloading the first of the potatoes, studying him, suspicious of strangers and instinctively protective towards Frankie.

"You seen everything?" she asked.

The boy started, glanced about him and strolled towards them as though he hadn't a care in the world. Halting in front of them, he watched them with a studied carelessness that was obviously not genuine, his eyes travelling from Rosa, to Joe, and finally to Frankie, who had also slowed to a stop now, conscious of an audience for the first time.

"You can keep your eyes off her," Rosa said quickly, watching his face. "She's not your type."

The boy sneered at Frankie's bony figure in faded jeans and T-shirt. "Gawd," he said, "I got something better to do. She's as skinny as a wishbone."

"Well, Cripes!" Frankie shoved her hands firmly on her narrow young hips. "Don't fret yourself about me, Mama. I'm not worried by that gadget. If he only knew it, he's tampering with death."

The boy stared coldly back at her. "OK, kid, keep your hair on. I'm no cradle-snatcher. I was watching your Ma."

Rosa's natural aggressiveness promptly reasserted itself. "Shall I stand still?" she asked. "Or can you manage if I go on working?"

The boy scowled. He was not used to being addressed like that by women – especially old women. In the areas where he and his gang had held sway, women of Rosa's age and standing had been in the habit of crossing the street to avoid him. He threw away his cigarette and moved closer.

"Wops, aren't you?" he said. "I don't take that kind of talk from Wops. You know what we did to the Wops in North Africa?"

Joe waited apprehensively. This sort of approach was all too familiar whenever he moved out of the area occupied by the Italian colony. "They still speak English your way?" he was always being asked.

Frankie edged behind him, nervous in spite of her ebullience, but Rosa was staring back at the boy, studying him, her face unchanged.

"You're not old enough to do anything to anybody in North Africa," she said at last. "My son was killed fighting the Wops and their mates. We're Australians."

The boy's hard young face fell. "Oh! Well, why didn't you say so?"

"You didn't ask."

Rosa's unchanging expression was disconcerting and the young man scowled again. "Ah, go bag your head," he said, at a loss for anything better.

"You've obviously not been very well brought up," Rosa commented. "Seems your Ma shoulda larruped you more."

The boy thrust his hands into his pockets and tried hard to stare her out, but, without his friends to add their noisy support, he was stuck for a reply.

"You going some place?" he asked at last.

"Why?"

"Just wanted to know. That's all."

"You the police?" Rosa asked.

"What's it to you if I am?"

"No, you're not the police," Rosa decided, unperturbed by the implied threat in his voice. "They got better manners. Besides, you're not dressed like the police."

The young man scowled again and fingered the lapel of his jacket, a cheap jacket flashily cut to hide its shoddiness.

"You're big like a policeman," Rosa continued searchingly. "But you're not a policeman. You come from Robert Rossi?"

"Who's Robert Rossi?"

"He's the bloke we – Oh, he's just a bloke."

"No, I'm not from Robert Rossi."

"Well, what the hell are you sniffing round here for then?" The boy was clearly put out by Rosa's direct approach and Frankie giggled, regaining her self-assurance. The lively mechanism of her mind, alert as a dockside sparrow's, brought out a favourite gibe, bubbling it cheerfully to her tongue as she saw him hesitate. "Don't be too rough with him, Mama," she said. "You're embarrassing the tripe outa him. He ain't tough. He only smells strong."

"A guy can look, can't he?" the boy said defensively, addressing Rosa. "You goin' on a trip? You're shoving stores aboard."

"What if we are?"

"A long trip?"

"What if it is?"

"Thought you might be glad of a passenger."

The reply was unexpected and Rosa's eyes met Joe's. Then she turned to the boy again, sitting down very deliberately and wiping her hands on her frock, so that the ginger cat crept nearer, half-expecting food. The tension was immediately relaxed. Joe sat down and Frankie cocked a thin leg over the winch and settled herself on the anchor cable.

Rosa was staring more amicably at the boy now. "Depends where you want to go," she said.

"Anywhere," he offered. "I'm easy. Just feel like a holiday. That's all."

"We're going a long way," Frankie put in and Rosa gestured at her sharply.

The boy eyed Frankie disinterestedly, a long leggy girl, then he ignored her completely and directed his answer to Rosa. "That's all right," he said. "Suits me OK."

"It's going to cost you something," Rosa pointed out.

"I got the dough."

Rosa hesitated. "You on the level?" she asked.

Joe, who had been watching them all this time, entranced, his black liquid eyes expressionless, started suddenly to life. He had been dreaming of someone to pay his fare – of good Australian pounds to buy drink. If they had to go to the islands on this mad adventure of Rosa's, OK, let them for the love of God take a passenger and earn money.

"Mama," he pleaded as he saw Rosa hesitate. "Take him along."

Rosa signed him to silence and addressed the boy again.

"We want cash," she pointed out. "On the nail."

"Mama – " Joe began to see his dreams of help and wealth and bottles of beer being thrust aside by his wife in the niceties of financial cut and thrust. The boy, however, was unperturbed.

"Don't trust me, eh?" He fished in a money belt round his waist and hooked out a wad of money. "What's wrong with that?"

"Looks all right to me," Frankie commented. " 'Less you made it yourself."

"It's good dough," the boy said, staring at Rosa with annoyance. *She* was clearly the force to be reckoned with and he continued to ignore the other two. "Silly old cow," he was thinking, frustrated by her lack of awe. "Stupid old biddy!"

Joe could see the anger on his face and he began to gesture.

"Mama – " he said plaintively.

"Well?" the boy interrupted. "Is it on?"

"Tell you what," Rosa said, and Joe turned away and tried to stop his ears to the haggling by clapping his hands over them with a ringing slap. "We'll take you cheap – "

"What?" Joe whirled.

"Cheap?" The boy was eyeing Rosa shrewdly, suspicious of kindness. "What's the catch?"

"Suppose you help work the ship?"

Joe looked up more cheerfully at the thought of someone younger and more energetic than he was to do all the pulling and pushing, to sit in the wind, to give him time for dozing. And at the same time to pay money. Not so much – but money, nevertheless. Ah, clever Mama! Clever Rosa!

The boy was considering the suggestion. "I'm no sailor," he said after a while. "I hadn't thought of working."

"Don't look like you ever did," Frankie said and he glared at her, annoyed to find himself on the defensive against them, despite himself.

Rosa was studying him out of the corners of her eyes, pretending to be occupied with a carton of tinned food while she tried to read the thoughts running through his mind. "We can tell you what to do," she said. "And you can go farther by working your passage. Farther from Sydney. Your money'll last longer. You pay passage money all the way, you won't get very far."

He thought it over for a moment. "OK," he said. "I keep most of my dough in my pocket and help with the ship? That it?"

Joe sat down abruptly. Between them, he thought angrily, they would soon arrange it that no money would be paid over at all. Mama, he muttered fiercely to himself, do not let him get away with a single halfpenny.

But Rosa was holding out her hand to shake the young man's. "That's a deal then," she said, and Joe groaned.

"You can wash the dishes," Frankie announced cheerfully. "They'll want me on deck."

"You'll take your share like the rest of us," Rosa said calmly. "You'll work your passage and do what we ask you."

"OK. How much you want?"

Joe looked up, cheerful again. "You pay us now? A pound? Two pound? To help out?" He held out a fat hand and grinned.

As the boy fished for his money again, glad to show it off, Joe's face lit up, but Rosa took the notes that were held out and shoved them into the pocket of her dress.

"I handle the money," she said firmly.

The young man watched as the silent rebellion smouldering in Joe's eyes clashed with the defiance in Rosa's and was quelled to uneasy fits and starts.

"Just one thing, though," he said. "When do you start?"

"Any time. Soon as you like." Rosa turned, speaking more to Joe than anyone else. "Soon as I ring up Lucia and tell her we won't be round for supper like we said."

"Now, Mama?" Frankie leapt up from the winch, prepared to work the *Tina* out on her own to get them moving.

Joe protested bitterly. With a passenger who was paying out good money, he had hoped to spend a few days longer in Sydney, postponing the evil hour when they must sail and using the money to its best advantage. "Mama," he said. "What-a the hurry? You can't go just like that."

"No such word as 'can't'."

"Mama, we got to get the things together."

"Nothing to get," Frankie chirruped. "Everything's aboard: pots, pans, clothes, bed. Only a few things Lucia's looking after and we won't need them."

"The sooner the better," Rosa turned again to the young man. "You better go and get your things."

"I got 'em."

"Your luggage, I mean."

"Ain't got any."

"Nothing?" Joe lifted his hands and let them drop to his sides with a slap. "Nothing?"

"Nothing."

"Funny holiday," Frankie commented, and the boy was immediately on the defensive again.

"Listen, you, you mind your own business and I'll mind mine. OK?"

Rosa watched him silently for a moment, then she gave her husband and daughter a push. "Get aboard," she said. "Don't argue."

The boy glanced quickly over his shoulder. "Might as well come aboard, too," he said. "I'll get below."

"OK," Rosa agreed. "We'll get the rest of the stores aboard. You going to give us a hand?"

"Now?" The reply was unwilling and grudging.

"We sign you on, don' we?" Joe turned and flourished an imaginary pen over an imaginary log book. "You think we let you off payin' and I do all-a work?"

Rosa took no notice, her ambition driving through the others' protests. "We can find somewhere for you to sleep later," she said. She was beginning to see the fulfilment of her idea in the young man's arrival and was anxious to be away. "You'd better make up a bed in the engine room. What's your name?"

His hesitation was noticed only by Rosa. "Smith," he announced. "That's it: Smith."

Rosa looked at him shrewdly. "Can't call you Smith all the time. What's your first name?"

"William. William Smith. They call me Willie."

Rosa looked at him a little longer, then she shrugged, an Italian shrug, philosophical and indifferent, accepting what he said for the truth, when she knew it was anything but. "Nice name," she said. "Nice simple name. Lots of Willie Smiths about. Easy to get lost in Willie Smiths. Better take off your coat and we'll get finished."

There were long banks of lavender clouds close to the horizon, dark against the afterglow, as the *Tina S* headed for the mouth of the harbour. Birds, shining glitteringly white an hour or two before, were now ghostly shapes that uttered lost lonely cries in the smoky monotone of evening.

The *Tina S*, like a matronly old hen, headed south for the open sea at the end of a long tow from Angelo Carpaccio's sturdy fishing boat. In the silence, they could hear the thump of the other vessel's engine and the slap and smack of water under the broad bow of the *Tina* as the wind tossed the waves into her bosom. In the air about them was the damp taste of the open sea and the salty smell of the waves. Behind them were the lights of Sydney with the sparkling span of the bridge with its winking aviation warning and the red diamond that marked its centre for shipping coming in from the Pacific. About it and below they could see the strings of lights that marked big ships and the moving clusters of the ferries trudging like bright beetles across to Cremorne and

Manly. Alongside them a buoy rolled and gurgled to the swing of the tide.

"OK," Rosa said, sniffing at the wind that was punching at the southern shores, shifting sand and drifting spray. "Here's where we let go. You got Tommy's atlas handy, Joe? When we turn north, she's going to run some if it really starts to blow."

Joe looked at her with black eyes big as ink pools. "Yes, Mama, I got the atlas. On the cabin table. Already Frankie has spilled tea over it." He indicated the cabin hatch from which wafted the odours of the bacon and beans Frankie was cooking for supper, whistling shrilly as she worked. "I ruled off the course. A straight line. It go over rocks and reefs, I bet. I don' know."

"Right. Tell 'em to let go."

Joe moved towards the bows and hailed the boat ahead. At once the thump of the engine fell to a mutter and, as the tow rope slackened and the wind whipped away the spray its bight slapped off the waves, Joe lifted the bowline he had tied in the end of it from the winch and dropped it with a smack on the water ahead of them. Immediately, Frankie's dark head appeared through the hatchway and she rested her elbows on the deck to watch.

"Here we go," she said, grinning up at Willie Smith. "Seasick yet, chum?"

The *Tina S* had already slowed to a wallowing roll in the long white-tipped swells when the other vessel came round alongside and a few boat-lengths away, still hauling in the tow rope.

"You go fishin', Joe?" came a voice, clear and crisp across the water.

Joe nodded. "We fish," he said shortly, his face expressionless.

"Hope you catch a lot. You goin' to haul 'em in by hand?"

Joe nodded again. "We goin' to haul 'em in by hand."

"Brother, you got a job there. Get a lot. Robert Rossi's wanting his money by the weekend. *Arrivederci*, have a good time."

"You go jump in the harbour, Angelo Carpaccio," Frankie shrieked.

The man on the other vessel grinned and waved to Rosa. "OK, Captain Mama. Keep that crew of yours away from the booze."

"Thank you for the tow and give my love to your Mama," Rosa called. "Now go and get on with your fishing."

Carpaccio waved and the other vessel's engine began to thump again, and she gradually drew ahead of the *Tina S* after the other trawlers as they steered for the fishing grounds.

"OK," Rosa said. "Off we go!"

"Right!" Willie Smith rubbed his hands and Rosa was pleased to see they were strong hands and that there was plenty of muscle under the striped city shirt. "Let's get." Now that he was committed to going, he was as anxious to be off as Rosa. "Let's start the engine."

"Engine?" Frankie guffawed. "We haven't got an engine. At least, not one that goes."

Joe indicated the sun-bleached canvas they had checked during the afternoon. "Sails," he said cheerfully. "You don' hear of sails?" He puffed his fat cheeks out and blew.

Willie stared at them, puzzled, only half-believing them, then as he realized they were serious, he nodded – satisfied, but still a little uneasy, still awkward and unfamiliar aboard the boat. He was spellbound by the ease with which the others used the ropes, and envious of the sure way they moved about while he was constantly thrown off-balance by the lurching deck.

"Suits me," he said. "You know best. Where do we head for first?"

"Brisbane," Joe shrugged. "Port Macquarie. Then we head out east."

"Where to?"

Joe scratched his head cheerfully. "Better ask-a Captain Mama," he suggested gaily. "She run the show, not me."

He moved aft to the wheelhouse, a square structure so small that when he squeezed in there to fist the wheel, his stooping back was against the paint-thickened boards and his belly was jammed hard against the spokes whose constant movement had rubbed his shirt and trousers threadbare against the bulge of his stomach and put a polish on the woodwork that even his neglect had never dimmed.

The vessel was purple against the western sky as they began to heave up the great sail, a billowing rectangle of canvas flapping and tugging at its fastenings. The water began to chatter and talk again under the forefoot and a slash of spray found its way across the bows. The creak of ropes sounded loud on the wind, which slanted obliquely across the land so that the roosting birds on the sandpits changed position to face it. As they headed towards the open sea, the canvas caught the last of the light like the underside of a seagull's wing, and even Joe was moved enough by the sight of it to hum a half-forgotten Neapolitan air.

Willie Smith stood in the bows, holding on to a rope whose function he didn't understand, staring ahead of them in silence, impressed by the width of the sea and the immensity of this new life he had embarked on. Then he turned and went towards the engine room.

"You forgot your jacket," Rosa called after him.

As she picked the garment up to offer it, there was a clatter and something fell from the pocket to the deck. They all stared at the object for a second, then Rosa kicked it quickly across the deck so that it slid into the scuppers and out over the side, dropping without a splash into the sea.

Willie bounded for the rail and stared at the darkening water that streamed away astern in a bubbling wake, then he whirled round on her. "You lost my gun, you silly old cow," he shouted, his young face going red and ugly. "It's gone down! I lost it!"

"We don't need guns on board here," Rosa said with an impressive dignity, while Joe gaped and Frankie hung out of the cabin hatch, her eyes goggling with surprise.

"That gun cost me a lot of money," Willie was shouting. "It was useful."

"So!" Rosa faced him, unmoved by his protests. "What were you going to shoot with it?"

"Why – " Willie hesitated " – birds and animals and things."

"You don't shoot birds and animals with guns like that."

"I've a damn' good mind – "

"Listen," Rosa said quickly. "If you don't like it, you better tell the police about it. We'll put back and you can go and report it."

Frankie was still gaping, and from the wheel Joe watched the clash of wills, his eyes flicking from one to the other as they faced each other, his chubby hands gripping the spokes until his knuckles were white. Willie was staring at Rosa, a tall, bulky woman with unwinking black eyes, then he lit a cigarette quickly and uncomfortably. "It don't matter," he said as he turned away. "I guess I'll manage without it."

Rosa watched him, her face expressionless. "What's your proper name?" she asked suddenly.

Willie turned on his heel. "I told you, didn't I? Smith. Willie Smith."

"That's not your proper name." Rosa's mouth had tightened and her eyes had grown sharp so that there was something intimidating about her that brought the truth out of Willie just as it always did out of Joe.

"Keeley," he said. "Willie Keeley."

"Whyn't you tell us that before? No secret, is it?"

"No, but – " Willie turned aft again " – it's just a name I don't go much on."

"I don't go much on mine," Joe said with a laugh that was falsetto with nervousness. "Salome Joe they call-a me in the 'Loo. That ain't so good either." He guffawed uneasily again, his white teeth flashing in the dusk, then his laughter died away abruptly as Willie disappeared into the engine room where they had given him a mattress.

Rosa stared after him, then she saw Frankie's wide eyes and bewildered expression.

"OK," she said. "Get below. It's time supper was ready."

"Aw, Mama – "

"Get below!"

Rosa raised her voice for the first time and Frankie ducked out of sight, and a moment later they heard the cacophonic symphony from the galley as she rattled the pans to show she was working.

Joe was still watching the dark square of the engine-room hatch with a gloomy fascination, then he turned and glanced quickly at Rosa.

"Mama – " he looked small and shrivelled, his face dark against his greying hair " – that a funny bloke."

"He'll do for us." Rosa hitched her woollen coat closer and peered towards the sea. "Beggars can't be choosers."

Joe was still staring at the hatchway, his brows twisted anxiously. "Mama, why's he in such a hurry to get away from Sydney?"

"Perhaps he's in trouble?"

"Trouble? The police, Mama?"

Rosa nodded and Joe's mouth dropped open.

"You see how his eyes go?" she asked. "Like this. Always like this." She wagged her finger from right to left horizontally. "Never up and down. Like he's looking over his shoulder all the time."

35

"He's a fine one to have aboard," Joe muttered. "He touch my little Frankie, I kick the living daylight outa him."

"He won't touch her," Rosa assured him. "He's not interested in girls. He's too scared."

Joe grunted. "Once, a long time ago in Italy, I was a soldier. I was often scared. But I never stop being interested in girls. We only want a mad-a dog aboard now and anything can happen. I don' like it. All-a time I do things I don' like."

Rosa rounded on him angrily. "The booze you've drunk's softened your backbone, I don't like it either but we've got to put up with it."

"You think he pinch something?"

"Maybe."

"You think he's all-a right?"

"We need money and he's got money, hasn't he?"

"Yes, but, Mama – "

"We need two strong arms and he's got two strong arms, hasn't he?"

"Yeah. I guess so."

"Well, he's all right."

Joe directed a final glance aft that was leaden with the suspicion in it. Then he lit a cigarette, looked hard at his wife's determined face and edged out of the wheelhouse. "OK, Mama," he said. "I go to look at Tommy's atlas now. Take her over."

Half an hour later, the *Tina S* turned north, passing near the stern of a P & O liner beating down into the blow from Brisbane, and headed past North Head and North Point. Dover Heights, a mass of glowing lights, its glare hanging in the sky, was over their stern. The Tasman Sea and the route to New Zealand was on their starboard beam. Ahead of them, as they fled easily before the buster, was the Pacific, mile upon blue mile of it.

three

One of the things that Rosa had failed to realize in the formation of her plan to hide the *Tina S* was that the world had become far too complicated and well-recorded a place for four people and a boat to disappear easily from its comprehension. Within five days, while the *Tina S* curtsied north beyond Brisbane with Rosa happily convinced that no one had noticed their departure, action was already being taken to stop them; and as they headed through the Great Barrier Reef at least two men were on the move into the Pacific across their path.

Richard Flynn studied all the reports on the Salomios and their boat that were available to him, and made a few preliminary inquiries in Woolloomooloo and King's Cross before packing a bag and taking a train north. He paused in Brisbane only long enough to get the first whiff of the islands from the poinsianas that looped and hung over old garden walls, and to discover from the wharves along the river curling through the city centre that the *Tina* had halted merely to draw fresh stores and leave another debt. It required wireless messages to find her track again and, having plotted it, Flynn took a plane east. As the *Tina S* reached the edge of the Coral Sea and the haunts of Byron, Dampier and Cook, Flynn crossed the thousand-odd miles of sweeping Pacific swells to reach Viti Levu, the largest of the Fijian group of islands.

Along the seafront at Suva, the capital, built like Venice on canals, ocean-going ships and island schooners were reflected in the quiet water as Flynn climbed out of his taxi by the docks and paid off his driver, conscious of the Indian's implacable unfriendliness towards him and Europeans in general.

The heavy air reeked with the smell of copra and Flynn's shirt was sticking to his back by the time he found the ship which had been chartered from Brisbane for him, a sleek little schooner called the *Teura To'oa*. She was moored astern of a cargo ship taking on a load of coconut flesh, and Flynn waved away the flies that filled the air as he stepped over a pile of greasy copra sacks and climbed aboard.

The owner met him as he dumped his bag on the deck, a shrivelled little man with a mean merry face full of crafty wisdom and lined with the wear and tear of sensuous pleasures. He had blue eyes and red hair going grey and a pink face that seemed never to have got used to the sun.

"Mornin', Major," he said with an aggressive friendliness that startled Flynn. "Seagull's the name. Captain Harry Seagull. Known in these parts as the Deep Sea Kid."

"I'm not a soldier," Flynn explained.

"You're a policeman," Seagull said, not in the least put out. "Both make life hard for honest guys. I'm a honest guy. Ain't any honest guys left in the world. Ain't even any honest dames. Not on your nelly, there ain't. Put your bag in the saloon. The boys'll look after it."

In an American accent that was so ripe it was patently phoney, he rattled off his conversation piece without appearing to stop for breath. He was whittling a piece of wood all the time he was talking, standing in front of Flynn in rumpled duck trousers, the top of his peaked nautical cap, like the toes of his rope-soled slippers, painted with silver paint.

Flynn opened his mouth to ask where he was to sleep but before he could draw a breath, Seagull was off again. "Got a passenger," he pointed out. "Don't normally take passengers, only this trip since I got one, might as well have two. Oughta get on well, the two of you. Things to talk about. Like to have things to talk about. Keeps the world going round."

"I thought *I* hired this boat," Flynn snapped, annoyed to discover the authorities in Brisbane had slipped up.

Seagull looked slyly up at him with his small bright eyes and grinned so that his ragged grey-red moustache curled upwards into his cheeks. "Going the same way. No harm. Take yourself off if you don't like it. I can always carry copra. Me, I'm independent. Plenty other boats about. None of 'em'll fiddle around for a cop, though. Only me. I'm a patient man. I do anything. I'd slit your throat for fifty nicker. Grub's at midday. Leave on the afternoon tide."

He wandered off, leaving Flynn breathless. Then one of the Fijian crew came up and took his bag and Flynn sat down on a cabin top, already a little exhausted. He had a feeling that in acquiring this little schooner for him someone had blundered badly. He couldn't imagine enjoying Captain Seagull's conversation very much after more than a day or two of it.

He took off his hat and began to mop his face. As the sun climbed higher into the sky, the moist heat grew more intense, and Suva settled itself into its mid-morning languor. Flynn glanced across the lagoon towards the native canoes with their sails of plaited pandanus mats. Beyond them was another schooner at anchor and beyond her still a brand new phosphate ship from the Gilbert Islands.

He hadn't been waiting long when the other passenger appeared on deck, a lean-featured man with shaggy hair and a tired-looking linen suit.

"You'll be Flynn," he said. "My name's Voss. Fred Voss. I'm a journalist."

Flynn frowned. "Seems there's been a bit of a mix-up somewhere," he said. "I hadn't expected to have newspapermen round me on this job."

"I didn't expect to have detectives," Voss grinned. "Somebody boobed. Seagull, I suspect." He sighed. "Five minutes with him and you feel as though you've been hit on the head with a road-mender's mallet."

Flynn said nothing and Voss lit a cigarette and offered the packet. "I'm sorry, old man," he apologized. "It was no choice of mine."

"That's all right," Flynn said, aloof and unwilling to exchange confidences. "Perhaps I can get another boat."

"You'll be lucky. There aren't any. I've tried already. Apparently we're getting too close to the hurricane season and they're all trying to lay up. As it happens, it might be for the best."

Flynn turned quickly. "What do you mean?"

Voss smiled again. "I'm sorry to appear as knowing as the Almighty," he said. "But I know you're a detective and why you're here and what you're doing. You're after a man called William Keeley and he's on a boat called the *Tina S* which you believe is heading out towards the Chesterfields and the New Hebrides and across to the Ellices. Right?"

"That's true enough," Flynn agreed cautiously. "How did you know?"

"Newspaper contacts back home and – " Voss grinned " – Seagull talks a bit, you know. There's a reward. Right?"

"Right," Flynn said, beginning to admire the other's efficiency. "Mr Keeley picked the wrong man. He picked someone with a powerful father. Strings were pulled and politics came into it. Five hundred pounds should talk big in the islands."

"True enough. In addition to half a million coca-cola bottles and a few babies, the Yanks left them with the idea that everything has a value. Someone on one of all the canoes, coasters and schooners in these islands ought to spot a two-by-four fishing boat with an unusual rig."

Flynn said nothing and Voss went on, looking vaguely apologetic as he spoke. "*I'm* after a human story – " he explained, " – these human stories, sometimes they make me want to puke – but this time it's a couple of old people and a kid trying to dodge a debt in a boat because they can't afford to pay. And, unknown to them, they have on board a young lout who's wanted for murder."

"Keeley?" Flynn turned quickly. "Are you following the *Tina S* too?"

Voss grinned. "That's it exactly. You're pretty quick. A big American magazine wants this story. There's a lot of money in it and I suffer from a cabbalistic fantasy that money's useful. And now, to improve on it, I discover Mr Keeley. I didn't know about him when I set off. Surely, since we're following the same trail, we can share the same boat in peace?"

Flynn sat down again and considered the position. "I'm not sure I'm keen," he said.

Voss shrugged. "Maybe I can help you," he suggested.

"How?"

"You're on the wrong trail. They're not running out to the Chesterfields and the New Hebs and the Ellices. They're turning south to New Caledonia and they're working north from there to the Loyalties and then the New Hebs."

Flynn looked at him. "How do you know? More contacts?"

Voss grinned. "Mrs Salomio left a message for her daughter-in-law before she left Sydney, telling her where they were going. The daughter-in-law got scared and told a neighbour who saw the possibility of earning some money and took her to a newspaper – the one I work for. That's why I'm here."

"Go on." Flynn's eyes were interested.

41

"Mrs Salomio said she'd write whenever she got the chance. There might be news in those letters. There'll certainly be postmarks. And Lucia – that's the daughter-in-law – he's going to take them straight along to the office when she gets 'em. She's being paid to. The newspaper will cable me what's in 'em. Between us, we ought to find the Salomios – for me – and in doing so – find friend Keeley – for you."

"Sounds fair enough," Flynn said slowly. "It's a bit unorthodox but let's give it a go."

Voss smiled again, relieved. "What's your part in the plan?" he asked.

"Liaison, chiefly," Flynn said, beginning to feel happier. "I've alerted police and port officials by radio – at least at those places which are big enough to have port officials and a radio. This is a 'must' job. We've got to catch Keeley. There's pressure on in the right places. There's been a report already of a boat that might be the Salomios, in the Chesterfields. It's my guess, they'll make their landfall in the New Hebs somewhere like Malekula or Efaté and eventually move up and across to the Ellices."

"What makes you think that?"

"I was born on Ocean Island," Flynn said simply.

"And I know the islands. That's why they sent me. And I know what I'd do if I wanted to keep out of sight, and if I had an old boat I couldn't trust to a long voyage."

Voss gave him a curious sidelong glance. "How are you proposing to get around?" He indicated the deck they were on. "This?"

"This," Flynn agreed ruefully. "I wanted police launches but they decided on this instead to save delay if we cross zones of government. Aeroplanes aren't much good when there's nowhere for them to land. Still, we've got the airlines keeping their eyes open and we've got radio. The *Tina S* hasn't. That's something. We know where they are. They don't know where we are. And if our reports are correct, they've only got sail. What else do *you* know?"

"Not much. Except one thing that makes this story big-time stuff. You know what they're navigating with? – a kid's atlas. A kid's school atlas and a bundle of throwaways bummed from the shipping offices."

four

While the *Teura To'oa* with Richard Flynn and Voss aboard was heading out to sea between the twin islands of Viti Levu and Vanua Levu, the *Tina S* was heading into the sun towards Efaté in the New Hebrides Condominium, a good five hundred miles to the west. Behind her lay the peaks of Eromanga.

The sea was an oily calm, except for long deep swells running up from the south-east, slow rolling valleys that set the masthead circling across the sky. The wind had disappeared except for occasional gentle puffs, and the slack jib slapped against the halyards with a wet sound that kept the gulls at a distance. The mainsail, clewed down for the night and not yet hoisted, lay in untidy folds along the boom.

Rosa sat peeling potatoes on the after deck with Frankie, who was nominally in charge of the ship, for Joe and Willie Keeley were still below, having spent half the night on deck in a rain squall repairing the main boom which had cracked when the *Tina* had got the wind on the wrong side of her and gybed, almost sweeping the indignant Joe into the dark water alongside.

Bitterly aware that odd jobs had never had a habit of cropping up while the *Tina* had been quietly gathering weeds at the wharfside in Sydney, the old man lay back on the iron bed in the cabin below, chewing a match, all he had to replace his long-vanished cigarettes, and watched the bright pattern made on the deckhead as the sun slanted up off the surface of the water and shone through the port in patches. He thought gloomily of how he had had to crawl out of the blankets in the darkness to saw a plank into strips and lash them round the cracked spar in a splint until it could be replaced, fighting against the buffeting of the spray which, every time the *Tina* had plunged her snout into the ink-dark seas, had whipped over in low vicious curves that rattled like hail against a jib wind-driven to the hardness of a sheet of metal, chilling him to the marrow and making his face raw with salt water. He had finally lost his temper with the job, he remembered, for too many years of laziness had taken away his native fortitude, and the derisive smile on Willie Keeley's face at his fumbling had infuriated him.

He studied the baroque and not very accurate front-porch barometer which had shared pride of place with Georgie's picture ever since Joe had stamped ashore in a half-drowned fury after being caught beyond Sydney Heads in an unexpected gale that had stripped the canvas from the *Tina*'s poles, and noted with satisfaction that it had risen a couple of points. As he climbed sullenly out of bed, he wished their ancient wireless set, whose flat batteries could pump out only a breathy wheeze, were able to cheer him with a little dance music to sing to, and, dragging on his shirt, his fingers still aching from the previous night's work, he heaved himself on deck.

"Nice job you made of it, Pop," Frankie said immediately, indicating the spar.

"I don' do it," Joe growled. "Mister Willie fix it. I don' see so good, so he take the serving mallet off-a me and do it for me."

His eyebrows performing gyrations on his forehead, he peered at the cracked boom and picked at the tallow he had applied. Willie's lashing, though inexpert, was secure.

"Mama," he said in grudging tones. "That kid is a born sailor. We are only a few weeks out and he is taking the jobs off me."

"I saw him do the shrouds two days ago," Frankie put in. "He got 'em in a knot like a Queensland hitch at first but he sorted it out in the end."

"When we set off," Joe went on, "it is Joe Salomio who is doing all-a work while he stand around like Lord Tom-a-Noddy and smoke cigarettes like he don' want to spoil his fancy suit. Now *he* does all-a work and *I* stand around." He patted the splinted spar. "It is all done up good just like rabbit-stew. It wasn't his fault she gybe."

"She wouldn't-a gybed if I'd had her," Frankie boasted.

"We wouldn't-a keep having to stop talking if you don' keep interrupting," Joe said without turning his head. "It could happen to anybody. It might happen to me. But he learns fast. I think we are lucky in some ways. If we're going to do this crazy thing, at least it's good to have someone young and strong with us." He paused thoughtfully. "But I don' like this trouble of his. You think he has any more guns and things?" He closed one eye at Rosa, crooked his forefinger and pulled an imaginary trigger once or twice.

"Think he has, Mama?" Frankie looked up, full of hopeful anticipation.

"I know he hasn't." Rosa picked up another potato. "I've been through all his pockets. I found a knife – a home-made one – and threw it overboard. He hasn't said nothing."

"A knife?" Frankie sat back. "Mama, has he got any more of them things? If he's in trouble with the police, shouldn't we tell somebody?"

"If we tell somebody, they'll find the boat."

Joe looked at Rosa, his eyes wide as he thought of the grubby thumb-breadths he had used to calculate current and drift and the maze of figures in which he regularly lost himself on the back of the ancient charts.

"Mama," he said sadly. "They find-a this boat, they are cleverer than Salome Joe. Yesterday, when I work out where we are, I find we are sailing down Bourke Street and heading straight for Riley's Bar."

He spat out his splintered match stick and faced Rosa once more. "Mama, he is getting inquisitive. Last night, he ask me again where we are going."

"What you say, Pop?"

"I tell him when the squall blow itself out we make for Efaté and pick up water at Vila. I guess that don' satisfy him, though. He'll want to know some more."

He stopped abruptly as they heard Willie whistling below in the engine room and they looked at each other and became silent, waiting for him to appear.

As he put his head out of the hatch, a shoal of flying fish broke surface in front of him in a flash of silver and blue, and he stared thoughtfully at the surface of the sea where they had disappeared. Willie was still a little surprised at the miracle of fish that took to the air – something he had never entirely believed in until a week or two ago, something that had given him as much of a shock when he had first seen it as had the first porpoises and the first piggy-eyed shark and the first wandering sperm whale that had surfaced near enough to expel its watery breath across the deck – things he had only seen in pictures before, without the vitality of life.

He hoisted himself on deck, trying to smooth the creases out of the cheap trousers he still wore with the jersey Rosa had loaned him, and glanced casually at the other three sitting together on the stern. He was no longer the frightened youth he had been when they set off. With every day that came and went, with every mile that passed astern of them, his confidence grew. The feeling that he was cleverer than the police, which had taken such a dip into fear in Sydney, was growing again and he was beginning to suspect he was more than a match for this slow-thinking, slow-moving old couple and their stringy daughter who were helping him to escape. Once more he felt he was master of his fate, the old Willie Keeley of the street corners and the dance halls, the Willie Keeley he had always imagined himself to be.

The seasickness which, to Frankie's unrestrained glee, had prostrated him for the first few days, had passed now and he could look her in the face and eat and, with eating and a steady stomach and legs that could balance against the roll of the boat, he felt better and stronger. The sunburn that had peeled the skin off his arms into raw patches had subsided too and even the cramped locker they had given him to sleep in, bare of decoration beyond the plain boards and the inert useless mass of the engine with its dulled copper pipes, had lost its first choking narrowness and even managed a surprising comfort and privacy he had never known in the tenement house he had lived in ashore.

Lighting a cigarette, he moved aft and sat down alongside the others, breathing deeply at the scented air. He couldn't remember a time before this when he hadn't been able to smell the wrack of traffic and the odour of garbage cans and old houses.

Rosa watched him dragging at the cigarette and squinting into the glare of the rising sun, her eyes blank as a curtain across her thoughts.

"Tea below," she informed him casually, picking another potato out of the bucket.

"It'll do later." Willie got to his feet again and walked along the deck, preoccupied with his thoughts, then as he came to the mast, he turned and faced them.

"Listen, Ma," he said. "Where are we heading?"

Frankie glanced at her mother and Rosa looked up slowly at Willie, her mind in a panic at the question.

"Efaté," she said cautiously. "Put in at Vila. Joe fixed the course."

"Then where from there?"

"Malekula." Rosa answered cautiously. "Ambrim. Espiritu Santo. I can't say."

"Don't you know?" Willie persisted.

Rosa put down her potato and wiped her hands on her frock, performing the unimportant movements with exaggerated care to give her time to think. "What you want to know for?" she asked.

Willie threw away the half-smoked cigarette and faced her squarely. "When I came aboard here, you said you wanted a passenger. Now you don't even know where you're going."

Rosa's eyes became opaque and guarded. "You said it didn't matter. You said you weren't bothered."

"I'm not. But I've been watching you the last two weeks. You've never done any trading. You've got no cargo. You just dodge around. I've seen you poking about with that old atlas of yours trying to decide where next. I'm not blind. I'm not growling either, mind you. I'm a lucky bunny. I wanted a trip and I got one. But where are you going? What's on, Ma?" He leaned over her threateningly, one hand on the cabin top to take his weight, his eyes cold in his brown face, his blond hair falling over his forehead.

Rosa looked steadily at him and for a moment there was silence except for the creak of the rigging and the chuckle of the bow-wave, and Willie began to bluster in his sense of inferiority before her calmness. "I don't like being kept in the dark," he said loudly. "I reckon I can look after myself."

"Yes," Frankie pointed out immediately. "You use a gun."

Joe's frightened eyes flashed in her direction but Frankie was staring aggressively at the boy, defying him to try any anger.

"All right," Willie was saying defensively. "All right. I've not got the gun now though, have I? Your Ma threw it overboard. I lost it, didn't I? I've not complained since." He turned to Joe. "Right. Now tell me what you're up to."

"Up to?" Joe's innocence was too good to be true. "We are up to nothing."

"Come off it, you old bum," Willie said, his voice rising and gaining confidence as he felt he was on sure ground. "Don't give me that. Why didn't we go alongside at Noumea? Why did we stand off and take on water with the dinghy and petrol cans? God, I got sick of rowing backwards and forwards. Why all them fibs you told that bloke about our papers? Why did we sneak off before daylight when he said he'd come back? Why did we keep clear of Port Patrick on Aneityum when we saw those yachts there? Why did we go to the far end of the lagoon at Lady Austen Island and get our food from the coons instead of going to the store where the white blokes were? Why do we always go the little places where there's nobody? We ain't been anywhere of any size yet?"

"You want to go somewhere big?" Frankie asked.

Willie swung round on her. "Too right I do," he said quickly. "But I'm not complaining. I just want to know what's on."

Rosa sighed deeply and picked up the potato and the knife again. Joe's jaw hung open as he waited to see what she would do.

"We aren't going nowhere," she said at last.

"Not going nowhere!" It was Willie's turn to stare.

"No." Rosa's shoulders had slumped. "We're dodging a bloke in Surry Hills. That's all."

"The cops?"

"We owe some money. We can't pay."

Willie laughed. "Dinkum?" he said. "Is that all?"

"It's enough, isn't it?" Frankie demanded.

"If we don't pay," Rosa explained, "we lose the boat. It's all we got. So we're hiding it."

Willie laughed again with relief at the thought of the Sydney police searching the streets of Surry Hills for him.

"Well, aren't I a silly cow?" he said. "I never guessed. I don't want to go ashore. I'll go with you – wherever you go. Listen – " he looked excited " – I got a bit of money on me. Not much, but a bit." He was silently thanking his lucky stars he had had the sense to carry his money about with him instead of putting it in a bank or hiding it like some of his cronies did. It would come in useful now and Willie was prepared to pay for safety, prepared to spend to prolong his flight. "It's only a few quid, mind," he went on cautiously, eyeing them sharply one after the other for a sign of greedy interest. "But it'll help. I don't want to meet people no more than you do."

"Why?" It was the first word that Joe had spoken for some time and it came out like a whipcrack, with Joe's dark eyes, wide and expressionless, resting fixedly on Willie's face.

Willie waved a hand airily, his features blank and uninformative. "Oh, nothing! Something like you. I owe a bit of money, sort of. Bloke wants to dong me for not giving it him back."

"You pinch it?" Frankie asked disconcertingly.

"Not exactly. Just a debt. I hadn't enough to pay him. That's all. So I nipped off. I'm dodging him. Like you."

"You gotta to dodge him all this way?" Joe asked. "Two-three thousand miles."

"He's a tough bloke, this one, and I'm not dodging no more than you are."

Willie stared defiantly back at them, his eyes reflecting the bright water, but as Joe opened his mouth to ask another question Rosa laid a hand on his shoulder and put a question herself.

"You're willing to go anywhere?" she asked.

"Anywhere you like. Why not? I got all the time in the world."

"You got no job?"

"Nope. I'm just kinda enjoying myself. Never been on a boat before. Except on a ferry across to Manly. Didn't realize it was like this. You get used to the quiet, don't you?"

Frankie gave a hoot of laughter. "You feel crook or something?" she asked. "You weren't so happy a while back when you were fetching up over the stern."

Willie grinned at her for the first time – in a way that dispersed his tense expression. "No," he admitted, "I wasn't. But I feel fine now. Don't know why I never thought of going to sea. It's not half bad."

Rosa was watching him shrewdly as he spoke, her mind busy.

"Look – " Willie lit another cigarette and, occupied with his thoughts, offered one to Joe – for the first time – and the old man snatched at it avidly " – how long you hoping to keep up this dodge?"

"Long as we can," Rosa said. "Why?"

"Well, they'll get you quick if you're not careful. Will they follow you?"

"Shouldn't think so. We ain't worth following. But if they recognize us, they'll probably try and impound the boat."

Willie thrust his hands in his pockets and stared over the water, a little startled as he always was to find there was nothing else in sight but the lifting sea. Then his brain became busy with thoughts of what he had left behind in Sydney and the desperate need to lie low. Into his mind raced scraps of stories he had read – mostly in pulp magazines and newspapers – and he whirled round on Rosa, his eyes glowing.

"Listen, Ma," he said. "Why not make her look like some other boat so they don't recognize her." He gestured at the empty swinging horizon. "There's all this to hide in. Why not do it properly? Repaint her for a start. They're looking for a grey ship. Let's paint her white."

"We repainting her for us or for you?" Frankie asked.

Willie evaded the question. "We can even paint a new name on her," he said. "Big. So they won't miss it if they look."

"Where we get the paint?" Joe asked.

"Anywhere. I'll buy it."

"That's what I mean. I don't got no money."

Willie ignored Joe in the excitement his plans roused in him. "Let's fix another mast up, too," he suggested.

"Another what?" Joe almost fell off the cabin hatch in his surprise. "Don't we got enough with one?"

"Aw, Pop," Frankie said irritatedly. "Give him a chance, can't you?" She was watching Willie now, listening carefully, her whole attitude tense and interested.

"Listen, man," Willie urged. "You got to box clever when they're after you and a bit of flannelling'll help a lot. Put up a new mast, like I say."

"First puff of wind, it fall down," Joe prophesied with a pontifical solemnity. "Mizzen masts always fall down."

"Shut up for a minute, you old fool," Rosa said, leaning forward, her eyes bright. "Go on, Willie."

Willie turned to her, reluctantly admiring her for her eagerness. "Listen, Ma – " his young face was alive now and in its excitement had lost its hardness " – why *can't* we make this boat look different?" He turned to Joe again. "What is she? What sort of boat? What kind?"

Joe considered. "She's a mongrel," he said. "She got a bit of a cutter in her. Only she ain't a cutter. If she'd got a bowsprit, you call her a sloop. Yeah, a sloop." He shrugged. "Only she ain't got no bowsprit."

"Well, why *can't* we have a bowsprit?" Willie had scooped the nautical term into his vocabulary immediately.

"Yes, Mama – " Frankie had begun to fidget with excitement as the idea caught her imagination " – I've read stories like this. Why shouldn't we have a bowsprit like Willie says?"

"And why *shouldn't* we put up a mast at the back end?" Willie added.

Joe shrugged again. "The main boom come round," he pointed out. "Like last night. Bic boc. Down come the new mast."

"Aw, Gawd!" Willie stared at him in disgust. "Ain't you helpful? Can't we shorten the boom?"

"No."

"Why not?" Frankie turned to her father quickly.

"The sail is then too big."

"Cripes!" Willie's voice was rising in its impatience. Irritatedly, he saw Joe's objections only as obstacles to his escape. Now that the idea was fixed in his mind, he was eager to translate it into fact. His eyes bright with excitement, he leaned forward towards Joe, his attitude vaguely threatening, trying to enforce the acceptance of his idea, not only with his words, but with his eyes, his whole being. "Listen, pally, can't we cut a bit of it off?" he asked.

"You start cutting her about – " Joe leaned back, smug in his knowledge " – she start to sag like a old lady's bloomers."

"Aw, Pop," Frankie shouted, suddenly as keen as Willie. "We could soon fix that."

"Yes, shut up, you old donkey," Rosa said. "Go on, Willie. I like what you say. It sounds good."

She made her voice sound enthusiastic though she was not deluded by Frankie's excitement or blind to the opportunism in Willie's voice. She knew his plans were only for his own benefit, but she decided to play a waiting game and profit as much from them as she could, for they fitted in well with her own plans to hide the *Tina S.*

Willie had turned towards her, reaching out for support.

"Look, Ma, these islands have got radio these days, haven't they? That puts 'em one up on us. Right. They're looking for one mast and no bowsprit – "

"But suppose they see a ship with *two* masts and a bowsprit?" Frankie ended, waving her arms while Willie grinned at her. "How about that? What'll they see then?"

"A bloody ole hodge-a-podge," Joe said happily. "With the knobs on."

Willie ignored him. The romance of the idea was beginning to take hold of him so that his young face was flushed with an enthusiasm that seemed to remove all the bitter lines there. "We can make another sail, can't we?" he asked. "We can fiddle this one some way to make it fit, surely."

"Sure," Rosa said enthusiastically. "We've got needles and sailmakers' palms and plenty of twine."

"OK, then, if we do that, what we got then?"

Joe looked at Rosa, paused with his mouth open as he thought twice about his reply, and said, "We got a yawl, I reckon. A funny yawl, but a yawl allasame."

"Right. These German raiders in the war – you've read of 'em in books – they rigged up dummy funnels and put fires in 'em to make smoke. They put up extra masts and built extra cabins and things."

"Then people thought they were something else," Frankie went on excitedly, almost like an echo. "Why can't we?"

"We ain't no German raider," Joe said. "That is why."

Willie began to get angry at last and his voice began to rise. "Listen, you old dope, we don't have to be a German raider to do it, do we?"

Joe stared back at him, blank-eyed and innocent-looking and Willie went on furiously. "Listen, you got more blow than Dingo Dick. If we want to disguise this old tub, there ain't no reason why we shouldn't, so stop getting in the way."

"Ain't no call for shouting," Rosa said quietly and Willie stopped abruptly.

"Sorry, Ma," he apologized, his voice dropping. "Only he kept on – " he swallowed his anger, seeing it would get him nowhere. "Listen, I was apprenticed to a carpenter until – well, once I was. I can do it with a bit of help."

"She look a damn' queer rig."

"What the hell does it matter so long as it helps?" Rosa suddenly lost patience with her husband's deliberate baiting and Joe blinked as she changed sides in the argument just when he had firmly believed she had come round to supporting him again.

Willie hurried on, eager to get her help while she still favoured him. "We just got to find somewhere quiet to lie up and repaint her," he pointed out. "And get a tree or something for a new mast."

"And another for the boom you cracked," Joe added, thinking of the hard work it entailed. "Also, as we ain't enough to do, we should scrape her bottom while we're at it."

"Good idea," Rosa said. "It hasn't been done for years. She'll sail faster then."

"I'll get the scrapers out," Frankie announced eagerly. "I know where they are."

Joe glared at Rosa as his sarcasm rebounded on his own head. "Sure," he said bitterly. "And put on a new keel. And paint the bilges. And fix a new engine." He paused and went on with a deeper weight of sarcasm. "But this is a great deal to do and there are only four of us. In the boatyard are riggers, carpenters, boat-a-builders, sail-a-makers, painters, labourers – " he reeled off the trades on his fingers, happily watching the odds mounting against them, until Rosa interrupted.

"We're not in a boatyard," she said angrily. "We're here. And all we want to do is repair her – "

"And maybe a new mast," Frankie put in.

"OK, a new mast. And there are only four of us. Better start thinking of somewhere to do it. We ain't all day."

Joe prodded himself furiously with a fat forefinger. "What-a you think I am?" he demanded. "King-a-Kong? You think I got the muscles of an ox?"

The argument that followed went on for some time before Joe's resistance was finally beaten down, and Willie grinned with triumph as he admitted he knew a place.

"You mighta got away with it, Pop," Frankie said, "if you'd tied Mama up and locked her in the engine room. Only I reckon you'd have got a ear bitten off in the scuffle at least. You got to do as she says."

Joe looked bitterly at the others. "We'll go to Aranga-vaa," he said flatly, oppressed by the thought of all the work that lay ahead of them. "If we can find it," he added more cheerfully, thinking of the uneasy courses he had drawn off with a piece of wood for a ruler and the times he had tried unsuccessfully to gauge their speed with Lucia's alarm clock and a bucket on the end of a line, the occasions he had prayed at night for a guiding light or a marked buoy to turn up and give him a position. "We can give Vila a miss – except-a perhaps for the paint – and run back towards New Caledonia and turn east. We got to avoid the big places but we got to stay near to land in case we sink. Port doctors and Customs ain't-a no good to us. Already, they ask too many questions in Noumea. We can lay up in Saddle Bay. It will be very hot. We will kill ourselves with work. We bury each other on the beach."

Rosa tossed her potato into the bucket with a plop and stood up, quite unmoved by Joe's prophecies of disaster.

"What are we waiting for, then?" she said, smiling.

Frankie skipped to the yards, followed by Willie, and as they strained together the great mainsail jerked up and filled out with the breeze. From the wheelhouse, Joe looked over his shoulder at the sun and spun the wheel until the shadows swung across the deck and lay athwart-ships. Then he glanced at the erratic old compass and headed the ship in a southerly direction.

"I get the atlas," he said. "And the 1907 charts and the shipping company adverts, and lay off a course. Another line. Over more reefs. Mama, we come through this, I keep off the booze for ever."

five

Aranga-vaa, in the half-circle of islands known as Dampier's Bracelet, which was the southernmost point where the buccaneer-explorer voyaged in his travels round New Guinea and New Britain, lay to the south-east of New Caledonia, to the south-west of Fiji and equidistant between the two. It was a crescent-shaped scrap of land that had once been the tip of a volcano before the sea had flooded in and filled the crater, and at one side it had been eroded by the waves so that the island now rested in the emerald of the ocean almost like a horse-shoe through the ends of which the Pacific rollers, driven by the South-East Trades, burst in a storm of green water and flying spray.

Its bay was broken into smaller inlets where the rain and the sea had washed away the soil and, above the water, the highest point of the mountain peaks lofted almost to a thousand feet in steep pinnacles of rock which, after halfway, became almost bare of undergrowth like a boy growing out of his clothes. On the lower slopes, the palms, the kauri pines and the feathery casuarinas were tinted with rusty lichens and backgrounded by evergreen leaves that were greasy-looking and as spatulate as an artisan's fingers. Into this humid undergrowth the light filtered through creepers that hung in lace-like curtains, and through the twisted arches of roots which stood up like the flying buttresses of some savage cathedral. Nearer to the lagoon, where the undergrowth was not so thick, there was the flash of rich blooms in the sunshine, the scarlet of hibiscus and poinsettia, the pale gold of candle flower and the wax white of frangipani. The peacock wings of butterflies added to the confusion of colour and scarlet-tufted birds dipped long beaks into crimson bells. By the water's edge kingfishers flashed like darts of blue flame and bronze-green lizards basked on the rocks.

Into this sunburst of loveliness, the *Tina S* erupted like a matronly old dowager thrust through a shop door at sales time. For a wild minute, with the swells becoming more mountainous as the sea bottom grew shallower near the reef, the racing waves swooped at her stern and lifted it high. The ears of her crew were filled with the clamorous dissonance of the surf as the old boat strained every plank in her rush for the entrance through the sizzling waters, then they crashed, with the sea boiling over the gunwales, into the silence of the lagoon.

Still staggered by the fury of the surf, Willie stared round him in the sudden stillness and his mouth dropped open with awe as the *Tina* rolled serenely up the lagoon in the early morning light, clawing her way in the slack breeze to where the foliage and the flowers kissed the water in sun-bright circles by a dark coral beach.

All about them, as they left the surf behind, was the silence, the moribund, unchanging silence of a forgotten island.

"Cripes!" He watched a sooty tern as it slanted down astern of them towards the sand, mewing as it fell in lonely echoes that called back to them from the shores. "It's a beaut'. It's a smasheroo."

While he stood staring at the island, he heard Frankie's voice shrieking at him from amidships. "OK," she was shouting. "Have 'em down, Dreamy," and he hurried after her to the yards and the *Tina*'s sails rattled to the deck with a screech of pulleys that echoed round the hidden valleys of

Aranga-vaa, then Frankie galloped past him like an awkward young colt to let go the anchor.

"You always let ladies do the work, you big-footed drip?" she demanded.

Willie grinned sheepishly and hurried to help her.

"OK, Wishbone! Get yourself out of it and let a man come."

He finished winding the anchor cable round the winch and took up a position in the bows again, gazing upwards, his feet in a puddle of water from the chain.

"Come on, softy," Frankie begged. "We haven't finished yet."

"Do you know what we got to do?"

"Sure I do. I been doing it on me own since I was old enough to spit."

"OK, do it a bit longer then. Now, run away, I got things to think about."

Willie was still standing in the bows, staring at the shore, when Joe came forward from the squat wheelhouse.

"The memory don' go so far wrong, eh?" he commented gaily, his hands working up and down over the stained patches on his pants. He stared at the tooth-like spires above them. "I read into that ole atlas things that ain't there."

He pointed towards the land. "We row a line ashore," he said, "and make fast to the trees. Then we warp her in close and put out some more lines, then when the tide drop she stand on her keel like the juggler with the ball on his back-a-side."

Willie was still gaping at the green slopes that rose to tremendous peaks which finally pierced the clouds, pointing heavenwards like the ruined spires of some gigantic natural monument, all his self-satisfaction gone in a feeling of minuteness before their immensity.

"What's biting you?" Frankie demanded, approaching them, wiping her wet hands on her trousers.

Willie indicated the island with a helpless gesture, at a loss for words to express what he felt. "Dinkum, I've never seen anything like this before."

"Well, you see plenty more," Joe said. "Across the Pacific are many places like Aranga-vaa."

Willie hardly heard him. He was gazing upwards again.

All the pleasure he had felt that he had bullied and persuaded them to fall in with his plan, had got them aiding his escape, had dwindled to a feeling of humility of which he had never thought himself capable.

As they had skirted the Great Barrier Reef and turned east for the New Hebrides in the early days out of Brisbane, he had thought he had seen all there was of beauty – coral beaches bright as parched ivory, with the jade sea threaded like lace through the nigger-heads of coral, an archipelago of tree-crammed shores where the birds hovered in black clouds that blotted out the sun – godwits, dotterels, warblers; and terns milling in their thousands like scraps of flung paper.

With Frankie, the child of the harbours and the beaches, to hang over his shoulder and whip up his sluggish enthusiasm as she shouted with excitement over each new miracle, Willie had long since lost his first blasé air of indifference until, days before they had made their present landfall, his jaw was hanging open with honest awe at the sights about him.

From Efaté they had bustled south to Eromanga and from Eromanga to Aneityum, then south-west between the Loyalties and Mare to the coast of New Caledonia and the Isle of Pines, doing the trip by the longest route but in the shortest hops so that land was never too far away if the struggling old *Tina* showed signs of giving up the ghost, as she very nearly did once when they ran ashore on a sandspit south of Mare and they all had to go over the side and shove her off again. From New Caledonia they had headed out into the Pacific again towards Matthew Isle and Hunter Isle, with

Joe watching his rigging with anxious eyes and Rosa guarding their rations like an old hen with her chicks; and Frankie, with her experience of the sea's fringe, dragging Willie off along every deserted beach they landed on, in search of eels, shellfish and shrimps, poking in rock pools down by the shining water's edge where their footprints were desecration's among the tide-strewn weeds and the tiny triangular marks of the gulls.

The beauty about them seemed to Willie to increase as they travelled and as he threw off the bitterness which, fed by ugly factory buildings in Sydney and old sad houses, had grown on his youth like a fungus. There had been a following wind all the way, which had made their work easier, and the sea had been calm with long slow swells lifting them gently so that they had seemed to be in an unreal world of light and movement. Islands in the distance had been green lifting rocks splashed with foliage and overhung with banks of cumulus they could see long before they raised the land out of the sea. They had been escorted for the greater part of the way by bands of hunting porpoises and, as they closed the islands, they saw huge man-o'-war birds circling the thousands of smaller fry that milled in the air, forcing them to drop the fish they had caught and, cheered on by Frankie's yells of encouragement, poaching them as they fell, glistening like drops of living water to the sea.

But now, all the things they had seen, all the teeming life that had crowded about them, seemed to have been caught up between the two long arms of the bay in Aranga-vaa. All the silence was here, all the peace – and for the first time in his life Willie was becoming aware of peace.

He started out of his thoughtful mood as Frankie grabbed his arm and pointed to the trees. "Look," she squealed. "I seen something moving. What is it, Willie?"

"It's a pig," he said. "It's a pig, Joe!"

"Sure, it's a pig." The old man shrugged. "Only wild pigs and rats live on Aranga-vaa. Ain't enough soil for anything else."

Rosa came forward to join them, thrusting them apart, wiping her face in the humid heat that snatched at their breath and brought the sweat to their bodies. "Well," she said. "You going to stand all day, staring? We got jobs to do, haven't we?"

They all gazed back at her defensively, then, as though that had been their intention all the time, they hurried to lower the dinghy into the water that shone like a sheet of glass over the enchanted world at the bottom of the lagoon. Willie climbed into the boat, his eyes aware of the fish that slid beneath them in gaudy layers down to the coral sand and the ink-blue rocks of the bay, and they began loading a heavy mooring rope, coiling it in serpentine loops in the stern. With the water lapping at the gunwales, they began to row towards the shore, Willie's eyes fixed again on the tremendous spires of Aranga-vaa, while Frankie sat in the stern paying out the rope with flat splashes into the water.

"How long you reckon we're going to be here, Willie boy?" she asked him, no longer awed by the aura of wickedness and cruelty that had seemed to hang about him at first.

"Dunno." Willie's eyes were still on those gigantic towers of rock and he spoke over his shoulder to her. "Few weeks, I reckon."

"How long will it be before we go home? – to Sydney, I mean."

Willie turned at last. "Gaw, I don't know. Years mebbe. Why, you going to miss your boy friends?"

"I've got no boy friends," she said angrily. "I don't want boy friends. I've no time for that sort of thing."

Willie grinned. "Scrawny bits like you always talk big like that, Wishbone. But they all come round in the end. You'll end up by going all gooey like the others and getting married and having kids. My sister was just the same."

"Nobody would want to fall for me," she said, suddenly quieter. "I'm too skinny. I got no shape and me hair's straight."

"Come off it, Wishbone," he encouraged. "You're only a kid yet. There's plenty of time."

She looked up, her heart full of friendliness to him for his encouragement. "You reckon, Willie? You reckon I will?"

"Sure you will. Why not?"

"It'd be nice to have some feller fall for you, I bet. Somebody nice like on the pictures."

"Or maybe a dirty big sailor like my sister got, who comes home drunk and knocks you about."

Her face fell, her dream shattered, all her friendliness dispersed by his thoughtless comment. "He'd better try it, that's all," she said in a low voice. "I'd fetch him one with the fry-pan."

By midday they had two lines made fast ashore and, with the anchor still out to kedge themselves off, had warped the *Tina* into position. By this time, she was resting on her keel on the dark sand and the dirty copper oxide above the waterline was beginning to grow in breadth.

"So – " Joe looked round him with satisfaction " – now we sit down and rest."

"Rest?" Rosa turned on him. She had taken off her dress to help with the pulling and the under-skirt that stretched across her broad frame was moist with perspiration and spotted with water. "Tomorrow, they might arrive to take her away. There's no resting yet…"

The look in her eyes forced Joe to his feet again and she moved to where Willie had spread their few poor tools on the cabin top and was trying to sharpen the chipped chisels and straighten the ancient saws.

"You going to manage?" she asked hesitantly, still a little dubious in his presence. His anger she could answer with its own kind, but his willingness to fall in with the plan left her puzzled and worried. "You got enough tools?"

Willie grinned, eager to be started. "All we're short of," he said, "is a decent cross-cut, some sharp edges, a plane, a mallet, a spokeshave, some nails that aren't bent, a carpenter's bench – "

A new spasm of doubt crossed Rosa's face. "Can we do it?" she asked.

"Sure we can. We'll manage without 'em, that's all." He gave her an encouraging grin that did her heart good and bent to work again while Rosa watched him, hope rising higher in her breast.

Long before the tide had completely receded, she had driven them over the side into the water and set them scraping the bottom, and by the time the sudden darkness came, most of what they had to do had been finished, and they climbed back aboard, weary and filthy and covered with the slime and weeds that had dripped from the hull.

Joe sat on the cabin top, slumped in weariness, more exhausted than he could ever remember, his blank eyes seeing warm seats on the wharfside at Woolloomooloo and the knife-backed cat hunting the sooty sparrows. Stretching his aching muscles, he looked forward to a comatose day of doing nothing, a dream from which he was rudely jolted by Rosa's next words.

"Tomorrow," she said, "we will start painting."

It took them longer than they had expected to daub the hull of the *Tina*. Without the assistance of a cradle or ladders, reaching was difficult and they had to lash brushes to boathooks and roll rocks across the shifting beach to stand on. By the time they had finished, another day had gone by and they were smothered with white paint.

"She don't look like the same boat," Rosa commented as she studied their work. "She'll sail faster, too."

"She won't sail so slow, you mean," Frankie corrected, peering through the splodges of paint on her face. "She didn't ever sail fast."

The following morning, assisted by Joe, who was swearing gloomily in Italian and good Australian, Willie set about knocking the box-like structure of the wheelhouse to pieces, setting the dust flying from long neglected corners and harrying the lurking cockroaches into the sunshine. Later, with the wheelhouse almost demolished, they rowed ashore in the leaking dinghy to search out a suitable pine tree for the new mast, while Rosa stripped off her frock again and sat down on the cabin top with Frankie to pull the sail to pieces, a back-aching job that tired their eyes and broke their nails.

By lunchtime, Joe had selected his tree and while he returned aboard to finish the wheelhouse, Willie felled it and began to trim it to a stout straight pole.

Ashore, where the foliage shielded him from the breeze that wafted in from the sea, the heat was intense and the flies swarmed about him, belabouring his head blindly as they buzzed around his hair. The bay was still and the land reflected mirror-like in the water. Above the spires of rock, the sky matched the grandeur of the island with a mass of cumulus that rose, blue meadow on golden mountain, high above the lagoon. Joe had stopped his hammering and was lying to recover his breath in the shade of the awning they had rigged on the foredeck with their shabby blankets. Apart from the occasional sound of a parrot crashing through the undergrowth and the plop of a fish, the place was clothed with the noisy silence of dead places that was a little breath-taking when the cries of the sea-birds were not echoing off the hills.

From the first day he could remember, Willie had heard the revving of trucks and vans in the streets about his home or the roar of sirens from the docks. Even at night buses ran right alongside his bed and the sound of the ships had come over the rooftops into his room. Aranga-vaa had a stillness, a sense of being poised in time, that made him want to hold his breath.

Rosa called him eventually for tea and, jerking out of the mood, he slipped into the water and swam to the *Tina*.

"Ready for a cuppa, chum?" Frankie shoved her head through the cabin hatch and greeted him with a tin mug as he climbed over the side, then promptly disappeared again like a jack-in-a-box.

"You don't forget nobody, do you, Ma?" Willie panted, wiping himself on his shirt.

"You're doing all the work, son," Rosa said seriously. "You need all the food."

He glanced at the pile of clippings by the cabin top where she and Frankie had sat all day with the sail.

"How's it go, Ma?" he asked eagerly, pleased at the progress they had made.

"Fine." Rosa straightened her back to hide her tiredness. "I'll soon have it undone. We're going to need all the canvas we've got."

As they sat back from their meal on the untidy table below the hurricane lamp, Willie wiped his mouth, mellow with a feeling of well-being, full-stomached and lethargic in the heat. He glanced at Joe picking his teeth with a match, and Frankie sprawled over the inevitable magazine, then for no reason at all his mind drifted comfortably back home, and he was pulled up with a jolt as the picture shattered and he saw the police at the doors in Surry Hills, questioning, prying, levering every one of his secrets from its hidden corner.

He was immediately obsessed by a sense of urgency and he stood up and began to collect his tools again. "I'm going to drill the deck for a new mast," he announced. "Coming, Joe?"

Joe looked up as Willie stripped off his shirt. "You only just-a finish one job," he pointed out. "Why you think God give you a backside? Don' you ever sit down?"

"Ain't tired." Willie paused with one foot on the ladder. "I'm going for a swim when I've finished."

"You like to get finished?" Joe asked quickly, his eyes bright and suspicious. "It is important?"

Frankie looked up from her magazine, watching them.

"Sure, it's important," Willie said. "We don't want anybody to recognize the *Tina*, do we?"

"That is more important for you than it is for us, eh?" Joe's eyes were blank and innocent again as he probed.

"No, why should it be?"

"I ain't ever seen you sit down. That's all. You got the ants-in-the-pants."

"Aw, leave him alone, Pop," Frankie said. "Leave him be. He's doing no harm wanting to work."

In his sense of resentment at the labour he had been forced into, Joe was trying hard to pick a quarrel. "I ain't ever seen nobody work like him," he pointed out loudly. "Only Fred Pellevicini when he pinch his brother's dinghy and paint it to look like some other guy's. He work like that."

Rosa rounded on her husband, her hands full of pots. "It helps us all, don't it?" she said. "Mind your own business."

Frankie watched her father subside into muttered grumbling, then she slid out from the table, wiping her hands on her pants. "I'll give you a hand, Willie," she said. "I'm coming now."

When they had gone on deck, Joe looked up at Rosa. "Mama, that boy drive too hard. There is something inside him."

Rosa slammed the dishes into the washing-up bowl. "Of course there is," she said. "Something that's not inside you: energy."

Joe's face wore a sulky expression. "Men who have that drive inside them are dangerous men, Mama."

Rosa slapped the dishcloth after the dishes. "Or successful men," she snapped. "Angelo Carpaccio's got that drive. He's successful. He owns two boats and an office with a telephone, and will own three boats and an office with a telephone before long. And he's only thirty-one. Robert Rossi's got it. He owns two boats – one of them this one."

The mention of Angelo Carpaccio and Robert Rossi made Joe feel homesick. He glanced through the porthole and saw only trees and the tangled greenery of the undergrowth across the water. Running his fingers through his hair, he shuffled in his seat as he compared it with the Sydney streets and the little office of Angelo Carpaccio. He licked his lips sadly, almost tasting the drinks he was in the habit of receiving there from time to time. "Mama, we are a long way from home," he said.

"And a good thing, too," Rosa replied, sensing his thoughts. "No bars."

"Mama, suppose-a this young man decide to kill us both and run away with the boat?" Joe's eyes rounded with agitation at the thought. "He could do-a the bunk and take Frankie. She is only the kid. She talks through the top of the head. She is enthusiastic. She is all we got, Mama, and with her he would know enough to sail the *Tina* now."

Rosa stopped with a handful of wet plates, and stared at the bulkhead in front of her, her face, shadowed in the growing dusk, suddenly doubtful and worried. "He wouldn't do that," she said.

"Why not?"

Rosa forced away her doubt and smiled, flattering him. "He'd run her ashore," she said. "He don't know his way around like you do, Joe."

Joe indicated the atlas on the table. "He has the atlas," he said sarcastically. "The wonderful atlas that tells us where the islands is and where the reefs ain't. Mama, I don' like it."

"There's too much you don't like," Rosa burst out, erect, matriarchal and commanding. "You don't like work. You don't like responsibility. You don't like risk. That's why we're here now. That's why we're hiding like a lot of criminals. Now shut up and go and help on deck."

When Willie had finished his work, he sat with his feet swinging over the side of the *Tina*, fiddling with a piece of wood shaving between his fingers. Frankie had her back to the mast, her knees under her chin. The palms ashore were profiled against the sky and every star in the heavens was reflected clearly in the lagoon in a firmament of diamonds. The amethystine night was loaded with the eddies of warm air that swung the island scents across the lagoon towards the cooler salt smell coming off the sea. From ashore came the snuffle of a rooting pig and the honk of the nightbird and, above them, the thin insect piping from the trees.

"Willie," Frankie said suddenly. "You married?"

Willie answered without moving his head. "Me? Married? Not on your life, kid. I got better things to do."

"OK. No need to roar like a grampus at me. I only wondered." She paused, trying to be casual. "You got a girl, Willie?"

"I had dozens. You can always get girls when you got money to spend."

"Money wouldn't fetch me."

"You're not a girl. You're only a kid. But you'll learn as you grow older."

Frankie studied her thin knees showing through the blue material of her jeans, and her bony ankles below their frayed turn-ups. The possibility of romance coming to someone as skinny as she was seemed very remote, she had to admit, and she was consumed with jealousy.

"If I was a man and I thought a girl was only after me for me dough," she said, "I'd drop her like a hot brick. And if I was a girl and he started telling me how much he'd got I'd tell him where he could stuff it."

"You fancy romance or something?" Willie asked, and she became silent, shamed by his derision. All the discomforts of making-do, of putting-up-with and going without on the *Tina*, all the vulgarities of the dockside and the hoarse hilarities of life had buffeted her without harming her, and underneath her self-confident raucous exterior there was an inarticulate naivety that came from being on the threshold of maturity. The film magazines she devoured were only a defence against the more brutal aspects of life, adding a scrap of colour to the little world she lived in behind the curtains of her bunk.

She answered Willie cautiously. " 'Course I don't fancy romance," she said. "But you can't buy everything for money. You can't buy love and you can't buy happiness. *You're* happier now than you were when you came aboard in Sydney. And it ain't spending money that's made you happier because you ain't spent any."

Willie turned and stared at her for a moment, startled by the wisdom of what she said and shocked to realize how right she was.

In spite of the ache in his arms and back, the ache of hard work, something he had never experienced before, he felt content, but he was puzzled to know the reason for it, for contentment was a new sensation to him, something that had never come to him when he had gasconaded round the alleyways of King's Cross with money in his pocket. He tried to put it down to the fact that his escape had been accomplished successfully, though he knew that could not be the only reason.

He was still working for his own salvation and no one else's, and he knew that every drop of sweat he shed brought him a little longer freedom. It had even crossed his mind several times to desert when their work was finished, up-anchoring when the others were ashore, and sailing the boat single-handed. The chance of failure would be no greater that way than it would be with them on board, and he was not afraid to try. But there was something in their need and the way they relied on him that shouldered the thought aside every time it rose to the surface. When it had first crossed his mind, he had felt that deserting them would not hit them too hard because, like himself, they had been brought up in an untrusting world; but the more he thought of it, the more he had doubts about it and even, to his surprise, about his own ability to make the break, for he gained too much happiness with them and too much satisfaction from Rosa's praise.

He knew she was the driving force behind everyone else. He had seen her too many times to doubt it, standing by the stove in her old felt slippers as though she were ashore and not in the heaving interior of an old boat, wedged against the bulkhead for safety, one eye on the swinging hurricane lamp that circled dangerously near her head, her fingers all the time on a handhold; tired because she found the movement of the boat hard on her feet and because her muscles were stiff with trying to keep her balance. But, for all her weariness, there had never been a complaint out of her. While everyone else on board was grumbling about the conditions or the weather or the food, Rosa had been like a rock, often unspeaking, rarely bad-tempered and never swerving in her decision to continue.

The few tit-bits on his mealtime plate had been provided from their monotonous diet at her expense, he knew quite well, while she stood – inevitably at the stove – to eat so that he shouldn't see what was before her. She had washed the only shirt he possessed and persuaded him to put it on in the evenings – "Because it suits you," she had said. "You're young and brown and it's so white." She saw that he had tea to drink in the hot mid-morning when he was thirsty – and had even rowed the teapot ashore when he was working there and Frankie was too busy.

There was something in her sturdy generous spirit that was prepared to give so long as Willie was prepared to do likewise, prepared to ignore his secrets so long as he was willing to help. Her attention had touched him in a way that had made him feel foolish and over-emotional when he had first experienced it, and there was something in her confidence that had sparked off an unexpected zest for life that made him more than willing to work.

Puzzled by his feelings, he stood up abruptly and threw off his shirt.

"I'm going for a swim, Wishbone," he said. "Coming?"

"Sure!" Frankie scrambled to her feet, as willing as he was to exchange her troublesome thoughts for movement. "Last one in's a sissy. I'll go over the other side."

They poised on the rails and dived out into the reflected stars, and as they struck the night-dark water, the picture there, with its inverted trees and mountain peaks and the glimmer of the yellow moon lifting over the rocks, shattered like a smashed mirror and dissolved into spreading ripples that caught the light in golden arcs...

When Rosa came on deck, she saw a glow of light in the engine room and laboured down the ladder to see what was happening.

Willie, his arms black to the elbows with old rank grease, sat on a box staring at the grimy pieces of the engine he had spread across the floorboards, while Frankie sat on the rolled and ragged blankets of his bed, her hair in long damp rat's-tails, her chin on her hands, watching Willie with an absorbed look.

"This is a nice mess," Rosa said, looking at the oil-black nuts and bolts. With Joe's words still in her ears, she turned to Frankie. "What are you doing down here?" she demanded.

"Nothing, Mama," Frankie said. "Only watching Willie."

"And what have you been telling her?"

Willie grinned. "That the sea's made of ink and the moon's made of green cheese. Come off it, Ma. She's able to look after herself and she's got more sense than you credit her with. She likes talking to me, don't you, Wishbone?"

Frankie nodded, her eyes fixed cautiously on Rosa.

"She's a kid," Willie went on. "I'm a kid too, if the truth's known. Mebbe that's it. She gets sick of old folks all the time. Give her a break, Ma. We're doing no harm. She only wants company."

Rosa had to admit the truth in what he said and she held back the rebuke on her lips. "OK," she said. "I'm not saying anything, am I? But it's time she was in bed and not poking about down here."

"Scared I'll make a pass at her, Ma?" Willie tormented.

"I'd hit you with a spanner if you did," Frankie said quickly.

"I'm not scared of anything like that," Rosa explained. "I'm scared she isn't getting enough sleep. She looks like a skinned rabbit. She's outgrowing her strength – "

"Mama, I'm not a child!"

"So long as I'm looking after you, you're always a child. Now get off to bed."

As Frankie crawled unwillingly up the ladder to the deck, Rosa turned to Willie.

"OK," she said. "Now what's going on? What are you doing?"

"Making the engine go." Willie looked up again and grinned. He had been secretly investigating it for days, working on it when they thought he was asleep. Useless, the engine seemed only a barrier in his path, for he didn't trust sails alone. Working, it could be an asset if the time ever came for it to be used.

"Just poking about," he added, seeing no further point in hiding his activities. "Seeing what's wrong with it."

"It's no good," Rosa pointed out. "It hasn't gone in a blue moon and even if you make it go, we've got no fuel."

Willie indicated a drum propped against the engine.

"I bought that in Vila with the paint," he said. "I didn't tell you. That's enough to start her."

Rosa frowned. "Starting her's no good when we can't afford any more fuel to keep her going."

Willie grinned. "Never mind. It's something to do."

Rosa suddenly looked interested and moved closer. "You can really make it go?" she asked.

"Sure." Willie smiled. "Dead easy. Just a question of time. It's an ordinary marine engine. Like any other. 1925, by the look of her, I reckon. Ain't much compression and the cylinder walls is worn. And there's one or two things cracked and missing here and there and the usual leaks. But I've got a vice down here and a few tools. I can do it. Plenty of horse-power. Bags of guts. And a big screw, Mama. Piece of cake, it is."

"You know all about engines?" Rosa leaned over him, watching his sure fingers.

"Sure. Motor cars mostly, but there ain't a lot of difference."

"But you said you were a carpenter's apprentice. Apprentices don't own cars."

"Other people do."

"And they let you drive?"

Willie glanced up and a smile spread across his face again.

"They never knew," he said.

Rosa frowned, shocked. "You mean – ?"

"I pinched 'em, Ma. I pinched 'em and sold 'em again. Did 'em up in an old shed and made 'em look different. There were a lot of us in the game. It's nothing new."

"That was dishonest."

Willie scratched his nose with an oily finger that left its dark smudge on his skin. "Yeah, I reckon it was," he admitted.

Rosa stared hard at him, thinking of her daughter, anxious that she should not learn too much about Willie's life.

"You been telling all this to Frankie?" she asked.

"Sure, why not?"

Rosa felt a spasm of anger. Frankie was a wild creature, living always in her dockside life on the edge of crime, but she was still, because of Rosa's influence, untouched by it.

"You shouldn't have told her. She's a good girl and the less she knows about that kind of thing the better."

Willie looked seriously at her. "You got her wrong," he said. "You got her all wrong. She's too old to tread on. She asks questions and she knows more about what goes on than you think. Ma, she's pretty smart with a spanner. I dunno where she learned but if I get this engine going, you'll be able to thank her for a lot of it."

Rosa was at a loss what to say. She looked quickly round the engine room. "You happy, son?" she asked unexpectedly. "You look it."

Willie stared back at her, conscious of the similarity of what Frankie had said, and tried again to sort out the unfamiliar emotions that had begun to come upon him. He grinned briefly and endeavoured to reply honestly. "Yes, Ma, I reckon I am – under the circs. Are you?"

Rosa smiled. She suddenly realized how like her son he looked – daring, impertinent and touched with the same spirit of adventure that had sent Georgie off to join the Navy. "Sure," she said. "I'm happy."

But her face looked taut and for some reason he couldn't have explained, Willie raised his voice to a ring of enthusiasm because he knew it would cheer her up. "I'm learning to speak Italian," he said gaily. "Just like Joe. Frankie's taught me. Listen: Uno, Due, Tre, Quattro, Cinque – Lunedi, Martedi, Mercoledi. Days of the week, see? I've learned to put on a whipping. I can sew canvas and I can splice a rope. I'll learn to splice wire soon. It's a piece of cake being a sailor, Ma."

Rosa's eyes clouded as she thought of her son for whom being a sailor had not proved a piece of cake, and he stopped as he saw her expression.

"Ma, what's wrong? You worried about something?"

Rosa sat down on a box, her heavy face troubled. She pushed Georgie to the shadows at the back of her mind with an effort as she answered. "It's *too* easy," she sighed. "Everything's gone so well. I get scared."

"Take it easy, Ma," Willie urged. "Save your breath for worrying when it comes bad." He peered at her in the yellow light. "You tired, Ma? You look it."

Rosa's relaxed face tautened and she forced a smile. "A little bit. We've worked hard and I don't sleep so well."

"Thinking too much?"

"I reckon so. I keep thinking of Frankie. The *Tina* sails all right, but them sails of ours look pretty tatty and I wouldn't like to run into a hurricane with her on board. Still, like you say, I'll take things as they come. We mustn't think of not succeeding. We've *got* to succeed. Tommy and Lucia are depending on us succeeding. And that means it's up to me. Frankie ain't very old and Joe's not so young as he was. He gives up more easy."

"I'll help, Ma."

"I know you will. Joe told me how clever you're getting about the boat." Rosa stood up and touched his cheek affectionately. "You're a good boy, Willie."

Willie glanced up at her. "Not really, Ma," he said soberly.

He watched her heave herself up the ladder and, alone once more, he sat without moving. Then he put his hand on his cheek where Rosa's fingers had rested and stared at the grimy pieces of the engine spread along the floorboards with wide puzzled eyes.

s i x

Rosa was awakened by the sound of feet on the planks above her head and the thump of a hammer. Guiltily conscious of over-sleeping, she sat up abruptly and threw on her clothes. As she hoisted herself up into the sunshine, she saw Willie already at work, cutting a hole in the deck with a chisel. Frankie was rattling the pots in the galley in a discord of discontent, eager to be in the sunshine among more exciting chores, and even her whistle had a plaintive note of frustration in it to mellow its piercing quality.

The land quivered under the wavering lines of heat, the thick foliage, mounting rank upon rank up the jagged slopes, oppressive in the stillness. Among the darker green Rosa could see the flare of hibiscus and the ivory of frangipani and, like a jewelled thread running down the slopes, here disappearing among the tremendous leaves, there reappearing over rocks, the little stream that ended in a warm pool above the beach where they had taken it in turns to squat naked with a piece of coarse soap, revelling in cleanliness and an abundance of water, after days of hoarding it on the run from Efaté.

Rosa pushed back her hair and stood by Willie, watching him.

"It's good to see young muscles," she said shyly. "When I was young I liked to work. Do you?"

Willie's forehead puckered. "I never did before, Ma. Dinkum I didn't. But I like *this* work. I reckon it depends on what you're doing. Being apprentice to a carpenter in a factory ain't much bottle but this is kind of different."

He straightened up. "Not far to go now," he said. "Then we can shove the pole in." He sighed. "After that we got to do the boom – we'll have to burn the wood off the hoops. It'll take time, Ma." He ended on a despairing note. "A lot of time."

"All's going fine." It was Rosa's turn to encourage. "We're already looking like a different ship."

"Just wait." Willie's enthusiasm leapt up again like a quick flame at her words. "She'll look like the *Queen Mary* when I've finished. I'm going to take that old exhaust stack from the deck and shove it out through the stern somewhere. It'll help us look fast. Then we got to give her a fresh name. What we going to call her?"

Rosa sat on the cabin top to consider, blinking in the sun that came up off the water and dappled the mast. "It's got to be a nice name," she commented. She looked up, her expression gentle and a little sad and proud. "I had a son," she said. "He was killed in the war. His ship went down in the Java Sea. He wasn't much older than you. I always remember him like you. His name was Giorgio. Joe chose it but I always called him Georgie so that when he grew up he wouldn't have an Italian name like Angelo or Giuseppe. So that he'd be more Australian and people wouldn't pick on him. Then, if he wanted, he could have altered his other name from Salomio to something good like Smith or Green."

She paused, staring at the deck between her feet. "But he didn't want to. He didn't care. He was a good Australian and a good Salomio. I'd like to call the boat *George*."

"*George?*" Willie was more moved than he thought he could be. "*George,*" he repeated thoughtfully. "That's a funny name for a boat. Wait a minute, though. I've heard of *Girl Pat* and *Boy Fred*. Why can't we have a *Boy George*? That's a good name for a boat."

Rosa smiled at him. "Sure. That's a good name. Let's call her the *Boy George.*"

The timbers of the *Tina S* were old but they were tough and the tools were blunt and it wasn't until the following day that they were ready to step the mizzen mast. As Rosa watched Willie lifting the pole into position, hindered rather than helped by Frankie, while Joe stood in the background shouting excited instructions, she felt thankful that they had him on board. He was doing in a day what would have taken Joe a week to do, and the job was better done when it was finished. Joe had all an old man's irritation with details and already Willie was learning fast about ropes and tackles and pulleys and he had a soaring enthusiasm that had withered years ago in Joe, an enthusiasm that had not seemed possible in the scared, boastful youth they had first met in Sydney.

Not pausing to rest, he scrambled below while Rosa and Frankie worked at the sails, and, with Joe to sit and draw lines and crosses and offer noisy arguments full of staring eyes and waving arms and waggling fingers, about why what they were doing was impossible, he lifted the floorboards to make a step in the keel for the base of the mast, and the boat rang to the muffled thuds of his hammering. They had fixed the pole in place, with all its lifts and stays rigged, by the time darkness fell.

"There you are," Willie said, standing back, the sweat streaming down his face. "What about that?"

"It is lovely," Joe said with heavy disgust as he headed to the cabin. "Now we are nothing no more. We ain't a yawl. We ain't a cutter. We only look like a Christmas tree."

More than a week had passed before they had rigged the bowsprit and the new booms – a week of sweating over the fire they had built ashore, straightening the iron bands they had burned off and reforging them to fit the remade spars, of beating out new ones from the stanchions of the old wheelhouse, a week of scorched clothes, fried faces and burnt hands. All of them laboured over the fire, Frankie leaping in and out of the bushes, fetching wood, running herself ragged in her enthusiasm. Rosa, in her underskirt, worked the improvised bellows; and Joe, his face streaming sweat, held on to the hot iron with a pair of home-made tongs while Willie toiled with the hammer.

It was a hard job, their bellows constantly breaking, their hammer barely heavy enough to forge the iron, so that Willie had to put all his strength behind it as he brought it down. And all the time, the intense humid heat of the clearing where they worked caught the sun and wrapped them around with the gagging closeness of the forest.

"Go easy, kid," Willie warned as Frankie, purple-faced and perspiring, her black hair plastered to her forehead, dumped an armful of wood alongside him. "Don't knock your silly self up. Or who's going to do the washing up?"

"Willie the Drip," she grinned, darting off again.

For a while, with the *Tina* turned inside out, they tried sleeping ashore in a lean-to of oars, canvas and palm fronds, but the night noises scared Rosa and the insects nearly drove them frantic, and finally they returned aboard to sleep among the shavings and the sawdust and the snippets of canvas and sail twine, and the ubiquitous cockroaches which their rerigging had made more active. Their bodies were bruised and weary with bending, their minds numbed with the noise of their own labour, and dizzy with the sunshine that smote like a sledge-hammer on their backs or, rebounding from the decks and the water, thrust like red daggers under their eyelids.

But, as the work proceeded and the decks were cleared of debris, even Joe's grumbling changed to snatches of song in a cracked tenor that was breathy with lack of use, and finally to an enthusiastic spurt of energy as he saw the end of all the hard work.

They finished repainting the cabin top and varnishing the new spars in three days. Then, while Joe held the dinghy steady, Willie carefully painted her new name on her stern. The old man's tongue worked between his lips and his eyebrows moved on his forehead in sympathy with the brush as Willie struggled over the lettering.

"That's good," he said, when they sat back. "That's a good name. He was a good boy, Georgie." He turned and addressed the lagoon. "You seen the *Tina S?*" he asked, spreading his hands. "The *Tina S?*" he answered himself shrugging hugely. "I ain't seen the *Tina S.*" Another shrug. "Only a big new ship called the *Boy George.*" A vast stretching of arms to encompass a liner. "A big, fine new ship with two masts and a bow-a-sprit. She was sailing for Tonga and the Society Isles."

Willie looked up quickly. "Why we going there?" he asked.

Joe grinned. "Because Captain Mama decide it is a long way from here and we can dodge into the Tuamotus if they get-a too close to us."

"What it like there?"

"Plenty islands. Plenty people. Plenty drink. Plenty food. Plenty girls. You like girls?" Joe winked slyly.

Willie grinned and, glancing at the lettering on the *Tina's* counter, dabbed on a final speck of colour with his brush and sat back to examine the effect. "Well, she's finished," he said.

They rowed away to stare at the reincarnated boat and admire their efforts. She had a patched appearance because of the fresh wood they had used, but the deckhouse and the exhaust stack had disappeared and the bowsprit for which Joe had already spliced and rigged the stays gave her a rakish look.

"She look-a funny now," Joe said thoughtfully, resting on the oars. "From the beam, she look fast. Then when you row round the stern and see her fat-a behind, she look as slow as an old sow in the family way."

"She'll do," Willie said, satisfied with their work. "Now, all we got to do is stock up on food."

"Perhaps from the store that ain't here? Perhaps from a refrigerator ship or something?" Joe indicated the empty lagoon sarcastically.

"No, you stupid old Wop, you. From what lives ashore. I'm getting sick of tinned food and we've got to make our stores spin out. They're going down too quick. We've got to start catching some of our tucker."

Joe slapped his chest, his good temper dispersed immediately as he suspected Willie of deliberately finding jobs for him. "Ha! So now, in addition to toiling like-a slaves on deck, we have also to find time to go looking for food."

Willie snorted. "Why not? We've got all day. All you do is stand around offering advice with your mouth flapping open like a barn door."

"I knock-a down the wheelhouse," Joe exploded, waving his arms as though wielding an imaginary hammer so that the dinghy was in danger of overturning. "I splice-a the ropes and rigging till my fingers ache." His hands worked an invisible spike. "I row-a the boat." He heaved an imaginary oar. "What else do you want?"

"It's not a hard job, Joe – sitting on your puss, holding a fishing line."

"I don't want to sit all day on my bum-a," Joe said, suddenly defiant. "Too much I am told what to do. By you. By Rosa. By Frankie even. Go here. Go there. Do this. Do that. I am the captain of this ship. I shall do as I please." He glanced at Willie's face and, oddly, it reminded him of Rosa's with its darkening expression and he was seized with a sudden panic at the certain realization that she would never be on his side if she were brought into the argument. "OK," he said, deflating abruptly. "I don't go, Rosa will find out. So I go. It is easier."

Willie took pity on him. "It'll be a change after the work," he said. "We're going to be busy between us. I've seen wild pig ashore. We ought to try and get one."

"How we kill 'em? Chase 'em till they drop-a dead of fright. Because – " Joe eyed Willie sourly " – I guess the wild pig can run faster than Salome Joe."

Willie grinned. "We'll shoot 'em," he said.

"What you shoot with? You lost your gun." A gleam of spite shone in Joe's eyes as he spoke and Willie flushed in a way that made him seem young and frightened again.

"Who said anything about a gun?" he asked. "There's a bit of sheet steel in the engine room. Maybe I can fix up some arrows with it. I've seen some saplings ashore that'll make crackerjack bows. I could fetch a pig down if I hit it in the right place. I can do the rest with a knife. I can sharpen one up and put a point on it."

"You pretty smart at making weapons." Willie had so completely thrown in his lot with them, Joe felt safe in making the dig.

Willie gave him a long look. "Maybe I am at that," he said. "And maybe it'll be useful to you now. I bet you wouldn't sneeze at a bit of fresh meat."

The following day, Rosa watched them climbing into the dinghy, Willie carrying the deadly little arrows he had fashioned, a big bow strung across his bare burly shoulders, and while Joe dozed off-shore in the dinghy, waiting for porgy and mullet to bite, a black dot on a surface so shimmering it hurt the eyes, Willie and Frankie plunged into the undergrowth after the young wild pig.

They headed inland, climbing the slopes with ease, scrambling over fallen kauri pines that had been choked with parasite creepers, stumbling over vines and thrusting chest-deep through the giant fern. Several times they startled the blundering parrots out of the trees above their heads, shrieking raucously, so that they started with alarm and Frankie jumped nearer to Willie in an instinctive movement.

"Come on, Wishbone," he said, pushing her away. "What you scared of – bogies?"

"Scared?" Recovering, she started to boast to hide her discomfiture. "I've seen things that'd turn your hat round. Keep going, Willie boy, I'm right behind you."

They had climbed through the first belt of undergrowth and could see glimpses of the lagoon and – occasionally – the *Tina*, foreshortened by the height and framed by the palms, when Willie halted and grabbed Frankie's arm.

"Hold it, kid," he whispered. "There's something ahead of us."

They crouched, tense and expectant, and a young black pig snuffled through the grass in front of them.

"Oh, boy," Willie breathed.

He hoisted the bow from his shoulders and, fitting one of the deadly little arrows, took aim.

"Hurry," Frankie whispered. "He's moving. If you leave it much longer, you'll only have his backside to go at."

The bow twanged and the arrow thumped into the trunk of a tree alongside the pig, which immediately squealed and bolted into the undergrowth again.

"Aw, nuts, I coulda done better with a catapult and me eyes shut," Frankie yelled as they crashed through the ferns after their quarry.

They climbed further, trying to follow the blundering path of the pig, then Willie halted again by a bank.

"I can hear it again," he said. "It's up top there somewhere. Come on, kid, I'll boost you up."

He took her by the arm and the seat of her faded blue jeans and hoisted. As he lifted, the threadbare material ripped and Frankie gave a shriek of alarm and clutched at her rear and Willie dropped her as though she were red hot.

He stared at her for a moment then burst into a roar of laughter. She glared at him red-faced, trying to perform impossible contortions to ascertain the extent of the disaster.

"That's it, go on, laugh, you great silly bonehead," she yelled. "Wouldn't think of doing anything to help, would you?"

"Do anything? What could I do?" Willie lay back and howled.

"Well, for a start, you could stop cackling like an old hen on a nest and see if you've got something on you to mend 'em with."

Still laughing, Willie fished in his pocket and handed her a piece of copper wire. "That's all I got," he chuckled. "Oh, Jesus, you look a fair sight!"

Still furious, Frankie twisted round again, trying to push the wire through the torn trousers.

"Take 'em off," Willie suggested. "You'll manage better."

"With you there? What you think I am?"

Willie waved a hand in disdain. "Go on. I got better things to look at."

She struggled for a few minutes longer, then Willie scrambled to his feet and, taking her arm, flung her face down on the bank and sat on her legs.

"Let me go, you great coot!" she shrieked.

He snatched the wire from her fingers and performed a hasty repair. "It's a fair rent," he commented. "It's a good job I'm not embarrassed easily."

"I am. Go on, enjoy yourself. Your eyes are sticking out like organ stops." Almost in tears of rage, Frankie twisted into an impossible position to glare at him.

"Ah, you're all skin and bone." He hoisted her to her feet with the damage repaired.

"Cripes, you've pulled it tight," she said, feeling herself tenderly. "It don't half dig in."

"Don't fret yourself, kid. You look like something off a Christmas tree now."

He gave her a whack across the behind and pushed her away and she twisted again to see herself stern-on.

"It looks like you've been playing cat's cradle," she said critically.

She paused and straightened up, her brows puckered with bewilderment. "Willie," she said, suddenly serious. "Do I act silly? I mean, do I behave like a kid out without its ma for the first time?"

Willie stooped to pick up the bow and arrows. "What do you mean?" he asked.

"You're always pulling my leg."

Willie rose and hitched the bow over his shoulder. "When a bloke pulls a girl's leg," he said, hitting on a home-truth unconsciously, "it's because he likes her. It's the one he makes passes at he don't like. He's a little scared of that kind and tries to show off."

"And you aren't scared of me?" Frankie felt disappointed. "Why should I be?"

"No, why should you be? I'm just a kid."

"I like you fine," Willie went on. "You're all right. You aren't always fixing your hair and complaining because it's too hot. You can keep up with me. You're the sort of kid a bloke likes to have around."

"I see." Frankie answered thoughtfully, at the back of her mind the wish that keeping up with Willie wasn't such hard work and the feeling that it would be nice if he'd ask her just once in a while if she were tired. "I just wondered."

"You don't want to worry about things like that," Willie urged, preparing to move on. "They're not important. Come on. Don't let's hang around. We might spot another pig."

He set off ahead of her, the old unrepentant prowling Willie of the Sydney streets who had suddenly become the self-confident hunter, all those instincts which had made him what he was attuned for the chase, all the single-mindedness and cruelty which had resulted in the fight that had put him aboard the *Tina* making him able to kill without compunction.

"OK, Willie!" Frankie suppressed a sigh that was young and bewildered and impatient. The child of old parents, she had been starved of youth all her life and while she wanted to keep up with Willie, to have him tease her, she also ached for an affectionate word from him, not just the brisk word of one skilful tracker of wild pig to another.

She trailed after him, dragging the stick and sack she had brought, suddenly with no heart for the chase.

Three days later, in the early evening, four weeks to the day since they had first sighted Aranga-vaa, the newly named *Boy George* hoisted her sails and turned towards the entrance of the lagoon.

They raised the mainsail first, narrower now that Rosa had cut a good four feet off its width, then the new jib they had made to Joe's instructions, an affair like a patchwork quilt, and finally the narrow little sail on the mizzen mast aft. With the wind in them, they bellied open, slapping at Willie and Frankie as they freed them. Slowly, the *Boy George* headed for the breakers at the entrance to the lagoon and made for the open sea, so that they all tasted the bitterness of brine on their tongues again and felt the dampness of the sea on their hands. Above their heads the sooty terns cried a farewell from their wheeling squadrons over the masthead, sharp and clear against the rolling masses of cumulus that hung on the mountain top.

"She looks fine," Rosa said happily, glancing about her at the trim vessel, her decks swept free of shavings. "She looks like a fully rigged ship."

"She sail like a fully rigged brick," Joe said contemplatively as he felt the pull of the wheel. "She rolls about like she got-a the belly-ache."

They all had stomachs satiated with pork from an uproarious celebration party the night before at which Joe had succumbed so much to the effects of food and the excitement that was obvious in Rosa that he had sung *Santa Lucia* to them from beginning to end. Below deck were the remains of two young pigs in salt and a few salted birds. Along the decks were strung strips of pork and fish drying to pemmican in the sun, and by the mast hung two stalks of bananas and bunches of drinking coconuts.

Rosa glanced round at the stream sparkling in the sunlight as it danced down the hillside to be lost in the lagoon. The bright flare of flowers was fading, disappearing into the darker greenery of the bush as they drew away. "We got to go easy on water now," she sighed. "I'm going to miss the baths."

She smiled at Frankie hanging perilously over the bows watching for the nigger-heads of coral that rose like monstrous cauliflower's under the surface. Her eyes were patient but there were lines of strain on her forehead and the wrinkles on her face seemed deeper. She was weary with the work they had done but uplifted by their success.

She watched the land slide past her, almost without it registering in her mind, her body slack and content, her hands heavy in her lap.

She looked across at Willie, well knowing how much they owed to his youth and enthusiasm, and there seemed in him just then some of the same pride that Rosa felt as he moved about the deck, his bare feet slapping the boards while he performed the few tasks attending their departure. He wore only a pair of trousers and his body was burned a golden brown, his fair hair bleached white by the sun. Knowing how far they had gone towards anonymity, Rosa felt a flooding affection for him and a fierce determination to hide him whatever his crime.

Almost as though he sensed she was thinking about him, Willie turned towards her and glanced back at Aranga-vaa. The steep spires of rock where the tenuous mist whirled through hidden valleys were dwindling now and the land fell away to the low reef on either side of the entrance to the lagoon. "Pity we couldn't stay," he said. "I enjoyed that place. But they'd find us if we did."

As the old boat whispered her way to the growling surf, he drew a deep breath and felt bigger than he had ever felt before. He had conquered seasickness and sunburn, and the need for cigarettes no longer troubled him. All the things that had once seemed so essential to his existence no longer had a place among his wants as his needs slipped into a new and truer perspective.

He decided he would view Sydney more clearly when he got back, and then he remembered he wasn't going back; he was never going back. The realization came as a shock to him and he felt a sickness at the pit of his stomach – a nostalgia for familiar narrow streets, and a tremendous desire to borrow a little more time to examine more closely the things he had never before had the desire to study or the sense to look at.

For a moment the black weight of knowing he was a fugitive oppressed him, then that curiosity he had always felt for the immense silence of Aranga-vaa caught his attention again and he forgot his unhappiness.

The sun was low as they passed through the reef on the ebbing tide. The light was fading rapidly and as the ship rose and fell on the open sea they lost all sense of being in a boat, of being anywhere but in a universe of sky and water.

The first porpoises broke surface ahead of them in a sparkle of light and formed up in escort as the terns began to thin out and return to the land.

"You know," Willie said – more to himself than to the others, his voice a little awed at the thought – "I feel as though I've never been alive till now."

Frankie turned, sprawling on the foredeck, and they all looked up at him, startled by the unexpectedness of the announcement. He stared back at them, then grinned foolishly and fell silent. As darkness came the stars were clear and bright. And the sea was wide and lonely and empty with only the old boat heading out from Aranga-vaa, growing smaller and smaller and smaller until she was only a dot on the wide surface of the water.

PART TWO

o n e

Going east from Aranga-vaa, north towards the Tongan islands and east and south again through the Cooks, you come to the George IIIs, a group of islands reaching out like a pointing finger to the Societies. They hang in the sea like a string of brilliants edged by blazing beaches, the giant rollers of the Pacific thundering on their outer fringe in a majestic diapason of sound, to send mounting crests of spray high into the air and set the whole chain of islets quivering to their roar. Inside their sheltering reefs of coral the lagoons are polished opal, and along the shore the palms bend their tufted heads to the direction of the wind like so many acolytes bobbing to an altar.

Over them, reflecting the colours of the lagoons, hang scraps of cumulus by which the ancient navigators from Tonga used to steer. Some of the islands have beaches a mile wide with sand so dazzling it hurts the eyes, others have coral gardens below the surface of the water in vivid greens, blues, yellows, purples and blacks. Others have pearls in their inland lakes. And others sharks.

The most distant of the George III islands is Fleet, and there is a village there and a store, all built of magnificent Norwegian wood taken from the wreckage of a timber ship which piled up on the reef in 1911 and still lies there, its bones just visible below the surface, half covered with coral sand, its weed-grown holds the halls of the purple parrot fish and the crêpe-skinned surgeons, its clouded ports their exits and their entrances.

It was at Fleet where the newly named *Boy George* made her first call for stores three weeks after leaving Aranga-vaa, chiefly because Joe remembered the George IIIs as a scattered and isolated group largely uninhabited by Europeans and not likely to be over-populated with officials.

"We got to have stores," he said. "OK, let's pick 'em up where there ain't no big-a-shots. On Fleet ain't enough to choose a football team. Last time I go only one guy live there. Villey or Villiers or something. He go there to dodge-a the nagging wife." Joe looked sideways at Rosa in the vain hope that the implication might encourage sweetness. "He like the sun and the birds and the quiet. Only the sun fry him and the birds don't ever sing and the quiet begin to drive him crazy." He shrugged. "He forget how far she is from the trade routes."

"That was years ago," Rosa said. "Maybe it's different now."

"We gotta to take the chance," Joe replied. "We gotta to get stores. The salt pig don't last for ever. If it's a different bloke, tough-a luck! We gotta to do some quick thinking. If it's the same bloke, he'll be so old now, we don't have to worry anyway."

Rosa still hesitated and Frankie joined in, reaching across the table to wag an enthusiastic finger at her mother. "Listen, Mama," she said. "Some time, some day, we've got to meet people. We can't just go on for ever keeping out of people's way. We've got to have stores. Well, let's go into Fleet and try out the boat on 'em. Let's go and see what they say about her. Let's go and see if they recognize us. If there ain't many people there, like Pop says, we ought to be able to get away smartish before they can do anything about it."

"Suppose they got a wireless? Suppose they're in touch? I wouldn't like to have 'em take the boat off us after all the work we've done."

Willie rattled the chart as he turned it round for Rosa to see. "Look, Mama," he said, indicating it with a fork. "There are plenty of small islands in the George IIIs, so we ought to be able to hide up again pretty quick if we've got to."

Rosa nodded at last, somehow convinced by Willie's slow drawl when Joe's staccato chatter and Frankie's noisy persuasiveness had left her unmoved. "OK," she said. "It sounds sense, I reckon. Let's go and see what they got to say about the boat."

They approached Fleet cautiously. They had passed through the scattered atolls of the Ha'apai group and skirted the perfect cone of Kao to Palmerston with its intense electric-blue lagoon, without seeing anything more than a distant schooner or a native canoe. While they lowered the sails and rolled gently to the blue swells that caught the sun as they swung down on the scrap of land before them, Rosa studied the island doubtfully, seeing it in her mind's eye swarming with officials and police and debt collectors, all anxious to impound the *Boy George*. She ran her eyes over the three-mile circle of rock and sand that rose at one end to a low scrub-covered hill.

"I ain't sure," she said doubtfully, her mind full of fears again. "I ain't so sure now."

"Aw, Mama," Frankie insisted, "we've got to try the boat on someone some time. Let's try here."

"Suppose they recognize her? They could stop us getting out of the lagoon."

"Mama," Joe pointed out, "there ain't enough people on Fleet to stop a match-a-stick getting out."

"It might have changed."

"Fleet ain't-a big enough to change that much."

Willie, who had been listening to the arguing for some time without talking, interrupted:

"Take it easy," he said slowly. "Let's sleep on it. Let's stay outside for the night. We can sail up north and come back in the morning for daybreak. That'll give Ma time to think it over."

As though that were the answer to all their doubts, they broke into smiles and Rosa looked at Willie gratefully.

"Maybe that's the best," she said.

"I gotta the idea," Joe said suddenly and they all turned towards him. "At the other side of Fleet is a spring on the steep side of the hill. It comes down in a pool and runs away into the lagoon. That's where they got the store. That's where we take on water if we want to. Only, also there is a beach below the pool *outside* the lagoon. Let's pick up water there. Two-three trips and we can fill the tank. That way we got time to look her over and think about it. Ain't-a too far to walk. We can go inside tomorrow."

They all applauded Joe's idea and hurried to hoist the sails again and make headway round the island.

It didn't take Joe long to find the beach that led to the spring and they loaded the dinghy with all the containers they possessed and rowed for the shore. Heaving the boat up the beach, they set off for the trees and began to climb, casks and cans slung about their bodies. But the slope was steeper than Joe remembered and he began to be amazed at himself for suggesting such labour.

"Maybe," he said, mopping the perspiration from his face, "we are now *all* crazy."

Half-blinded with sweat as she plodded upwards, Rosa anxiously watched Willie and Frankie pressing on ahead, their young muscles carrying them beyond the other two as they competed against each other to see who could set the pace, Willie striding out unthinkingly, Frankie determined not to be outdone and thrusting painfully through the bushes he pushed aside with ease, struggling to keep up with him until Rosa and Joe were out of sight behind them.

The spring wasn't far from the beach but the path grew more rocky and eventually Frankie began to stumble.

"Let's rest," she panted. "I can't go no further. I'm going to bust."

"Come on, kid," Willie said, not taking his eyes off the path ahead. "You got no stamina. Not far now. Keep it going. Give us your hand. I'll give you a heave."

With Willie half-dragging her behind him, they stumbled through the thinning undergrowth until he stopped dead. A long way behind, they could hear Rosa and Joe blundering after them and Joe's voice raised in a wail of despair.

"Nearly there," Willie said, still holding Frankie's hand. "I can hear the water now."

He practically dragged her the last few yards upwards until they stood on the brink of the pool together, Frankie drooping against him, laughing hysterically with exhaustion.

"Gawd," she panted. "You go at things like a steam-engine. You oughta take it easy."

He laughed back at her, then their eyes met and Willie became conscious of having his arms round her while she leaned against his chest.

She was staring at him, admiration in her eyes, and his laughter died abruptly as he looked back at her a little breathlessly.

Frankie opened her mouth to speak. "Willie – " she managed at last.

Willie said nothing, as though he hadn't heard her.

"Willie – " Frankie said again " – what you gawking at?" and Willie started abruptly and frowned. Then he pushed her away quickly, almost roughly, and bent to the water so that she could have bitten her tongue off in sheer misery.

"Willie," she whispered. "What's the matter?"

"Nothing, kid, why?" he said sharply. "Come on, we got to hurry."

Frankie knelt alongside him, shyly trying to glance up at him under her eyebrows. But Willie's face was expressionless and discouraging and in the end she gave it up, wondering if she'd been imagining that first warming look of gentleness.

They had finished filling their containers long before the other two had arrived, and Frankie started to arrange hers about her, thinking with dismay of the rocky path downwards.

" 'Strewth," she said slowly, feeling the weight on her shoulders. "I never knew water was so heavy."

Willie looked round, then he slowly put his own containers to the ground again and crossed towards her.

"Here," he said. "Let me have a couple of those."

Frankie looked up at him, her eyes resting on his face.

" 'S'all right, Willie," she said. "I can manage. I'm not complaining."

"I know you're not. But they're too heavy for a girl. I'll carry 'em."

"Honest, Willie, I can do it."

"I'll carry 'em, I said," he reiterated gruffly. "A girl can't go lugging things about like that."

Without a word, Frankie lowered her containers to the floor and Willie felt their weight one after the other, then he took the two heaviest and placed them with his own.

"Willie, honest – "

"I'm trying to help you, aren't I?" he said sharply. "Now dry up."

"Yes, Willie."

Meekly, Frankie hitched the remaining containers about her body, Willie helping to fix the ropes and arranging his shirt over her shoulders so they wouldn't cut the skin, then they sat on the brink of the pool and waited for Rosa and Joe.

They were both still preoccupied with their own thoughts as they up-anchored again, their tank full, and circled the island towards the village inside the lagoon.

The old ship bowed her queenly way into the pass, rolling as the current and the waves threatened to drive her on to the fangs of rock, like an elderly stage star acknowledging cheers, even the surf unable to chivvy her into lack of dignity.

Purposely, they dropped anchor as far as possible from the village and immediately two or three native pirogues set out from the shore and hurried towards them, skimming rapidly across the mirror surface of the water.

"OK," Frankie said nervously, as she watched them approach. "Here we go. Who's going ashore?"

"Willie," Rosa said at once. "He's the smartest. He'll not drop anything out we don't want dropping out. He can keep his mouth shut and spy out the land at the same time. 'Sides, he's got the money and he knows how much we can afford to spend."

"What'll I say?" Willie asked, his eyes on the pirogues. "They're bound to be curious."

"Tell 'em we're trying to get to America. Anything you like. Kid 'em on a bit. Tell 'em we're going all the way. You can think of something. You know where we've been. Go and have a look at the charts before they come, then you'll know what you're talking about."

Willie looked at her, then at Frankie. "You reckon it's best for me to go alone?"

"You scared?" Joe asked quickly.

" 'Course he's not, you old fool," Rosa said. "Go on, Willie. If Joe goes, he'll let the cat outa the bag straight away. When he opens his mouth, he sounds like he oughta to be poling a gondola."

The pirogues were manned by islanders, fair-skinned men with flowers in their hair who, as soon as they came alongside, offered them a lift ashore.

Rosa pushed Willie forward. "Go on," she said as he climbed over the side of the *Boy George*. "Tell 'em the rest of us got work to do. Tell 'em a good story. You can do it fine. If it's OK here, I'll get 'em to take a letter for Lucia."

Willie sat in the stern of the leading pirogue, tense with the responsibility of aiding their disguise by what he had to say, then Frankie waved to him from the high bow of the *Boy George* as they drew away.

"Go it, Willie," she shrieked. "Give it 'em good!"

Willie grinned and waved back, the tenseness in him snapped, and turned his eyes towards the village in the distance.

As they drew closer, he could see a white man waiting on the beach, and Willie began to wonder what he was going to say, what questions he was going to ask, and tried to concentrate on the story forming in his mind as he stared at the terrifyingly brilliant sand that hurt his eyes with its glare as it caught the centre of the sun and flung it dazzlingly upwards.

"Pleased to meetcha!" He could hear the man on the beach shouting in a high cracked voice as they drew closer to the shore. "Pleased to meetcha."

The man was wading out towards them now, grinning all over his face and waving. "Glad to have you here," he was yelling. "George Villiers is always glad of company."

Willie felt better as he heard the old man's name. So Joe had been right, he thought, and perhaps it wouldn't be so difficult after all.

"Saw you off-shore last night," the old man was saying. "Wondered what the hell you were doing. Picked up water, they told me. Why didn't you come inside the lagoon and get it here? Coulda had a meal with me."

Shabby and withered with the heat, his trouser-bottoms soaked, he met Willie as he stepped ashore in front of the store, doing an excited double-shuffle that kicked up the fine sand in little puffs, gambolling round him like an elderly puppy, offering him drinks, hospitality, food, supplies, anything he required, garrulous to the point of embarrassment, until his very effusiveness put Willie on his guard.

"Sorry, can't stop," he said as they crossed the beach. "Got to pick up another passenger in Papeete. Just dropped in for flour and tinned stuff and salt and kerosene."

Old Villiers' face fell with disappointment and his excited shuffle stopped. His eyes stared back at Willie out of a well of loneliness. "Can't stop? But everybody stops here. I always put on a meal. Nobody's in a hurry here. I rely on people for news."

"Sorry!" Willie was adamant, feeling the responsibility for the *Boy George* weighing heavily on his young shoulders. "We're all out for speed."

"What ship are you?"

"*Boy George*. Trying to get from Auckland to Los Angeles." Willie was enjoying the story he had made up and he brought it out with zest, still not too old to have lost the joy of hide and seek. "We just come from Palmerston," he said. "Heading for Tahiti and then the Marquesas before we make the crossing. Two of us aboard, that's all."

"Can't you come round for a sundowner?" Villiers pleaded. "Just for the evening. I can promise good tucker. Bring your friend. Bring anybody. Glad to see 'em. Always glad to see people."

"Sorry. Just come to take on supplies. You got supplies to sell, I suppose."

Villiers nodded eagerly, obviously snatching at anything that might prolong the stay. "Sure. Plenty. Pleased to be of assistance. Take all you want. Anything else? Charts? Courses? Tell you my friends along the way if you'd like to call on 'em. Only got to mention my name. Can't you even come in for a drink?"

As Willie persisted in his refusal, the old man's eyes clouded and he began to sulk. "Don't see many people here," he complained, his voice almost a whine. "I keep looking. I see everything that passes. Haven't seen anything of an old sloop, have you? Name of *Tina S*. Got two Italians and a kid on board. Been told to watch out for her."

Willie hesitated before offering a cautious reply and made a point of keeping his face averted. "Nothin' at all," he said. "We kep' off the trade routes."

Villiers was studying his face intently. "You a film star or something?" he asked unexpectedly.

Willie stared, startled by the question, then he grinned quickly. "Sure. You seen any of my films?"

"Not that I remember. But I must have seen your picture in the magazines I get sent out from Brisbane or something."

"That so?" Willie felt a jab of the old fear and turned his face away as though he were squinting back at the *Boy George*.

"Felt certain I knew you," Villiers went on more cheerfully. "Face's kind of familiar."

He peered across the lagoon to where the *Boy George* lay at anchor. The bowsprit they had rigged gave her a rakish look when she was lying beam-on.

"Fast-looking ship you got there," he said.

"Fast as hell," Willie agreed. "How far away are these people in the *Tina S* supposed to be?"

Villiers shook his head. "Dunno. Somewhere around."

"Who's been asking for 'em?"

"Police. Message came over the radio to look out."

"Where are the police now?"

"Cook Islands. That's where the message came from. Resident Magistrate put it out, I guess. Two-three weeks ago. Can't say for sure. Time's no object here. Tavita Ohoa – he looks after the store for me – he got it on the receiver. He was with the Yanks during the war and he learned radio. Resident

Magistrate makes him an allowance now. Only sending station this end of the George IIIs."

"Think they'll find 'em?"

"They got a good chance. Why don't you stick around and help look for 'em? You can stay here. Good spot." Villiers glanced at Willie, hopelessness in his eyes. "Get things squared up before you move on. Have a good time."

Willie showed no sign of wavering and, as the islanders loaded their canoes with flour and canned goods, Villiers stood on the beach and watched him disconsolately, his thin shoulders hunched despairingly, his fists in his ragged pockets. Then Willie shook his hand.

"Thanks for all the help," he said. "If we make Los Angeles, we'll send you the papers. It'll be in all the papers. We sure got away from here fast, thanks to you."

Villiers watched the native canoes skimming across the lagoon, his heart empty within him. The talk of Los Angeles made him feel miserable. He still had memories of big cities, though they were faint enough now to have only the substance of mirages. He heard the shouts of laughter from the vessel lying out in the lagoon and, wondering what the joke was, unhappily decided they were laughing at him and began to worry again where he'd seen the boy who'd come ashore.

Going to his verandah, he ruffled through the pages of the magazines that reached him in the hope of finding some clue to his identity. But, his mind already vague, he saw no connection between the stilted official descriptions he had received over the radio and the brown-faced healthy young sailor who had bought stores from him, no connection between the uncertain accounts of the matronly *Tina S* with her single mast and wheelhouse and the newer looking boat across the lagoon with her yawl rig and rakish bowsprit.

On board the *Boy George*, Willie was relating his adventure ashore. "Asked me if I was a film star," he said and they all rocked with laughter. "I told him I was and asked him if he'd seen any of my films. Any of my films! He never recognized the *Tina*. Said what a fast-looking ship she was."

"Fast!" Joe slapped his fat thigh. "If he only knew. She waddles across the ocean like a drunken Latvian coming down Bourke Street."

Willie grabbed Frankie's hands and they began to waltz round the foredeck, while Joe began to clap his hands and stamp. "Mama," he said over his shoulder, "it just shows. He don' know who we were. We've done it fine."

Willie's posturing subsided slowly as he saw the trouble on Rosa's brow and Frankie let go his hands. Rosa was staring thoughtfully at nothing, and Joe's clapping and stamping slowed to a stop.

"What is it, Rosie?" he asked. "Don' it show we disguise her good?"

"Sure it does," Rosa said slowly, her voice flat and heavy as she flapped the air with a piece of cardboard for a fan. "But it shows something else as well. It shows they're looking for us. They're not just sitting on their backsides in Sydney waiting. They've come after us."

She looked at the sheet of cheap notepaper in her hand, the beginning of the letter she had hoped to send to Lucia, and screwed it up into a ball and tossed it into the sea.

They all watched it bob lightly away on the tide, all of them conscious of a feeling of deflation as their pride in their disguise was drained away in a sense of anxiety.

Joe stared at Rosa, his dark eyes amazed. "All that way," he said. "Just for a old-a boat and a bad debt."

Willie had turned towards the stores they had bought from Villiers and he poked at a carton of beans with his toe. "Don't you kid yourself," he said slowly. "It's not you they're looking for. It's me."

Joe looked quickly at Rosa and became silent. Frankie's smoky dark eyes grew big and puzzled, her thin face and figure making her look younger than her age.

"We'd best get away from here quickly," Rosa said and their laughter had completely disappeared.

"Get away from here?" Joe's face reddened. "Don' we only just come? Don' we ever going to stay nowhere? Don' we ever just laugh and sit around? Don' we ever get-a no fun? Don' we ever go ashore and have a drink?"

"What you going to buy drink with?" Rosa asked.

Joe looked sheepishly at Willie and began to rub the palms of his hands up and down across the seat of his pants. "I think perhaps – " he paused and licked his lips " – perhaps a small loan. Since we have so much money – "

"The money's for stores," Willie said shortly. "Not booze."

"Ain't no reason not to spend a little of it," Joe wheedled.

"I don't want to."

"Always 'I don't want to'," Joe exploded, flinging his arms upwards. "You come on my boat. You eat-a my food. You use-a my sails. Why 'I don' want to'?"

"Because I say so and it's my money."

"You got proof-a that?"

"It's in my money belt. That's good enough."

"Oh, no, it ain't good enough – " Joe began, but Rosa silenced him with a gesture.

"Look," she said. "While we're arguing the toss, somebody ashore there can be in touch with the police by radio or something. Let's head for Tyburn and turn for the Societies. We can keep to the south of them so we aren't seen."

"OK, Captain Mama." Willie grinned and spoke gaily to break the sudden tension. "You're in charge."

He glanced towards Frankie, and Rosa was quick enough to catch the expression on their faces as their eyes met; and the anxieties she had felt as they had pushed on ahead of her up the slope to the pool the previous day crystallized into an unexpected fear.

"Come on, kid," Willie said. "Let's push on."

"Push on," Joe grumbled, as he shuffled towards the wheel. "Always 'push on'. Christmas ain't-a far away and we don' even get the drop of booze. Just push on. Soon we push on so much we drop-a off the edge of the earth."

Old Villiers watched them leave from a wicker chair on his verandah, shaking his head in exasperation. He was still ruffling through the magazines as he squinted across the water to where the sun caught the sail, making it white against the darker clouds hanging over the islands to the east that showed above the sea in a line of palm tufts and coral fragments.

t w o

It was a week before it suddenly dawned on the old man on Fleet where he had seen Willie before. He had spent seven sleepless nights worrying about it, racking his tangled brain as though he were searching into a junk room, restlessly shifting the rubbish there from side to side in search of a treasure. Then, when he was working in the office at the back of his store, he suddenly dropped his ledgers and dived for the shelf where he kept all the out-of-date newspapers that came to him from Brisbane and, flinging them open and casting them aside one after the other in a rumpled heap, he stopped dead at last, kneeling on the floor, his eyes fixed on a group of pictures on a centre-page spread. Willie's face, blurred to dimness in a pumped-up snapshot, stared back at him from a frame of Rosa and Joe and the old *Tina S.*

Villiers crushed the paper into a ball and, stumbling down the wooden steps, set off running on his spindly legs towards the hut of Tavita Ohoa.

"The police," he was yelling. "Get your set going and contact the police."

Villiers' incoherent message – somewhat garbled – reached Robert Flynn at Papeete. In the *Teura To'oa* he had searched from New Caledonia to the New Hebrides before eventually heading in disgust for Tahiti.

His brain still numb from a new demand for increased charter rates from Captain Seagull, who had not realized just how long his boat was to be required and was in consequence determined to get as much as possible for it while he could, Flynn had been in Papeete some time, contacting the outlying islands by radio and trying to decide his next move, when a motor car called to take him to the Préfecture de Police.

Half an hour later, he hurried out into the sunshine and took a taxi back to the hotel where he had left Voss, heading along the crowded waterfront where everything from a Hong Kong junk to the wealthy yachts that came in from America lay alongside. They were passing the trading schooners, lashed beam to beam in a maze of rigging, bowsprit after bowsprit pointing to the open sea away from the pink-flowered acacias that shaded the sea-wall, when a lorry loaded with food from Australia backed across the road and the taxi came to a stop. In his haste, Flynn paid off the driver and hurried the rest of the way on foot through the American tourists and the French servicemen who whistled at the dark-skinned girls.

He found the journalist among the ramshackle buildings that were hidden with cascades of flaming bougainvillaeas and hedges of hibiscus, sitting in a little café half obscured by oleanders and occupied in gesturing with a fly spray at a half-caste Tahitian waitress.

As he approached, Voss looked up, waved away the girl and ordered drinks for them both.

"We've got some real news at last," Flynn said, dropping into a chair and mopping his face. "I think we've found the Salomios. Some old joker on Fleet in the George IIIs has spotted them."

"The George IIIs!" Voss sat up and put the fly spray on the floor beside him. "God, and we've been searching round New Caledonia! They must have been hundreds of miles away while we were putting up with that lousy hotel where the bugs ate the pattern out of your hat band and that damned man tried to sing like Jean Sablon every other night. How do you know?"

Flynn thought bitterly of all the wasted miles they had covered; of weeks of patient, useless searching; of the airless streets of Noumea where they had listened to the flat Asiatic pipes mingling with the blare of jazz and the Melanesian voices intoning 'I got sixpence' with no knowledge of what it meant; the dusty hotel rooms with faulty fans chattering in the ceilings like nagging women as they stirred the thrice-breathed air; all the islands they had visited, questioning the priests and the native gendarmes who lorded it over the islanders, the schooner captains whose gin they had sipped, and the government officials.

"How do I know?" he said. "They put in for stores there. That's how."

"But the last we heard they were in Vila doing a bit of hard rowing to pick up food! Daughter-in-law Lucia in Sydney got an airmail from Vila."

Flynn looked up, his neat bulk in direct contrast to the other's untidy leanness. "Well, now they're hundreds of miles away," he said. "They've disguised the boat. They've stepped an extra mast."

Voss sat back, staring at the blue half-circle of jagged peaks of Moorea across the bay. "What do we do now then? Send out a new description? Because if they've rigged an extra mast there's nothing to stop 'em taking it down again if they feel like it." He picked up the DDT spray and gave a few experimental squirts at the flies around him which paused only for a moment before returning refreshed to the assault.

Flynn was staring at the table. "I never thought I'd be reduced to this," he said bitterly. "I feel like a hack man on a beat again. You wouldn't think one slow old boat without radio or engine could put it across us with all the equipment we can muster, would you?"

"There's one thing you forgot when you alerted all those police and officials and listening stations," Voss pointed out. "The other side's got brains, too. They're doing a bit of dodging."

"I expect Keeley put 'em up to that." Flynn looked cheated and angry.

Voss waved the DDT spray at a fly. "I wonder if you're meant to club 'em with it?" he mused. He turned to Flynn. "I expect he did," he said. "He's got good reason to. It's getting a bit protracted, isn't it?"

Flynn sat up, recovering his confidence. "Don't worry," he said. "You'll be back in Sydney before long."

"Think so?"

"Someone on the *Tina* will crack. People from big cities can't sail round these islands for ever, never seeing anyone, never talking to people, cooped up on an old boat, dodging civilization all the time. It's just a fact that exists about the islands – just as you know there are sharks at Penrhyn and none at Manihiki. It's something we all dream about but it doesn't work. It might be the old man. It might be Keeley. But someone'll crack sooner or later."

Voss swung round to face him and pointed with the fly spray. "I'll bet it's later rather than sooner. Mama Salomio's a tough old bird. *She* won't crack and she won't let anyone else crack."

Flynn frowned: "I hope to God we get 'em before they reach the Tuamotus," he said. "The islands there look like the Milky Way. They're not on a plane route either so we could write off our arrangement with the airline pilots to keep their eyes skinned. The whole thing becomes more difficult altogether. Besides – " he paused " – the Tuamotus are notoriously dangerous and if they run ashore there – and they *could* with only an atlas and a few throwaways to navigate with – the whole lot of 'em could be lost."

Voss eyed him curiously. "And you wouldn't be satisfied to see friend Keeley quietly drowned?"

"*I* would. But the mother of the kid he murdered would rather see him hanged, I'm sure."

"And the Salomios?"

"I don't want the Salomios drowned in the Tuamotus any more than you do," Flynn said. "But not for the same reason. To you, they're a story. To me, they're assisting Keeley to escape. I want them as much as I want Keeley. Quite apart from the fact that they're dodging their debts, they're breaking the law."

"Do you realize how far they've come, Flynn?" Voss asked quietly. "I was working it out when you arrived."

"I know how far they've come all right," Flynn said shortly, thinking of the money and the time that had been wasted. "It's a hell of a long way!"

"They could become the best-known couple in Australia," Voss said, flipping at his newspaper. "We could get everybody screaming for photographs – even in America, and that's big money. Lucia could sell the family album, if we could persuade her she's got a saleable commodity. We'd have to get an option on all the pictures, of course," he mused. "An appeal fund for them would go down well, too."

"Do you usually run appeal funds for people who don't pay their debts?" Flynn asked sarcastically.

Voss raised his eyebrows. "We do more," he said. "We run polls and reader surveys and we'll probably run one now to decide if the police in their mercy should follow like avenging angels or leave the Salomios alone merely because they've got guts. All the same – " he broke off and glanced at Flynn " – if some adventurous kid had sailed as far as these two old jokers – and in a leaky boat, too, he'd have got his name in the papers, wouldn't he? Why shouldn't they, at their age?"

"Why shouldn't they? It's just a pity they had to take my man along with 'em, that's all."

"Makes a better story," Voss grinned. "You've got to blow 'em up a bit. If they hadn't thought of it, damned if I wouldn't have suggested it. Boy, with this angle, I can get the great reading public *screaming* for its before-breakfast blood-and-thunder in no time. *Demanding* the latest on them. If they keep it up much longer, they'll be as famous as Josh Slocum. Everybody'll take 'em to their hearts."

"Will they take Keeley as well?" Flynn asked dryly.

Voss smiled. "Nobody would care two hoots about Keeley. I'd take good care to make it clear the Salomios don't know who he is. And, if I guess right, so would all the other newspapers."

"You can't be certain they don't know."

"No, I can't. But better men than me have told whoppers. Even Simon Peter fenced a little."

Flynn began to get angry. "In other words, because of this newspaper campaign that's being prepared, I've got to catch Keeley without upsetting the great reading public. You'll make it damn' difficult for me. I'd rather find him without all this damn' nonsense clogging up the issues. You seem to have lost sight of the fact that the Salomios are hiding a murderer who stabbed a harmless if rather stupid kid."

Voss subsided slowly into his chair and Flynn stood up, leaning on the table to point. "The sooner it's finished the better – before the whole of Australia starts to swoon with emotion. We'll get the radio hams on the job. There are plenty of them in the islands. All the schooners carry radios. They use 'em mostly to order their whisky, but for once they can use 'em on behalf of law and order. I'll have every damn' pair of eyes in the islands looking for 'em. They can't go on for ever. Time's on our side."

"Is it?" Voss eyed him through his cigarette smoke. "With Seagull cutting up rough? He knows we can't get anything else with the hurricane season on us. If he picks up any business, he'll leave us flat. He's always fiddling with that blasted pedal wireless in his cabin, talking to his buddies. Time's not on our side. It's on *theirs*. If they get out beyond the Tuamotus they'll make for the Marquesas and if they make the Marquesas, they'll try America. Bless 'em, they'll never do it. But if they do, *if they do*, Flynn – you've had 'em. Murder or no murder. The Yanks'll love 'em. They love the underdog there. If Bonnie Prince Charlie had fled to America instead of France, there'd still have been Stuarts on the throne in the Old Country. You've got to move."

Flynn's smile had grown hard. "I've moved," he said triumphantly. "I did a lot of moving while I was at the Préfecture de Police. The French are going to search the Marquesas, the Societies, the Tubuais and the Gambiers. I've got things churning at last." His voice rose slightly as Voss stared back at him. "They're doing most of it by enlisting the islanders' help. There'll be launches and schooners and native outriggers looking for 'em. There'll be every blasted boat that floats. And I'm going to take the *Teura To'oa* into the Tuamotus and search there myself. I've already contacted the Governor by wireless. I'll drive that old bastard, Seagull, till he drops apart. The Salomios have got to keep going," he concluded, "and, God help 'em, bucking the trade winds all the way as they are, it's going to be tough."

three

Up to the point of leaving Fleet Island, luck had been with the Salomios with no worse incident than when Joe's dubious navigation had been in error and the grease spots that Frankie's boisterous cooking had spilled on the charts had been mistaken for islands. The weather had been kind with sunshine and following winds that didn't strain the old boat, and by sheer luck they had kept out of the way of the authorities. But now, as officialdom got its back up, the weather began to turn against them also.

They ran into a calm with air so dead the clouds were mirrored exactly in the water by day and the stars by night and the horizon disappeared in a misty haze that left them apparently suspended in mid-air over a silent ocean. The sails drooped limply, giving no shade to the sweltering decks, and the pitch rose in slow bubbles between the planks. The drinking water was hot in the tank and, overside, nosed by the foraging sharks, were the empty tins they had thrown away a week before, without a ripple big enough to overturn them, glinting all day in the water until they grew so sick of them they thrust them under with the boathook.

When their nerves were ragged with the rattle of blocks and the sound of empty sails slapping from side to side, a faint doldrum whisper appeared and the canvas filled and the old boat began to move again. But no sooner had the wind arrived than it backed to easterly and they had a run of head winds and squalls which tested the *Boy George* to her limits.

The rain which came with the squalls flattened the great Pacific swells to a calm but soaked them all to the skin for, with her seams opened by weeks of hot sun, the old ship leaked through into their living quarters and even their bedclothes were cold and cheerless. Puddles formed on the floorboards and the air was misty with a dampness that seemed to hang about below-deck like a fog.

The fresh-water tank began to leak and the supply they had taken on at Fleet with so much labour had been halved before they discovered it. The constant rain squalls provided an answer to the problem, however, and they put out on deck all the containers they possessed and rigged big baths out of old sails. But these and the barrels and buckets they had lashed at various points made movement difficult until, eventually, nerves began to get frayed and quarrels came quickly and arguments started, even Rosa and Willie, who had never argued before, disagreeing over their course.

When they halted for the night in the lagoon at Tyburn, another of the George III group, they found they had anchored over a shallow and awoke to find the boat on her beam ends, with all the lockers bursting open and the stove hanging from its moorings. When the morning came, they discovered they had lost one of their precious buckets overboard from the deck.

Two days later, the *Boy George* gybed in a sudden squall so that the mizzen boom whipped round and the little mast Willie had so painstakingly rigged carried away its stays and cracked. They had to put back into Tyburn again and cut and trim another young pine for a new one.

"I knew it would be no good," Joe said delightedly. "Always they are no good."

As they left Tyburn a second time a heavy following sea was running and the *Boy George* groaned aloud as she rode like a surfboard on the foam-crested combers, constantly increasing her speed without warning and swinging to port or starboard as she slid into the deep troughs, while the water came in bucketful's over the stern.

They lowered the mizzen sail which eased the motion a little and the watch that night was dry. The next day the sun was warm again and there was a strong breeze so that they were able to get most of their clothes and bedding on deck. It was while everything was flapping in the breeze like a regatta and they were all feeling happier at the prospect of warmer clothes, that Willie chanced to glance astern and noticed a tremendous roller filling the entire horizon. It was made up of several smaller waves which had run into each other and, as it came sweeping up on them, the *Boy George* dropped further and further into the smooth hissing trough that ran before it.

"Jesus, Mary and Joseph!" Rosa interrupted the Hail Marys she had been saying on their behalf ever since she had first sighted it and whispered a prayer to herself as it roared up on their stern. "Take care of little Tommy."

Frankie was below in the galley and there was no time to get to her, and only Joe was calm, one hand on the wheel, one eye on the vast following wall of water, correcting the *Boy George* as she tried to slide off to port. Before any of them expected it, the whole tremendous weight of the sea collapsed on the decks, the solid green crashing across the planks with the fury of an avalanche.

Rosa heard Willie's shout – "Frankie!" – then, coming to the surface through the boiling spray, she saw Joe, only his head and shoulders visible, still struggling with the wheel, the only one of them who knew what to do, while Willie clung to the stays forward, fighting the drag of the water that raced across the decks and ahead of them in a yeasty smother.

Fortunately, it was over in a moment and the waves behind appeared to be normal enough, and with the water sloshing round his ankles, Willie leapt to the cabin hatch. Dropping below, hardly touching the ladder in his hurry, he found Frankie sitting on the floor with the dishes and the remains of the food across her legs, spluttering and dazedly pushing the hair out of her face.

"You all right, Frankie?" he asked, lifting her to her feet. "You hurt, kid?"

She gazed at him dizzily for a moment, then a smile that transformed her thin features spread across her face and her eyes lit up.

"Willie, you came to fish me out?"

On deck, as the water streamed noisily out through the scuppers, Rosa wrung the water from her clothes, then her eyes fell on the spot where their strings of washing had been, and with a wail she scrambled to her feet.

All but three of their precious blankets had been swept away, together with most of their spare clothing and all the containers which had been on deck. The mainsail had a split down half its length and what remained of their bedding huddled in sodden bundles like small dead bodies in the scuppers.

"The blankets," she shrieked. "The blankets! See if you can find the blankets!"

"Never mind the blankets," Joe roared. "Get-a the sail down before she tear to ribbons."

Rosa hurried to the halyards and sent the sail rattling to the deck, while Joe whirled the *Boy George* about on her course.

They found one blanket still afloat half under the water and an old coat of Rosa's, but all the rest of their belongings had disappeared.

They were in low spirits as they turned towards Tyburn Island for the third time. The disaster which had come on them from nowhere seemed twice as crushing, following as it did on all their good luck.

Joe was the first to voice his thoughts. The soaking they had received made him think back across the thousands of miles to Sydney with its sun-soaked slopes and the alleys of Surry Hills with their leaning tenement houses, the rattling corrugated iron fences and the homely smell of ham-and-beef shops. He suddenly realized just how far from home he was, how far from the cronies who gave him comfort when Rosa pressed him too hard, and he felt like bursting into tears. Surry Hills wore a cosy glow just then, for distance lent enchantment, and Joe remembered only the warmth and the familiarity.

"I want to go home," he said. "I got fed up."

Rosa looked at him, her face hardening. "Home?" she said, a warning immediately in her tones.

"Don't we all have enough?" Joe demanded bitterly. "What am I? Christopher Columbus? Captain Cook? I belong in Sydney. I don' like being here."

"Just because you're wet. Just because we've had a bit of trouble." Rosa's voice was getting thinner and lower.

"A bit of trouble!" Joe's hands started to flap. "A bit of trouble, she say. We lose the mainsail – " He described a parabola with his arm to indicate the wave and made the sound of tearing with his tongue.

"We can mend it," Rosa snapped.

" – we lose all our clothes." Joe threw imaginary coats and skirts into the sea as his excitement grew. "We lose our blankets. We don't got no water – " he stopped dead as water made him think of drink and he realized on the instant just how much he had missed his daily ration of beer, the sneaked schooners and demis he scraped together that Rosa never knew about, the Saturday sousing he liked to indulge in and the Sunday lie-ins when he slept it off.

"We ain't got nothing left," he wailed. "We ain't got nothing!"

"Shut your mouth, you old fool," Rosa stormed, her eyes flashing. "We can mend the sail. We can manage without clothes. We can manage without blankets. We can collect water in something else. We can ration it."

She turned to Willie. "What do *you* say?" she asked fiercely. "We *can* manage, can't we?"

Willie looked up from the floor where he was collecting broken crockery with Frankie. "Sure, we can," he said calmly, sitting back on his heels. "So long as we go careful."

"Ha!" Joe seized on the point. "Now we start getting to go careful. And already I ain't-a touched a drop of booze since we left Sydney."

"Booze," Rosa snapped. "That's all you ever think about – getting drunk on other people's charity! You've got no backbone."

Joe shrugged. "I don' need no backbone," he said. "Just a strong stomach."

Rosa glared at him, tears coming to her eyes, and Willie got to his feet quickly and laid a hand on her shoulder.

"Cheer up, Mama," he said. "We'll manage. We got to manage."

"I'm thinking of the stores," Rosa said. "We can't afford to hang about."

Willie shrugged. "We still got some money," he said. "Even if we hadn't we shouldn't starve. There's food everywhere on the islands."

Rosa's face went red. "There's one thing that's for sure," she said. "We're not going back." She looked at Willie. "If we go back, the cops'll get you, won't they?"

"Yep," Willie said very quietly, and Frankie's eyes became bright and scared-looking. "I reckon they will."

"Was it bad what you did?"

Willie's eyes were on the deck. "Yes. It was a bit," he said.

"You pinch something, Willie?" Frankie asked timidly.

"No. Not exactly."

"You hurt somebody?"

"That's it, kid."

"Bad, Willie? Real bad?"

Willie nodded. "Sort of."

Frankie didn't pursue the subject any further. She had experienced enough of life in the dock areas to know when not to enquire too deeply.

Rosa also had her suspicions but she thrust them hurriedly out of her mind.

"Don't worry," she urged him, colouring a little. "They won't get you."

"Thanks, Mama," Willie said.

Joe stood up again, red-faced with jealousy. "So that's the reason." He thrust out a fat dramatic hand. "*He* got-a more importance than me, eh?"

"Yes," Rosa snapped. "Him and the boat and Frankie. All I've done all my life with you is pull you out of bars and borrow money to take the place of what you've spent. *You* ain't the reason. Make no mistake."

She was suddenly hard and unforgiving, as they had not seen her before – without the spark of pity for her husband that always redeemed her quick temper.

"Take it easy, Mama," Frankie said uneasily, and Joe put out a hand in a calming gesture.

"Now, Rosie," he began hesitantly.

"You can shut up," Rosa continued. "And you needn't paw me. If you aren't man enough to stick it, we'll leave you behind and I'll be glad to see you go."

Joe sat down abruptly.

"Right!" Rosa got control of herself again. She stood up and looked around her, shuffling her feet in her old slippers. "We better get on with sorting things out a bit."

While they lay in the deserted lagoon, Rosa sat down to repair the worn and fraying sail, patching the huge rent with scraps of canvas she unearthed from the boat's lockers, a wearying job that required all her courage to persist with it, for she knew well that it would inevitably split again because the canvas was old and rotten. Eventually, it would have to be replaced and they had no means of replacing it, but she preferred not to think of that as she laboured with palm and sail needle and twine and resin. They could face that problem when they came to it.

The sodden blankets and clothing were strung about the shrouds to dry while Joe, grumbling and making awesome prophecies of disaster, went out with the dinghy fishing and Willie and Frankie went ashore with the bow and arrows he had fashioned at Aranga-vaa, one of them carrying a sack, the other the razor-sharp knife. Always they returned with food of some sort and as she found they were not drawing on their meagre stores, Rosa's spirits rose a little. Coconuts and bananas and fish, with the occasional eggs Frankie found or the birds Willie caught, kept their diet reasonably varied; and their water supply improved so much with the containers Joe made out of coconuts that hung like a bunch of grapes from the mast that Rosa felt a flooding of affection for them all.

"Christmas, day after tomorrow," she announced. "I reckon we ought to celebrate."

The next morning, while Frankie emptied the ship of every scrap of paper they possessed and cut it into paper chains stuck together with a paste of flour and water, Joe secretly went ashore and found a little pine tree, which he raised in the end of the cabin.

"Ain't-a nothing to hang on it," he apologized to Rosa, his dark eyes large and humble. "But I reckon it help to make it seem more like Christmas."

"Joe," Rosa said, overcome by love and the desire to mother him. "Joe, it's beautiful!" She paused and went on quietly. "Joe, old dear. Don't let's fight. It's my fault, I know, always goin' on. Only it's tough and if I give up we all give up. That's why I keep picking on you!"

"That's all right, Rosie." Joe gave her a peck on the cheek. "I know what it's all about. If I didn't get so tired, mebbe I'd never open-a the trap, anyway."

While they were talking, they heard Willie's shout from the beach, and when Frankie went to fetch him with the dinghy they found he had killed a wild chicken, probably the last remnant of a vanished habitation.

"It's a bit skinny, Mama," he said with a grin as he held it up for her in the cabin. "But if we spit out the bones and the gristle, she'll do for dinner."

Rosa stared from one to the other of them, then her gaze wandered over Frankie's paper trimmings and Willie's chicken and finally rested on Joe's tree. There were tears in her eyes as she turned to face them again.

"You are all so good," she mumbled. "Something from each of you. Now, it begins to feel like Christmas."

That night, caught by a mood of nostalgia, they sang carols on the foredeck and tried not to think of busy streets and brightly lit shops when all they could see was the empty lagoon and the silent ridge of palm-tufted land.

The following day, to go with the trimmings and the chicken and the tree, Rosa fished in the bilges where they kept their spare canned food and found a tin of peaches. Frankie was frantically trying to make something of her hair, struggling with comb and scissors and water in front of the spotted mirror.

"Mama – " she turned frantically to where Rosa crouched, scarlet-faced and sweating, over the oven in the galley " – where's me frock?"

"Search me," Rosa said.

"Whyn't I ever wear a frock?" Frankie demanded angrily. "I never wear a frock."

"Far as I know, you've not got one," Rosa said, straightening up and grinning at her. "Last time I tried to make you wear one, you bit me. I've never tried since."

Christmas dinner was a riotous affair, for Rosa produced a bottle of home-made wine she had been storing under the bed for months, and they all tried to pretend they were tipsy on it.

"One more bottle like that, Mama," Joe said gaily, "and I ain't-a responsible for me actions."

He leaned over and kissed her heartily full on the mouth and Frankie, scrubbed to the point of shining, stared hopefully at Willie. But he was laughing at Rosa's blushes and didn't appear to notice.

During the afternoon, Rosa and Joe fell asleep and Willie and Frankie swam over the side, one of them always on deck watching for sharks. In the evening, after a meal at which Rosa allowed extra sugar and produced a cake she had made, a very plain cake devoid of icing but a cake nevertheless, Willie followed Frankie on deck and sat beside her on the stern.

"I've been saving my bit of Christmas till now, Frankie," he said quietly.

Frankie turned to him, puzzled, and he fished in his pocket.

"It's your birthday soon," he went on. "Mama told me. In January."

"That's right. I'll be seventeen."

"Well, I've made you a Christmas present and a birthday present all in one."

Frankie was trembling as he held out his hand, and with fingers that suddenly seemed clumsy she took from him a tiny wooden cross he had carved.

"It's only got sail twine to put it round your neck," Willie apologized. "But I plaited it nicely so it'll look better. It ain't worth much but I spent a long time on it."

Frankie found it difficult to speak at first. "Oh, Willie, it's beautiful. I'll treasure it always." Her eyes were bright with moisture as she looked at him.

"I've been saving my Christmas kiss till now, too," he said. "Pity we've got no party decorations to make it nicer."

He spoke casually but his voice was a little unsteady.

"Put it on, Willie." Frankie held out the cross and bent her head. As she straightened up again, Willie kissed her on the lips.

There was no passion in the gesture, just gentleness and affection, but Frankie sat back, satisfied, her heart full.

"I reckon this is the nicest Christmas I've ever spent," she said.

They lay in Tyburn several more days, unable to venture out because of a wind that raised the combers on the reef to huge proportions and made the opening into the lagoon impassable, and every evening after dark, after pumping the bilges, Willie took one of the lamps into the engine room and continued to tinker with the engine.

"Haven't we nearly finished fiddling with this old thing?" Frankie asked.

"Nearly," Willie told her. "One day, kid, I'm going to get a job fixing engines. I got a way with 'em, I reckon, and I could make money and perhaps open a garage – or a boatyard."

Frankie's eyes searched his face, taking in every contour, proud of his skill yet vaguely jealous of an old inanimate engine that could so hold his interest, while she was granted only spasmodic attention.

"You'd like a steady job, Willie?" she asked.

"Sure I would," Willie said fervently, then he put down his spanner and stared at his hands, startled at the enthusiasm in his tones. "Yeh, sure I would," he said again, more firmly, as he picked up the spanner once more and went on working.

"Settle down and all that?"

"I guess so."

"Maybe get married – " Willie looked up as she tried to edge him back to that exquisite moment on Christmas night " – in time, I mean," she added hastily.

"Maybe," Willie said. "Why?"

"Oh, nothing!" Frankie pushed her hurrying thoughts to the back of her mind and concentrated on looking absorbed. "I just wondered."

"But that'll be a long time yet," Willie said. "If I got a garage or a boatyard I'd have to work hard to make it go, wouldn't I? A man's got to work to make his mark in the world."

"Yes, sure he has, Willie," she agreed earnestly. "If I was you, I'd get down to it and never let up till I'd fixed myself a place. *Then* I'd maybe look round for a girl."

Willie stared at her, a half-smile on his lips, and she gazed back at him, her black eyes wide and innocent. "Yes," he said. "I reckon that's what I'll do. That's a good idea, kid. But first of all I got to fix this engine. I want to surprise your Ma."

They had already decided to leave Tyburn the following morning and Joe was lying on his back in the cabin, thinking of all the bars in Bourke Street and trying to imagine them one after the other all the way from the waterfront and all the cronies he was likely to meet in them. He liked people and crowds and happiness, and the loneliness of his present existence, with no one about them but the few island fishermen who came into the lagoon to watch their nets or make fish traps, only served to make him feel more solitary.

Rosa was sewing her old coat with sail twine, for she had long since run out of cotton. It made a poor job and she realized just how shabby the garment was becoming. Her mind began to dwell on clothes and the shops in Sydney, and her thoughts travelled across the years to when she was taking Georgie for his first grown-up suit – in the days before Joe grew too fat and lazy and they still had money to enjoy.

Then she began to think of the lonely Christmas they had just spent and began to compare it with the boisterous parties they had once had, surrounded by dozens of dark-eyed noisy relatives. Then she smelt the incense at the church and heard Father Gilhooley's grating voice again and saw the brass candlesticks and the candle flames glittering like stars. And the Young Men's Association and the Children of Mary fighting with each other at the Corpus Christi festival, bass against falsetto, for possession of the hymns, and Georgie in starched white and lace winking at her from his place as an altar boy, unimpressed by the solemnity of the occasion so that she was at first shocked and then warmed by his gaiety. Then she saw him as a young man making eyes at Lucia across the church when he should have been paying attention to the responses, and finally in the dark blue of his naval uniform, grave and gay together, as he told her he was leaving. And all the time, as she thought of him, his face kept fading and she kept seeing Willie's instead, just as irrepressible, just as grave, just as angry and sulking when he couldn't have his own way.

She was still struggling in her mind to separate the two, to push away the image of Willie, blond and big and handsome, that she kept seeing in place of the slight dark Italian boy who was her son, when the *Boy George* seemed to jerk once, twice, and again, and she relaxed that the deep-throated coughing noise she could hear came from the engine.

Joe was sitting up on the bed now, staring at her, his eyes big and round, the flat grey hair that had once been black and kinky standing up straight round his bald patch like a halo.

"Mama," he said. "The engine. It goes."

With his finger he executed the wavering circle of a turning wheel, then they both dashed for the ladder and heaved themselves up on deck to see the little round puffs of exhaust smoke exploding through the stern, where Willie had led the pipe when he had removed the smoke stack from the deck.

They found him in the engine room, a grin on his face, his arms black with grease to the elbows. Frankie, half-obscured at the other side of the engine, grinned over the top at them, a smear of oil across her face.

"Mama!" she shrieked as she saw Rosa appear. "We got it going. Willie fixed it after all."

Rosa stood with her hands on her hips, smiling, while Joe skipped up and down, staring at the engine, his mercurial temperament lifted by this new success.

"You cure-a the leak?" he asked gaily and Willie nodded.

"And the water pump? You make her work too?"

"Sure. Ten years' growth in it for one thing and the valve washer all worn out. I made a new one."

"What with?"

"An old shoe sole, Pop," Frankie said. "I found it for Willie in my locker."

"Is that all that was wrong with it?" Rosa was staring angrily at her husband, suspecting him immediately of laziness.

"Hell, no, Mama! Lots more than that. The whole thing's had it really, but I made it cough a bit. Won't last for ever but she goes."

Rosa looked at him for a moment, then her face fell and she switched off the engine. The sound died with a few despairing coughs and they were in silence again.

"It's gone!" Joe's head appeared from under the engine, "It's no good again."

"I switched it off," Rosa said flatly.

"Aw, Mama, why?" Frankie demanded. "It'll probably take us hours to start it again."

Willie said nothing, but on his face was a look of frustration and hurt.

"It uses fuel," Rosa explained, her face blank and determined as she faced the disappointment. "We haven't got any money to buy any more. Save it till we need it."

Willie shrugged and Joe watched them, still on his knees, as they argued. "OK, Mama," Willie said. "But let me get it going properly first."

"It'll help when there's no wind," Frankie pointed out. "I got sick of hauling her round in the dinghy to find a breeze last time."

"Makes it safer going through the reefs," Willie went on.

"It uses fuel." Rosa's gentle face was hard as it always was when she argued with Willie – as though she had to keep a tight hold on her emotions in case they ran away with her and made her give ground. "It uses plenty."

"I brought a drum aboard. I told you I did."

"If you use it all up, it won't be there if we ever want it urgently."

"Won't be much good if it is there, if the engine won't start, Mama," Frankie said.

Rosa thought about it, then she nodded and Joe began to beam again. "OK," she agreed. "You get it going. Then you stop it till we need it."

"I'll have to keep starting it, Mama." Willie picked up the spanners and began to put them away. "Now and then. Just for a bit from time to time. To make sure she's working. But I'll tell you what – while I'm at it, I'll charge the batteries of that old radio you got down there. They're all right. Only want hotting up. Then you'll be able to hear the news and listen to a bit of music. There's a dynamo – if it works – and I oughta be able to fix up something."

Frankie's eyes lit up. "Oh, boy, boogie woogie!"

"I can do without music," Rosa said, feeling that any additional comfort was something they ought to do without under their straitened circumstances.

"Mama, music'll do us good," Frankie pleaded.

"I'll only run the engine while I'm tinkering with it," Willie promised. "It'll be enough to hot up your batteries again."

Rosa thought about the weak sound they got from the ancient radio and decided that a little music might give the boat some semblance of home. "OK," she said finally. "Just a bit then. It'll be nice to hear the news."

As Frankie hooted her delight, Rosa realized she was thinking of Surry Hills again, and Lucia and Tommy, and she pushed the thought briskly out of her head.

"We got to get away from here," she said. "The wind's dropped."

"It won't stay dropped, Mama." Joe was thinking of how the work increased when they left the shelter of the land. "I watch the clouds. The air is full of cock-a-tails."

"All the more reason to go while we can," Rosa said. "I've seen canoes in the lagoon. They might have told somebody. We got to go. We've been here long enough."

four

The bad weather which had started while the *Boy George* lay in the lagoon at Tyburn, although it caused them considerable discomfort from damp and cold, saved them from being caught in the growing net that Flynn had thrown out from Papeete.

The wind that sprang up almost as they slipped through the reef prevented the island fishermen from making their way to Fleet where Tavita Ohoa's transmitter could sound a warning and, by the time they could safely travel, the *Boy George* had made her getaway to the north-east and to the south of Tahiti. There, she narrowly avoided a copra schooner taking her time from the neighbouring islands to Papeete and bustled before the wind like a hurrying old hen over the horizon just in time.

It was at this point that the wind changed again and for a week as it became worse they buffeted head-on into it, through the Tubuais, struggling to make headway north-east. Then the wind grew stronger from the north and the fat old ship just wouldn't hold her course and they had to run before it under a rag of jibsail.

Through two days and nights, they ran south-east, with no certain knowledge of where they were. Only luck kept them from running foul of the reefs that sprinkled the sea, for always they managed to see or hear the surf and claw off before they struck. There was nothing they could do to make the unhandy *Boy George* pull up into wind and, unable to help themselves, they fell asleep in their exhaustion, still driving south-west along the fringe of atolls, while Flynn in Papeete cursed his infuriating luck.

When the wind had dropped sufficiently for them to turn east again, they found themselves off a large palm-fringed atoll with a mile-long lagoon the colour of a kingfisher's wing, where immediately two or three native pirogues came out to meet them.

In a conversation conducted in pidgin English, they managed to discover that the island was on the southern and western edge of the Tuamotus, so they said they were the schooner *Tiapi* bound for Pitcairn and shooed the islanders away with gifts of rice and an old frock of Rosa's.

Willie watched them go, staring after them at the wide white beaches beyond them shimmering in the sun.

"We ought to stock up on food while we're here," he suggested. "Might not get another chance and we shifted a bit at Christmas. She's nice and lonely here and we ought to try ashore for eggs and things." He looked round at Joe. "Howja catch turtles, Joe?"

"You going to catch turtles?" Frankie stared at him in amazement. There seemed to be no end to his imagination and inventiveness.

Willie looked down at her. "Sure. Why not?" he said. "We can eat 'em, can't we?"

"We can eat-a them," Joe agreed. "But what you think you are? A turtle he is pretty strong. He is fast like a racehorse. It is hard for the islanders to catch 'em. You think you are cleverer than the islanders?"

"No." Willie was unperturbed by Joe's baiting. "But we might catch a little one. I'll have a go. If I don't do it the first time, I'll try again. We've got plenty of time."

For three days, his skin glistening with salt from his repeated duckings, he waited off the beach with the dinghy, with Frankie to act as driver, trying hopelessly to chase the turtles they found in the water up the flat and shining beach. They ran splashing through the shallows, yelling with laughter, till they were both drenched and breathless, and had to sit down to recover from their exhaustion. Then, in the end, with Joe's instructions still in their ears " – keep him away from the deep water. Don't let him swim – " they were lucky enough to corner a small female and chivvy her up the beach away from the sea until she was in water too shallow to escape. With Joe's shouts coming like a distant echo across the wide beach to them, they flung themselves together on top of her, splashing in a fury of movement in the water so that the bright drops rose in rainbow fans against the sun, struggling until they had her on her back, her flippers flapping helplessly. Still holding tight to their catch, they laughed until they were tired, sprawling and entangled in the water.

Finally, Willie lifted his head off his arms, still grinning, and saw Frankie's face close to his, its brown skin dewed with splashes of salt water, her hair over her forehead.

Abruptly, he leaned forward and putting his hands on her shoulders, pulled her closer and kissed her hard. She looked startled – this was no Christmas kiss – then she brought round her arm in an instinctive resounding clout that came all the way from the wharfside at Woolloomooloo and the days when she had had to keep the friendly drunks at bay. Willie rolled over in the shallow water, his ears ringing, and sat there, the wavelets lapping at his feet.

For a moment, Frankie stared at him angrily, then she scrambled to her knees at his side, panic-stricken at what she had done and terrified of the consequences.

"Gee, Willie, I'm sorry! Did it hurt? Honest, I'm sorry. Only it scared me for a moment. Those old bums back home used to try that. You didn't kiss me like that last time." A look of wonder was crossing her face now. "Willie," she said. "You kissed me properly!"

He slowly rose to his feet, brushing the water off himself. "Sure thing," he said. "Why not?"

He looked at her a moment as she knelt on the sand, her clothes plastered to the contours and curves of her thin young frame, then he hoisted her to her feet and kissed her again, a long kiss to which she responded wholeheartedly, her whole impulsive being flowing out towards him.

"Willie," she whispered joyously, flinging her arms round his neck.

But the warmth suddenly went from him and, unexpectedly, he pushed her away and bent over the feebly flapping turtle.

"Willie, what's the matter?" Her voice was flat with disappointment.

"Nothing," he said, frowning, his eyes angry and preoccupied.

As he knelt down, she knelt beside him, indifferent to her saturated clothes, trying fumblingly to help, still breathless and apologetic and scared of him all at the same time. "Gee, Willie, was it because I donged you? I wouldn't have if I'd thought – truly, I wouldn't – only – well, I've never been kissed that way before – not to *mean* anything."

Willie looked round at her, his eyes puzzled, then he bent to work again.

"That wasn't a kiss," he said gruffly, his eyes on the turtle as he tied its flippers. "You ought to see me give a real one."

"Yes, Willie. I bet that'd be nice. All the same – " she stared in front of her unseeingly " – that was real enough for me."

"Gah!" Willie was busy knotting the cord now. "I didn't mean it."

Frankie stared back at him, her expression changing. Her young heart, untutored in adult emotions, shrivelled inside her at his words and her mind suddenly blackened at his treachery.

Willie saw the look on her face. "Here," he said quickly. "Don't stare at me like that. What's got into you, kid?" he asked brusquely.

"Nothing, Willie." She moved nearer to him and knelt by the turtle, still helping but without enthusiasm now.

"You don't want to go falling for me," Willie went on. "You want to pick a nice bloke."

Frankie's anger was subsiding a little. "*You're* nice, Willie," she said. "You never laugh at me like the others always did. You've always been kind to me – helping me and playing tricks and things."

"I didn't mean that," he said irritably. "I meant someone who'll work hard and look after you."

"You work hard, Willie. You're always working. You look after me. You always lift heavy things for me."

Willie shook his head, as though he were trying to clear his brain of confusing thoughts. "Frankie – " he tied the last knot and they started to drag the turtle up the beach towards the dinghy " – I mean a nice young bloke who works in an office and wears a collar and tie. Some bloke who'll stand you to the pictures and buy you things. Chocolates and so on."

"Wouldn't *you*, Willie? I mean, if we had any money to spare and you could buy chocolates here."

"Aw, hell – " Willie had a driven look on his face. " – Frankie – "

"Soon I'll be old, Willie. We aren't young for long." There was despair in her tones, the despair of the inexperienced at the thought of age. His indecisive answers frightened her and she saw herself too old for love before she had enjoyed it. "What's the matter, Willie? Is it something I said?"

"Frankie – look – " Willie seemed desperate " – I like you. I like you more than any girl I've ever met. But, listen, you're only a kid. And I'm no good for you. I'm not the right kind."

"Willie!" Frankie's large eyes were fixed on his face. "A girl doesn't think of things like that. I don't, anyway. And you did kiss me, Willie."

"A kiss is nothing. I told you, I didn't mean it."

Willie turned brusquely away from her. "Listen, Frankie," he said over his shoulder. "I shouldn't have done it. Just get it out of your head. There's no good can come of it. Wait till you get home and then look for some honest bloke who'll be good for you."

"Aren't you honest, Willie?"

"No!" Willie's head was flung back and the word was torn out of him. "You know I'm not. I'm rotten. Now shut up."

The following morning, they hoisted their anchor and let the breeze blow their bow round towards the entrance to the lagoon.

Frankie was watching Willie as he let the anchor cable clatter to the deck. Her face was sulky and there was a frustrated look in her eyes.

"From now on we gotta to stand watch all-a time," Joe announced, blissfully unaware of her expression, as he moved aft towards the wheel. "That ole barometer she swing about like a monkey-up-a-stick. We get too damn' near the hurricane season."

Willie turned to the sail and caught Frankie's look, young, rebellious and uncertain.

What he had said to her on the beach had come from his heart but, as he saw her thin face, doubtful and unhappy, he hadn't the will to stand by it.

He glanced towards the stern and saw Joe was out of earshot. Rosa was below, crouched over the stove.

"On your feet, kid," he said quietly. "Work to do. And don't scowl like that. You've got a nice little dial when it's

139

not looking like you want to kill somebody. I didn't mean it, what I said on the beach. Honest, I didn't."

"But you meant it when you kissed me, didn't you?" Frankie hissed back. "You can't kid me. A girl can tell."

"Yeah," Willie said as he took hold of one of the yards. "I meant it. Only don't start getting serious. You're too young to get serious."

Her face lit up, once more full of hope, her black eyes larger and darker, her face suddenly more mature, and she scrambled to her feet and took hold of the rope with him. Willie smiled at her and, without saying anything, put his hand over hers as they pulled.

As they began to trudge north again in the deteriorating weather, they found the rain squalls had their compensations in that they were able to maintain their water supply and even managed to bathe in the downpours, lathering themselves all over in the rain, with Joe and Willie pushing the coarse soap under the width of the sail to Frankie and to Rosa who squatted half-naked and burning-faced with embarrassment on the other side.

The days went by with no sign of pursuit and, as the feeling of being harried died a little, they began to feel better again, varying their diet with turtle and occasional tinned food, and even able to put up with damp clothes and the absence of comfort in the straining old boat.

Frankie was sustained through the hardship by the warm glow that ran through her every time she thought of Willie. Nothing was suddenly too much trouble for her and she performed the most menial tasks happily, her shrill whistle cheering them all, her eyes bright, her thin face alive with happiness. Even Joe was affected by her ecstatic behaviour.

It was while Willie was on watch on deck, inevitably with Frankie listening to him talk, that Joe heard an unexpected broadcast from Papeete that for the first time gave him some idea of the odds they were now facing.

It came from Radio Tahiti, in French, and made no reference to Willie, but only to Joe and Rosa and Frankie and their ship.

Joe listened to the dispassionate voice coming from their newly envigoured set, describing their voyage from Sydney to the Barrier Reef and beyond, detailing the points where it was known they had been seen – Efaté, Noumea, Fleet Island and Tyburn. One eye on Rosa, to whom French was a meaningless babble, he listened carefully to the announcement, his rusty border patois good enough to make out the meaning. He had heard the first words without realizing what they were about, but he sat up so sharply as he caught his own name that Rosa put down the coat she was sewing and started to ask questions.

Joe fiercely signed her to silence. "Mama," he pointed out. "He talks about us."

Rosa stared at him disbelievingly.

"Mama," Joe said angrily. "Don't I understand French? Don't I talk with Mama Piaf back home?"

Rosa still stared, still not quite believing, and Joe began to translate hesitantly. Rosa sat up and even Joe – fat, lazy, home-loving Joe – began to feel a twinge of pride as he heard the distances they had travelled.

"Mama," he said. "Perhaps we are cleverer than we think."

Then the announcer went on to describe the growing search. The crews of American vessels and even aeroplanes were keeping their eyes open round Pago Pago in American Samoa; the French – as Flynn had described to Voss – were hunting through the Marquesas, the Societies, the Tubuais and the Gambiers; and the British through the Ellice, Gilbert and Tongan groups. Australian and New Zealand ships were also helping and even the Dutch authorities had been persuaded to assist in case the *Boy George* had doubled back towards the Coral Sea. No mention was made of Flynn's personal search among the Tuamotus to the north of them.

As they listened to the growing array of the opposition, Joe's face lost its first rosy look of pride and grew longer and gloomier as he translated for Rosa, who said nothing, sinking back in her seat, her face expressionless, silently rubbing at a bunion at the side of her foot.

As the announcer went on to the next of his news, Joe stood up.

"Mama," he shouted. "They hunt us like the jack-a-rabbit. French, Americans, English, Dutch, New Zealanders. Even Australians. Why don' we go home?"

"Because, you old fool," Rosa said slowly, "we'd lose the boat and Tommy would get nothing and you'd end up in gaol. That's why."

She looked up through the hatchway to the stars that whirled round the truck of the mast, and stared at the black square of the sail that carried them through the night, then she put her hand on the ladder and heaved herself up.

Willie was sitting by the lashed wheel. He had his back against the mizzen mast and was busy with his own thoughts. He could feel Frankie's thin shoulder against his, and occasionally her hair, hacked enthusiastically short for Christmas, brushed his cheek.

He glanced down at her, trying to analyse his emotions. In spite of their difficulties he was happy. He was accepting a challenge for the first time in his life and his existence among the alleys of King's Cross and Surry Hills was far enough behind him to be only a blur. He had seen thousands of miles of the greatest ocean in the world. He had seen islands like jewels set round the glossy mirrors of lagoons where the coral shone in blacks and blues and reds and jades. He had seen the biggest fish and the biggest birds, and had pitted his strength and courage against the weather.

Occasionally he thought of home but, unlike Joe, never with regret. Occasionally, too, he thought of the fracas which had caused him to be aboard the *Boy George* sharing his life with three Italians whom he had once regarded simply as Wops and not as human beings, but when he did he thrust it hurriedly from his mind until, with the passage of time, he had almost convinced himself it had never occurred. Almost, but not quite, for Joe was given to probing and even Frankie's adoring curiosity kept raking it back into the daylight.

He frowned. The complication of Frankie was something that had never occurred to him when he had put forward his plan to disguise the *Tina*. Now, the very thought of living out his life in this fugitive abnormality seemed to be out of the question. But he had undertaken the venture for Rosa and he could think of no good reason for abandoning it. From being allies only out of necessity, he and Rosa worked together now because they needed each other, because they drew strength from each other's plight and sustenance from each other's encouragement.

He was jolted from his thoughts as he heard a footstep on the deck. Quickly, he jerked the dozing Frankie to life and began to talk in a loud voice about nothing at all. But Rosa had seen them clearly against the night sky starting guiltily apart.

She lowered her heavy body to the deck beside them with a wince. They smiled at her, but her first words brought fear to Frankie's eyes and removed Willie's grin as they drew back the thoughts he tried so hard to avoid.

"They're after us, Willie," she said. "They got everything but the Navy out." She spoke slowly, oppressed again by the feeling of being harried, chivvied from island to island with their meagre shelter and meagre sources of food, and she saw Frankie's hand creep into Willie's.

Joe looked accusingly at them. "That bloke been on the radio," he said. "I wish you'd never mended it."

"What happened?" Frankie asked. "What did they say?"

Rosa told them, leaving out nothing.

"Only place they aren't," she said, "is here."

"We got trouble," Joe chipped in gloomily. "We certainly got trouble. And all-a time the weather don't get no better. I get scared to look at that old barometer."

Rosa spoke thoughtfully. "Why couldn't we go to America?" she asked, her mind already seeking new routes of escape. "They'd leave us alone there. We could all start afresh."

"Ain't no good, Mama," Joe said. "These sails won't stand up to a trip like that. We're bucking the trades all-a way. Besides, we have to stop in at the Marquesas for water – and they're searching the Marquesas. He say so."

Willie sat still, his back against the quivering mast, feeling the life of the boat as she pushed her blunt nose through the water. "Well," he said slowly, "if they're every place else but here, the best thing for us to do is stay where we are."

"Ain't much around-a here to keep us alive," Joe observed gloomily and, as though to give weight to his words, his bulging stomach uttered an arpeggio of discontent.

"Where there's plenty to keep us alive, there'll be plenty of people," Frankie pointed out.

"That's true enough," Willie agreed.

"You afraid of people, Christopher Columbus?" Joe asked with heavy sarcasm.

"You don't think they'd organize a search like this," Willie said without turning his head, "just for an old tub and a couple of old people who owe a few quid, do you?"

Joe became silent, then he looked up sharply and said, "What-a you done that it's so important you got to be found?"

"Enough to make it important."

Willie felt Frankie's fingers clutch his tightly in encouragement, and when he offered no further explanation and Joe persisted, Rosa hurried the old man below.

"Ain't no good shutting me up like I got the clamp on the mouth," he protested vehemently. "That boy, he is no good. You see him with little Frankie – cuddling and mushing."

"I saw him."

"She was holding his hand."

"I know. She's growing up fast. But he'd never harm her, I swear."

Rosa began to light the stove to boil a kettle. In her mind was still the fear that had appeared in Frankie's eyes at her news, and the hope when she had mentioned America, the disappointment when Joe had pooh-poohed the idea. For years she had tried – not entirely successfully – to pass on her faith and her own limited learning to a child who had come too late to be completely within her control. She had seen her grow up only partly schooled and wild as the gulls that flew across the beaches and shores she loved so well. For years the warm maternal giving that was in Rosa had been quenched by the death of her son under the guns of the Japanese in the Java Sea, and she had not had the strength nor the youth to rouse it again for Frankie. But now, as she remembered the look in her eyes, the look of a newly adult woman, that affection sprang again like a fresh fountain.

"Rosie," Joe was saying, "they want the American Navy and the French Navy and the British Navy and the Australian Navy and the New Zealand Navy and every goddam' navy that ever was to look for him, then he done something bad. Real-a bad."

Rosa turned on him furiously, slamming the kettle to the stove top with a ringing clang.

"Shut your trap, you spineless old booby," she stormed. "Or I'll fetch you one with this."

Joe stared at her as he sat down. Bad temper from Rosa was something he was used to, and threats were nothing new to him, but Rosa with tears running down her cheeks was something he hadn't seen for many years.

five

The following evening, when Willie was alone on watch and Frankie was grumbling over the dishes, slapping dirty water all over the galley floor in a noisy protest, Rosa left Joe sitting in sulky silence in the cabin, wishing he had tobacco for his pipe and a schooner of beer.

"Or even home-made wine," he pleaded out loud. "I don't argue at that. Sometimes I drink it. Even methylated spirits. I never drunk it before but I try now, Lord."

Rosa sat down beside Willie in silence and for a long time neither of them spoke. The Southern Cross swung over their heads and the light from the sky illuminated the spars. Only the slightest of breezes sent the long slow swells lifting across the sea, their curves gleaming under the stars. About them was the incredible silence of loneliness and great spaces – with just the faintest undertones of moving water and the chuckle of the wave against the *Boy George*'s bow. Once they heard the mew of a gull across the darkness and knew they were not far away from land, where the birds shifted uneasily in their sleep on the spits of rock and sand.

When Rosa finally spoke her voice was hesitant. "Willie," she said quietly. "You and Frankie: what's going to happen?"

Willie looked round at her without speaking and, encouraged, Rosa went on. "You like her, don't you, Willie?"

Willie nodded slowly. "More than that, Mama, I reckon. She's a nice kid."

"That's all she is, Willie," Rosa said, a plea in her voice. "A kid."

"I know that, Mama," Willie answered stiffly, a touch of pride in his tones. "You got nothing to blame me for."

"I know, Willie. I'm not complaining. But she's all I've got now."

"I know that too, Mama. She's too good for me. I try to keep away from her, only it's not so easy. When she's got her mind set on something, she takes a lot of shifting off it. You know that. And this is only a small boat. Mama – " he turned towards her " – I declare to me God I've only kissed her. That's all. I know what you feel about her. And I know what I am. I wouldn't saddle her with that lot," he ended bitterly.

He sat in silence for a while, then he looked up at Rosa again. "How about putting me off on the first decent-sized island we touch?" he suggested. "I'll be all right and they'll let up on the rest of you then."

There were tears in Rosa's eyes as she replied. "You'd starve to death," she said. "And Frankie'd get so skinny with grieving you'd not see her sideways. No, Willie, while the boat sails, you stay with us."

"Joe doesn't want me."

"Joe hasn't been asked." Rosa folded her hands in her lap, listening to Frankie singing in a croaky monotone above the clash of dishes in the galley. The breeze blew a wisp of hair against her face and she felt she could reach up and touch the swinging stars, and her soul soared out to them, praying for a little happiness in a life that had not tasted much of it.

"Willie," she said after a while. "What did you do that's so bad all these people is out after us?"

Willie sat with his hands in his pockets, feeling the cool wind on his back, watching the sea sparkle with phosphorescence on either side of him, throwing its glow on the bulge of the sail.

"I was a silly cow," he said after a while, not moving his head or changing his expression. "I killed a bloke."

Rosa sat motionless, shocked a little but not surprised, then she shook her head. "That was bad," she said. "What happened?"

Willie shrugged, unhappy and harried as all those uneasy memories began to chivvy him again. "I dunno. I was having a cuppa coffee in this dive when these two come in. Big car they had. Him and a little sheila, both smelling of money. He'd had one or two. He said I was looking at his girl – "

"Were you?"

"Sort of. She was pretty. Prettier than you ever see 'em round King's Cross or Surro. I couldn't take me eyes off her. He saw me and started getting noisy about it." Willie spat in disgust over the side. "The silly cow, making all that fuss about a sheila. In the end, he tried to draw me one off and I did him. He started it. Dinkum he did, Mama. He went down like a log and I ran. I didn't wait to see. I took their car."

"But that was a fair fight."

"I'd got a knife," Willie muttered.

"The one I threw overboard?"

"Yep. That was the one."

"You stuck it in him?"

"He shouldn't have kept coming at me," Willie said quickly, his voice high with indignation. "He wouldn't leave me be. I stopped him, that's all. It was fair enough."

"Not with a knife."

"No," Willie said more calmly. "I reckon not." He thought for a while before continuing. "Don't know what made me do it, Mama. Honest, I don't."

"What would your mama say?"

Willie laughed bitterly. "She wouldn't care. It never worried her if I didn't come home for days."

"What about your pop? Wouldn't he leather you?"

"Always out. Always in the bars. He wouldn't notice."

"Why did you carry a knife round with you?"

"The other blokes did."

"Did *they* stick them in people?"

"Not much. In fact – no, they didn't." Willie didn't resent her questions and was trying to answer them as truthfully as he could. "We all flashed 'em around a lot. We used 'em to carve our initials on trees and fences. We often said we'd stick a bloke but we never did – only me. Silly cow, I was. Sometimes, we got a bloke in a corner and cut his tie off or ripped his suit up a bit if he was one of the other crowd, frighten him a bit, make his pretty clothes look bad, but we never stuck anybody."

"Only you did."

"Yes, I did." Willie seemed depressed and for the first time angry. "Hell, I dunno why though! I just did."

"I reckon," Rosa said with a weighty finality, "that it wasn't your fault."

Willie looked up at her, grateful for the reassurance to his crowded spirit. "Honest, Mama? You reckon I'd get off if they caught me?"

Rosa hesitated before replying, choosing her words carefully. "I dunno about that," she said, and Willie's shoulders drooped again. "We'd better take no chances. But I reckon if your mama'd been good to you and your pop'd helped a bit, you wouldn't have carried that knife and then it wouldn't have happened. My Georgie never carried a knife. I'd have larruped him if he had. Once I caught him lying to me and I lammed the living daylights outa him."

She was silent for a while. "Willie," she went on at last, "I hope they never find us. I hope we go on for ever."

"That'll be fine for Frankie," Willie said bitterly. "It'll be a smashing way to spend her youth."

"I'd thought of that," Rosa said. "But we can worry about that later. She's content enough. Listen to her singing. This is all she's known. Why should she want anything else when she's happier now than she's ever been? I reckon I still hope they never catch us."

Willie drew a deep breath. "We can't do it, Mama," he said. "Some time it's got to stop. We haven't the money."

Rosa sat up straighter as his words brought to her for the first time the inevitability of their defeat. From nowhere she remembered a film she'd once seen about people trying to escape from the Nazis in the war. She hadn't entirely understood the significance of it then, but now she began to understand the emotions of a hunted people and their wretchedness at having nowhere to rest.

"Willie," she said slowly, "I wish we could find some place – somewhere nobody knows us – somewhere we could be still. So we don't have to keep moving all the time. I'm not complaining, but it'd be nice to have a home again instead of this old boat. I get to feeling so cramped. I get sick of climbing over things and the ladders get me joints. And the cooking in old bits of wood in a can to save kerosene. I've not cooked anything decent for ages, it seems. And there's Frankie, falling out of her pants and nothing to change into."

She stopped dead, as she realized her wish for stability and security was becoming a complaint that contradicted her wish to go on, and she stared at her feet, blinking rapidly as the tears crowded into her eyes.

"I reckon it's my fault," Willie said quietly. "If I hadn't been with you, you might have all got clean away. They wouldn't have chased you. And Frankie wouldn't be acting the way she is."

"You've done all right, Willie," Rosa said quickly. "And Frankie's come to no harm. She's just grown up a bit, that's all. If it wasn't for you, we wouldn't have gone on so long as we have. I guess all we've done is spend your dough and get in the way."

151

The weather began to deteriorate again as they ran further north into the Tuamotus. Heavy rain squalls came pounding down on them from the south-east and as there was little wind apart from these, they had to make the best use of them.

"I don' like being around here," Joe said uneasily. "Too near to dark and I don' know where we are."

"Oughtn't we to shorten sail?" Willie asked as he shinned down from the masthead where he had climbed to watch for reefs.

"Maybe," Joe looked over his shoulder, steering by ear alone. "But we oughta get outa here a bit. Too many reefs and she won't claw off."

It was dark before they were aware of it and the old boat was pitching badly, plunging into the swells and shuddering as she threw off the weight of water. Then with a crack like the rattle of artillery, a new squall was upon them and the flapping sails filled and the *Boy George* tore north-west as though all the devils in hell were after her, lurching from crest to crest of the cross-swell, the main boom whipped to the full extent of the sheets. The wind was still blowing from the south-east and the *Boy George* was yawing heavily as they ran along a mile-long cluster of coral rocks that lay just under the surface of the water, smashing the waves into flying splinters of spray.

"Push her to starboard," Willie shouted. "She'll thrash herself to bits."

"No," Joe shrieked back, his head cocked for the sound of waves on an open shore. "We got-a too near the reef. Don' let her fall off, Frankie."

"No, Pop," Frankie shouted from the wheel. "I got her tight."

Not quite certain of what they were doing, Rosa was staring from one to the other from where she clung on by the mast.

"If we'd only got charts," Joe wailed, "instead of old MacGillicuddy's pipe-lighters."

"Charts won't help us now," Willie said tautly. "It's too late for charts."

They could only huddle on deck and stare at the surf rushing closer, then Willie noticed the reef with its pounding foam was passing more and more towards their quarter and he began to shout with excitement.

"By Christ!" he yelled. "We're going to scrape past."

The surf was roaring in their ears, throwing up gouts of spindrift to the sky, and Willie was actually yelling that they were safe when there was a tremendous crash and all four of them were flung to the deck as the *Boy George* shuddered to an abrupt halt. The weight of the wind in her sails flung her masts forward and, with a crack that sounded above the noise of the sea, the mizzen mast snapped off short and the top half of the mainmast came smashing to the deck.

The bowsprit they had rigged lay at forty-five degrees to the scudding clouds, and the stern was almost under the waves that washed over Frankie where she was lying by the wheel. The boat was moving slightly to port and starboard still but she seemed to be tightly held by the reef beneath them. The upper half of the mainmast, still secured by the shrouds, hung over the ship's side, hammering at the planks and covering the deck with rope and canvas that flapped wildly in the wind.

By the time Rosa had picked herself up from the deck, Frankie was already scrambling across the wreckage, clawing at it frantically with bleeding fingers.

"Willie!" she shrieked. "Willie! Where are you? Mama, for God's sake, he's overboard!"

Joe was struggling to his feet now and clambering up the wet deck after her.

"We don't never ought to have come out here," he shouted as he started to drag at the wreckage. "This ain't like fishing off Sydney Heads."

"He's here," Frankie shrieked. "I got him. Oh, Pop, hurry!"

The agony in her voice tore Rosa's heart apart and she scrambled after them and helped heave the debris across the deck. Blinded by the rain and buffeted by the stinging blows of the canvas, they got Willie out, dazed but unhurt, and as soon as he came round, he saw the wreckage and struggled immediately to his feet.

"The engine," he said. "Let's get the engine going."

He was slithering crab-like across the deck to the engine-room hatch when Joe stopped him dead with a shout.

"Get-a this lot clear first," he said. "Or we get her round the propeller."

Frankie was diving for the axe when Rosa's yells pulled her up short. "Not overboard! Not overboard! We've got no more sails!"

"Jesus, Mary and Joseph," Joe moaned. "We'll be drowned! Cut it loose!"

"Not overboard," Rosa insisted. "Not overboard!"

The wind had dropped as suddenly as it had sprung up but the waves were washing against the stern and down the length of the boat, sloshing into the cabin and against the three struggling figures on the foredeck. While Rosa and Joe held his legs, Willie managed to reach over the side and secure the rope that Frankie passed him to the broken end of the mast. Then the four of them, cursing and falling over the loops of wire and the folds of wet canvas, heaved the broken spar inboard.

"Get the mizzen squared up," Willie yelled, struggling towards the engine-room hatch.

All the saints Rosa was busily invoking under her breath as they worked came to their assistance at last for, with the seas threatening to roll the *Boy George* over on her beam ends, the ancient engine started at the first swing and the thrust of the screw held her more steady against the coral.

Joe hurried to the wheel and they put the *Boy George* astern, her keel grinding murderously off the reef. Slowly, they manoeuvred her about and put her dead slow in the opposite direction, the engine coughing sturdily below, while Willie, his face drawn and anxious under the blood that was smeared from a cut on his temple, watched over every clank and rattle of the old machinery.

Rosa stood in the bows, staring ahead into the darkness.

"Good St Christopher guide us," she was muttering to herself. "Good St Christopher protect us now."

Within half an hour, with the rain slashing down in another squall, the bows had struck again, flinging them all to the deck once more.

"We gotted in the middle of a reef somehow," Joe moaned.

"Thank God the wind's dropping again," Willie said. "Let's have a look at the chart."

"We oughta be here," Joe said, jabbing a thick finger at the stained paper down in the lopsided cabin among the littered pots and pans and the stove torn from its moorings. "Only, this chart is so old she is no good. Look-a here."

He pointed to a scratchy pen-and-ink picture of a sailing ship bowling through a reef which was set in a corner of the chart with the words, "HMS *Pelorus* Entering Harbour."

"I bet old MacGillicuddy got this one at Martin's Pawn-Shop," Frankie commented. "Or mebbe the School of Art."

Joe bent closer to read the fine lettering, his eyebrows performing a *pas-de-deux* on his forehead. " 'Dangerous ground not much-a surveyed'," he intoned carefully. " 'No survey of these waters'." He swung the chart round and peered again, his voice rising in alarm as he read. " 'PD.' That means 'position doubtful' and it is over a reef, Mama.

The chart is dotted with Mister PD. We do everything that is wrong. No wonder we get stuck. We oughta be swimming now."

For another hour they raced the engine, trying to manoeuvre the boat about for a passage to safety, then as the wind slackened to nothing again, they dropped the anchor and Willie and Joe lowered the dinghy and rowed round the light Rosa lashed to the stump of mainmast, probing for a deep passage through the coral.

"There's nothing deeper than a fathom," Frankie wailed as she hauled in the dripping lead line for the twentieth time. "We're stuck."

"Let's chance it then," Willie shouted back above the noise of the waves. "Let's go ahead. If we can't go back, we might as well go forward."

They pulled to the *Boy George* and Willie started the engine again.

"Come on," he muttered. "Don't you go letting us down, y'old bastard."

"Starboard a bit, Frankie," Joe shouted from the bows as the engine started to cough. "Then steady as you go."

Rosa said a decade of the Rosary quickly and called on St Christopher again.

Willie shoved the engine into gear and the *Boy George* jerked forward.

"We sink," Joe panted, staring over the side. "Try again."

Once more they crunched and ground their way ahead another few yards, rumbling and quivering as though they were an old tram on broken wheels.

"Again," Joe shouted more cheerfully. "Soon we sink. Try again."

For an hour, with heart-stopping grindings, they moved forward in lurches and stumbles, their keel hardly ever free of the broken coral below.

"I hope we're not much longer," Willie muttered anxiously. "We're down to the last pint or two of fuel."

"Never mind-a the fuel," Joe shouted gaily. "Again. This-a time we drown for certain."

They were all hanging over the side, staring into the water for obstructions when the *Boy George* met with no more resistance and floated decently upright in calm water.

"We're across it," Frankie shrieked running from the wheel to where Willie lay half-out of the engine-room hatch. "We're in a lagoon. Oh, Willie, you were right. We've done it."

She flung her arms round his head and shoulders and hugged him.

"Sure, we're across it," Joe said, his high spirits disappearing as he became aware of his aching feet. "Now we pump her out. Then, when we can't get out again, we sit back and starve."

six

The squalls which drove the *Boy George* across the strand of coral left Flynn cursing his luck in Papeete, whither the *Teura To'oa* had been driven back by the rising wind, a fact which brought on a blazing row between Captain Seagull and the impatient Flynn that was concluded with threats and left them both determined never to set foot on the same deck together again.

"We had 'em cooped up in Tyburn," Flynn said furiously, "and now, thanks to that old fool, we've lost 'em again."

He was sitting near the overgrown coral sea wall, under a frangipani tree that starred the ground with ivory blossoms, sitting where he could glare at the *Teura To'oa* moored with her stern to the quay among the vista of masts and rigging and cabin tops, the solitary light that shone from Seagull's cabin porthole dusting the moving water with diamonds. Voss sat smoking silently, watching the Tahitians in denim trousers talking in groups to the girls.

The sun was slipping rapidly behind the steep hills and the valleys above Papeete wore an ever-changing pattern of light and shade. With the sunset, the shadow of the stumpy spires groped towards the slopes at the opposite side of the bay, and crept higher and higher until only the mountain tips where the clouds swirled like smoke were touched to gold by the sun. And then even they were dark, and the saw-edge peaks of Moorea, nine miles away, disappeared into the night.

As Flynn watched, the lights of the honky-tonks and the bars began to appear and behind them in the poorer streets, the lamps of the shanty quarters and the Chinese stores. A jukebox started up somewhere in a jangling French tune that marched across the quiet air like an advancing army until it was cut to pieces by the chatter of a mini-bike.

"Papeete's not so romantic when they turn on the radios," Voss said.

"What did you expect?" Flynn demanded. " 'The Pagan Love Song'?"

Voss grinned and Flynn stared at the flame of his match as he lit his cigarette, then he savagely obliterated it.

"Damn Seagull and his lousy boat to everlasting hell," he said. "I've never been nearer to taking Keeley in. I suppose the old fool's picked up some trade and wanted to be back here to clinch it. I've heard he's preparing to disappear as soon as the weather clears. We had them in the palm of our hand. Now we don't know where they are."

"Perhaps they're at the bottom of the sea."

Flynn stared at Voss, shaken from his anger by the other's expression.

"Not they," he growled uncomfortably. "A blow like that wouldn't sink 'em. They'll be all right. If that damn' silly radio announcement hadn't been made they wouldn't have gone scuttling deeper into the Tuamotus."

He stood up and stared at the *Teura To'oa* for a while before continuing. "I've been with the police to the radio station," he said eventually. "They're going to make a series of announcements about the search. And they're going to send it out in English and repeat it from Fiji so that if they've got a radio – and we know they have – "

"Sure, we do," Voss commented, without looking up. "Lucia told us they had. Or, at least, they had when they left Sydney. Mama hasn't mentioned it since."

Flynn glanced at him. "Well, now they'll hear a new broadcast. This one will tell them we're concentrating on the Tuamotus and that we're searching everywhere but the Societies round Tahiti. That'll send 'em scuttling back here where the islands are well populated and nice and close to each other."

Voss watched him silently, saying nothing.

"And this time," Flynn ended, "we'll tell 'em about the reward that's offered for Keeley."

"It'll never work," Voss said immediately.

"Why not?"

"Because Mama Salomio isn't that kind, I'll bet. After all this time with that kid aboard, she'll be bursting at the seams with maternal instinct. God help 'em, women wear themselves out with emotion. But I'll bet he's a better kid than he was."

"OK. If it doesn't work with the old lady," Flynn said confidently, "it'll certainly work with the old man. He's just the type to be interested in five hundred pounds."

Voss said nothing and Flynn took his silence for disapproval and broke out defensively. "I've got a job to do," he said. "If your son had been stabbed or beaten up or robbed and the police allowed themselves to get sentimental over the man who'd done it or the people who were helping him to escape, you'd feel pretty sick, wouldn't you? There isn't room for sentiment in the police force."

Voss bowed slightly with his head. "*Touché*," he admitted. "You have a point there. But I can't help feeling just a little admiration for the Salomios."

"Hell, neither can I," Flynn snorted. "But as far as I'm officially concerned, they're a set of interfering busybodies and I wish Keeley had never heard of them. By God, if he hadn't, he'd have been in custody four months ago now and there'd have been at least one pair of parents a lot happier because of it. But the blasted newspapers have completely clouded the issue by playing up the Salomios."

"It's made a wonderful story," Voss smiled, undisturbed. He took two or three newspaper clippings from his pocket and showed them to Flynn. "Look at these: 'Salomios Sail To Glory,' *Sydney Sun*; 'The Courage of the Salomios,' *Morning Herald*; 'Where Are They Hiding?' *Brisbane Courier-Mail*. Notice that? '*They*.' No need to mention their name any more. They've become simply '*they*'. Everybody knows 'em now. Look – " He flipped through a whole bundle of clippings and sat back, watching Flynn's reactions. "Melbourne. Adelaide. Perth. Everybody's interested. New Zealand papers too. *Wellington Post. Auckland Star.* Dunedin. Christchurch. See this? *Fiji Times and Herald*. Even the Americans in Honolulu and Los Angeles. Even the French in Noumea. I can't read French but I can see 'Salomios' there in the headline."

He stuffed the clippings away and lit a cigarette quickly.

"They've reached London and America, Flynn," he went on happily. "They'll soon be pushing the politicians off the front pages. Believe me, it's the biggest thing since the end of the war. From being an old couple in debt they've become famous. They'll be met by the Lord Mayor when they get home."

He paused before continuing. "It might interest you to know that the money they owe on the boat has been offered by some philanthropic old jerk who owns a couple of sheep farms. All this has done his old heart good. The pioneer spirit's not dead, etcetera, etcetera, blah, blah, blah. And he's not alone in his sentiments either. Have you noticed that there are now three other newspapermen in Papeete?"

"I have. What do they intend to do?"

"Apart from attending the Préfecture de Police for news – which they certainly won't get before you and therefore before me as well – they're waiting for the *Teura To'oa* to leave harbour. And when she does, they'll set out after her. That'll be fine if we're not aboard as it seems we won't be."

"How do you know all this?"

"They cornered me in a bar – last night when you were in conference with the police on the next move. Pity they didn't realize that there's nothing I like better than being cornered in bars. Besides, I can afford not to worry. I'm always one jump ahead of them. I've got Lucia in Sydney."

"She hasn't come across much lately."

"They're probably out of touch with post offices, or money, or both. Or they're scared. Probably a little of all of them. Especially since that broadcast. It could be that Mama's started getting wise to us. We'll have to watch that daughter of hers in Brisbane in case she sends her news via her. Fortunately we'd thought of the daughter as well as the daughter-in-law."

"And now you've got *all* of them neatly parcelled up and working for the paper?"

Voss looked over his shoulder at Flynn. "We've even started the poll I told you about," he said gloomily. "We've removed Lucia, by the way, and taken her with the boy out of reach of the other newshounds."

"It's a dirty game," Flynn said slowly. "You're making capital out of their suffering."

Voss wagged a finger. "Flynn, you're jumping through *my* hoop now. But, take it easy, they're suffering far less now that they've got some money in the bank and plenty to do and see than they were when they'd no money in the bank and nothing to do but sit and bite their nails. Lucia's going to be all right."

Flynn frowned. "Sometimes, you seem so anxious for these damned Salomios and all their hangers-on I wonder whose side you're on."

"Yours every time when it comes to personalities," Voss laughed. "Theirs, when it comes to sentiment. If only they'd write a few letters and give us some real stuff. They're playing cautious now and I live for lost causes. They mean good solid circulation. That's why the Charge of the Light Brigade always packs 'em in. That's why all the readers in Australia and even further afield are jumping out of bed every morning and fighting each other for the paper as they've never done before. The Salomios are a lost cause. They can't win. We all know that. But we're all wishing like hell that they could and hoping by some miracle that they will."

seven

The night seemed a lifetime of anxiety and there were times when the crew of the *Boy George* thought the dawn would never come. They huddled together with their stale cups of tea in the unlit cabin over the littered table, their feet among the damaged crockery, the dislodged stove, and the pans that their crash on the coral had flung to the deck.

All the time, as the water sloshed about her feet, Rosa kept asking herself if this tremendous task she had set herself was worth while, a thought that had begun to occupy her mind more and more in the solitude of darkness before sleeping. It had all proved so much bigger than she had expected, so much more difficult, and at times even her stout heart wavered at the thought that it had to go on and on – and on. They could never go back.

She needed help and advice. She needed the church about her with its coolness and the warm light of the sanctuary lamp and the Latin mutter of the priest. If she could have walked round the corner and sat in the bare green waiting-room of the presbytery with its smell of dust and its picture of the Pope and waited for Father Gilhooley to come in and take the weight of responsibility off her shoulders, she would have felt sustained.

"I'm sick of climbing ladders and looking through portholes," she said out loud. "I'm sick of kerosene stoves and water out of petrol tins. I want a house and stairs and a gas stove."

As the others looked up at her, startled, she pulled up short, throwing off her sea-weariness.

"I got to forget that," she reproved herself sharply under her breath. "I got to forget all that." Sighing deeply, she rubbed her hand across her mouth and brushed her hair back. As she remembered Lucia and Tommy back home in Sydney, she forced the feeling of defeat from her mind and set her face resolutely against the odds.

Her eyes rested affectionately on Joe sitting huddled on the bed opposite her – irresponsible, gay, ridiculous Joe, bewildered by all the hardship, Joe who could never have saved them from poverty – and on Willie dozing on a box his young strong face smoother now that the weather and a little decent responsibility had ironed out the mean lines.

His arm was protectively round Frankie, who curled against him like a puppy seeking warmth, her young face pinched with weariness. Looking at them together, heartbreaking in their youthfulness, Rosa felt even more determined to go on, and was surprised to find that Willie's cause had become as important to her as her own, for she knew what he had done back in Sydney was too big to be judged by her alone.

When the eastern horizon faded to a dirty grey, it showed skies that were still scarred by ugly squall clouds, but the violence had gone from the waves. They crept on deck in the first light, their eyes full of the sand of too little sleep, and surveyed the damage. The *Boy George* looked a derelict, her decks a mass of halyards, wire shrouds and torn canvas.

"There's one thing," Willie said, "she's not leaking. There's not enough water to drown a mouse in the bilges and I pumped her out last night."

"I heard you," Rosa said heavily, remembering the squeak-clank squeak-clank that had broken through her dozing.

"Rudder's had it, though," Willie continued. "She's all splintered to hell and gone and the ironwork's bust. But – " he pointed across the water " – there's a pass over there where we can get out if we can get her going."

"The Lord had mercy on us," Rosa said.

"We need-a more than the Lord's mercy." Joe was surveying the decks. "We need a boat-a-yard just now."

Willie was gazing across the lagoon to where the encircling land rose a little. "There's some trees there," he said quickly and Rosa's heart leapt at his undefeated spirit. "Straight ones. Why can't we rig new masts?"

Joe laughed harshly. "This ain't-a no match-a-stick of a mizzen. This a big pole. We can't lift a big pole with the hands and the backs."

"Oh, hell, man," Willie said irritatedly. "You always look for the things we *can't* do first. We can hoist it up somehow."

"I am too old for lifting and straining." Joe sat down heavily on the cabin top. "I get sick in the belly. Rosie, I done it once. I'm too old to do it all again."

"Pop – " Frankie put her arms round the old man's neck " – come on, just try once more."

"Joe," Rosa pleaded, "just a little more. We'll think of something then. Just a little more, though, so we can get out of here." She turned to Willie. "Can we get to the other side of the lagoon? And can we fix her without having to pay for a boatyard?"

Willie looked serious, then he grinned. "Mama," he said "the days when we could afford a boatyard have been gone long since. The money's getting low now, you know."

Rosa sighed. "OK," she said. "If it's like that, we'll do it on our own."

Willie dropped below and bent over the engine. For a long time it refused to start but eventually its reassuring cough cheered them. With aching muscles, they heaved up the anchor and began to move slowly across the smooth water,

Frankie in the bow with the lead line searching for sudden shallows or the purple shadows of the niggerheads. Several times they had to retrace their course as they ran against banks of rock and finally, while the trees were still two hundred yards away, the engine spluttered and died abruptly.

"Fuel's gone," Willie said.

"We go," Joe replied, his spirits rising a little. "Still we go."

They ran on under their own way for a while longer, having to lower the dinghy and labour over the oars for the last hundred and fifty yards. Fortunately for them, the deep water ran close inshore and they were able to anchor again within a few yards of the trees.

"Done it," Frankie yelled gleefully. "We've done it."

While Willie and Frankie went ashore, Joe set about clearing the deck, untangling the ropes and wire and flaking them along the planking. They had none too much spare rope now and no spare canvas, so Rosa carefully folded the sails and put them below in the cabin with the sail needle and palm and resin on top of them. Then, between them, they secured with a heaving line the broken mast they had heaved inboard and levered it into the water again to float alongside, sweating at the effort, Rosa's clothes straining across her broad back as she laboured to help the grunting, unhappy Joe.

Meanwhile, ashore in the dying wind, Willie had cut down two young trees slightly more than half the length of the proposed mast and skidded them down the beach to the water's edge.

"Now we can make sheer-legs," he grinned at Frankie as they stood ankle-deep in the shallows. "Hoist 'em up tomorrow. Day after, we can cut a mast and use the sheer-legs to drop it in place."

They sat on the beach to eat the fruit they had found and drink the milk from the coconuts the squalls had brought down.

The wind had disappeared completely now and the clouds had cleared and the last of the sunshine was falling in jade greens and salmon pinks on the curling breakers that rolled up outside the reef. Over the spit of land, they could see the stump of the *Boy George*'s mainmast touched to gold.

Aphrodisiac scents sighed in to them from the meadows of the sea weighted with salt spray, finally losing themselves over the lagoon where the terns still plummeted down after fish.

Willie sniffed the air and lay face down on the sand to stretch.

"It's going to be hot tomorrow," he said. "Hell, kid, we're going to sweat."

Frankie stretched out alongside him, twitching her ragged pants straight. "Think we shall do it, Willie?" she asked with desperate anxiety. "Put her to rights again, I mean."

"Sure we shall," Willie said confidently. "We've done it once. We'll do it again."

Frankie frowned doubtfully, then she smiled at him. "If you say so, Willie, I reckon we will. You're smart with boats. You ought to do well with a boatyard."

Willie turned towards her, his face close to hers, his bare shoulder brushing her sleeve. "I'd have to work hard, kid," he said. "No time for anything but work."

"I'd wait, Willie."

"You'd have to wait a long time. You'd be old like you said."

"Would you mind, Willie?"

He searched her face, while her eyes followed his, her lips half-open, moist and young.

"No," he said with a firmness that made her feel humble and uplifted at the same time. "No, I wouldn't, Frankie. It wouldn't make any difference to me how you looked."

"Oh, Willie!" Frankie gazed adoringly at him and, twining her arm tight round his, she hugged it. "Willie, I do love you – "

She was startled by the depth of the passion she felt, and a little frightened for, though she was ready for love, she was not yet old enough to understand this exultant singing thing that stirred her to her very soul and soared over all the difficulties that were in their path.

She lay back on the sand, fingering the little cross he had given her, and stared at the sky that shone in fading blue slits through the tattered banners of the palms curving out from the shore.

"I never knew being in love was like this," she whispered. "I've seen Mama and Pop – you can't imagine them being in love and holding hands, can you? I've seen other people fighting and bawling. Or I've seen 'em going down alleys looking kind of shifty. I never realized being in love was beautiful. It seems so natural here, Willie, to love someone."

Willie leaned over her. "You've grown up, Frankie," he said quietly. "Your face's changed even. You look prettier."

"I *am* prettier," she said confidently. "I feel prettier. You made me prettier, Willie."

She put her arms round his neck. "Willie," she asked, "do you ever feel frightened?"

"Sometimes," he said feelingly.

"About us, I mean. Sometimes, I can't bear to think about it – like it's all going to break and fly to pieces in my hands."

Willie smiled at her, gently, indulgently, and she went on, trying to put her feelings into words.

"Every night I pray," she whispered, "that we'll find somewhere safe. Not an island – I'm so sick of islands and sea, Willie – but somewhere where there's no one to come between us. No police, nobody who knows anything about you. Somewhere we can feel we don't have to go on running, where we can grow up and get married and live like human beings."

Willie was silent and she went on as though, having released her feelings, they were flooding out of her unchecked.

"What's the use of all this hard work," she asked, "if we've got no happiness? I don't want to take any chances about might and maybe and perhaps. I want it now. So I've got something to remember in case anything horrible happens."

Willie frowned. "I wish I could give you some happiness, Frankie, but – hell, I'm in no position to give anybody happiness. All I can do for you is take it away."

She put her fingers gently on his lips, and rubbed her cheek against his shoulder, then she lay back and stared steadily at the sky again. "I said just now," she murmured, not looking at him, "how it was beautiful to be in love. But sometimes it's awful too, Willie. It is for me. It makes me awful scared. Oh, Willie," she said. "There seems to be so little time."

She held him to her fiercely and her voice grew stronger with determination as she began to feel things with a woman's instincts and cast off finally and irrevocably her childhood indecision and doubt.

"So little time, Willie," she whispered. "Don't let's waste it."

It was another day before they got the stump of the old mast out. The tumbled waters outside the reef had calmed to long swells and the lagoon lay still and torpid on the windless ocean, so that the four on the *Boy George* sweated as they worked, in their nostrils the odour of sun-baked coral. Joe and Rosa took turns on the winch handle that heaved the rope through the apex of the sheer-legs, while Willie laboured flat on his face in the suffocating bilges, knocking out the wedges and chocks that held the stump secure to the notch in the keel, with Frankie stretched out behind him to pass him tools. It was heart-breaking work under the floorboards but at last they could move the stump in its socket, and several days later – panting days that exhausted them – the new mainmast was secured.

"She look once more like Captain Salomio's pride and joy," Joe said proudly, staring up at the long straight pole piercing the sky. "When Noah build his ark, he ain't got nothing on you, Willie." And to Rosa's delight, they heard his breathy tenor struggling with *Vesti la Giubba* –

The others were infected by Joe's happiness. "We'll have a feast tonight," Rosa said. "I'll open a tin of steak – we've not got so many left – and some fruit. Peaches – how's that?"

Willie was looking sombrely at them and Rosa caught his uneasiness.

"What's the matter?" she asked. "Something wrong?"

Willie nodded. "Sure is, Mama," he said. "I been wondering how to tell you. I got to looking over those cans we stored in the bilges while I was down there. The sea water's got into em – the lot. There ain't one that ain't blown up like a dead cow."

They stared at him, stunned. "We got no canned stuff left?" Rosa said.

"Not a one, Mama."

Joe threw up his arms, his enthusiasm dispersed immediately. "And we don't got no money either. That-a finish it. I want to go home."

"Shut up, you old fool," Rosa said. "We're not beaten yet."

"No – " Joe eyed her unhappily " – but we ain't so far off now."

Their meals from then on were sparse affairs and Joe, as he miserably wiped the grease from his plate with a piece of bread, scraping up the last flavour of fried pork, was in a rebellious mood and ripe for revolution.

They had already cut down the tree that was to become the mizzen mast when the radio, weak with failing batteries once more, brought them Flynn's new message. The chirp of the loudspeaker had brought them a little cheer in their isolation and they listened to the announcer's cheerful voice, eloquent of comfort, with a feeling of friendliness. Then, first in French and then in English, he began to give out the message which had been specially prepared for them by Flynn.

Joe was catching cockroaches, a regular job of his when they became too bad, solemnly parading about the cabin with a tray bearing the kerosene stove held near the cracks in the ancient deckhead, so that the cockroaches, yellow and rustling from twenty years of crumbs and scraps of crayfish, tumbled out in scorched, dead dozens.

He lowered the tray slowly and listened, one fat hand on his hip, his eyes round, his stomach protruding through his worn vest.

"They know where we are," Frankie said, putting down the dog-eared magazine she had read a hundred times now. "I bet they've known all the time."

Rosa's reaction was just as Flynn had expected. "We've got to get away from here," she said.

Joe slammed down his tray. "Where the hell-a we go to?" he demanded furiously. "Always we go. I get sick of going." He sat down on an upturned bucket and began to sulk.

"We've got to head towards the Societies," Willie said. "They seem to be everywhere else."

Rosa sighed, thinking nostalgically of the crowded streets of King's Cross, shabby, faded, noisy, but never refusing them shelter. Like all women, she needed security and the absence of roots was undermining her confidence.

"Whichever way it is," she said, "there's one thing – we can't stay here."

"I like it here," Joe said angrily. "It is fine here. We might as well starve-a to death here as some place else."

While they were arguing the announcer was still talking, unheeded until they were pulled up short by his next statement.

"With the Salomios on the rerigged *Tina S* is a man whom the Sydney police wish to interview. He is William Keeley, of Sydney, and a reward of five hundred pounds has been offered to anyone who can give evidence of his whereabouts – "

Willie leaned over quickly and switched off the radio. Frankie watched him, her face tragic.

"OK," he said bitterly in the silence which followed, his features robbed of their youth. "Now you know for certain that it's me they want, not you."

"You musta done something big if they pay-a that much just to find you," Joe commented.

"Shut up," Rosa said sharply, remembering her brief conversation with Willie, that monosyllabic discussion that had told her so much about him and yet so little.

"Listen," she went on. "Why *can't* we go to America?"

"Mama, I told you once. Because we ain't-a got the stores. We ain't-a got the boat for a trip like that." Joe had turned towards her, stamping his foot to impress his points on her. "Because we aint-a got the sails."

"Can't we try?" There was hopelessness in Rosa's tones as she pleaded with him.

"No, Mama. For a trip like that, you gotta to have money. You gotta to make preparations. Two-three months." He shrugged. "You gotta to have a boat – not a old string-a-bag like this one."

Willie had been watching them as they argued and as Rosa turned away, defeated, he stood up. "I'm going on deck," he said flatly. "I got a lot of clearing up to do."

Rosa watched him go in silence and as Frankie made to follow, she caught her by the arm.

"You hear that?" she said, unbalanced by the worry crowding in on her. "You hear what he said? He's on the run. The police are after him. Why did you go and fall for a boy like that? Whyn't you pick a decent boy? Now what do you think? – after you hear that lot."

"Mama – " Frankie's eyes were big and surprised, " – I knew. I knew all the time."

"You knew? How did you know?"

"He told me so himself."

"When?"

"Weeks ago. One night on deck. It don't make any difference."

"You little fool!" In her distress, Rosa swung her daughter round savagely and sat her on the spare bunk. "What good can come of it? You're only a child."

"You weren't much older when you married Pop," Frankie said firmly, jumping up again. "Lucia was only seventeen and a half. I'm old enough to marry anyone. And, anyway, I promised I'd wait. I promised I wouldn't get in his way while he was getting himself some money."

"You did, did you? You've been talking it over – you and him?"

"It was my fault," Frankie cried. "I started it. Don't go on at Willie. He hadn't anything to do with it. He told me to go away. He kept on telling me. But I didn't want to. Mama, I don't ever want to go away from him. And I'm not going to let you make me."

She stared back at Rosa defiantly, prepared to do battle for the thing she believed in, for the first tender thing that had ever arrived in her wild young life.

Rosa looked haggardly at her daughter, then she turned slowly aside and Frankie flew up the ladder after Willie.

Joe watched his wife for a moment, then, taking advantage of what he thought was an argument in his favour, he leaned forward and spoke in an insistent whisper as Rosa wearily began to sweep the neglected mugs from the table to the tin she used for washing up.

"You hear that, Rosie?" he said. "Five hundred pound reward. No wonder he buy stores. No wonder he change the boat – two masts," he snorted. "No wonder he always keep on working. Five hundred pounds, Rosie. Five hundred pounds."

"So what?" Rosa kept her back to him so that he shouldn't see the misery in her face. She knew what he was going to say even before he said it.

"Five hundred pounds, Mama. That pay off the boat and give us something in hand. We live comfortable on that till Tommy grow old enough to take her over. We ain't a chance, Mama. You know we ain't. I get hungry. We all get hungry. We got nothing left. No money. Soon we have no food."

"I don't want no blood money." That ingrained instinct in Rosa that came from living all her life in the dock area, that instinct that told her all policemen were enemies, made her stand against the infamous suggestion that she should inform on one of her own kind.

"If you don't shut up," she went on, "I'll hit you with the coffee pot."

Joe sat back on his bucket silently. He was sick of hard work and sicker still of their diet of bananas and coconuts and fish, and even sicker than that of the absence of anything stronger to drink than the brackish water from the tank.

"Mama," he whispered softly. "All we gotta to do is send the letter – the cable – anything. We could put in somewhere on some excuse and get one of the islanders to take-a the letter to the nearest radio. Give him the half-a-nicker for his trouble. I know where he keep it. I've watch where he put it. I've seen it – "

"I suppose you've helped yourself too?" Rosa swung round from the washing-up tin and glared at him so that he jumped.

"No, Rosie. Honest-a-true. But I know where he keep it. We can take-a the quid or so."

"Judas," Rosa spat at him. "Informer! Thief! One more word, that's all. Then the coffee pot."

Joe shrugged and slumped against the bulkhead, scowling. "Mama," he muttered. "He is the criminal, isn't he? Perhaps the murderer. There is nothing wrong in telling the police about that – "

He rolled backwards off his bucket with a howl as the coffee pot came round in a sweep and hit him at the side of the head, showering him with luke-warm coffee. The bucket shot from under him with a clatter and as his behind hit the floor he roared again, then Rosa flung the whole tin can full of greasy water, mugs, plates and all, across him.

Willie and Frankie put their heads in at the hatch, in alarm at the shouting.

"What's happened?" they demanded.

"Nothing," Rosa said calmly, beginning to pick up the mugs. 'It's Joe. He slipped. Knocked the coffee pot outa me hand. That's all. Ain't that right, Joe?"

"Sure," Joe agreed gloomily, spluttering and gasping on the deck. "Sure, that's-a right."

"We got a bit excited," Rosa went on in a flat voice.

"Excited? What is there to be excited about?"

"We're going to America. I've decided."

"What?" They almost fell into the cabin.

"Whatever happens, we can't do no good here."

Joe sat among the debris of the washing-up and gaped.

"But, Mama – " Frankie stared at her " – we've hardly any money left."

"So what?" Rosa stood with a mug in her hand, hardly seeing them. "We've come all this way without any money. Why shouldn't we go the rest of the way? We'll find somewhere like Panama. They'll have us. They'll not ask questions. Or somewhere in South America. There's nothing to lose."

"Mama – " Joe managed to speak at last " – I won't go." He jumped up, showering dishes and water to the deck. "All that way. We never get back to Sydney again."

"What difference does it make? We'll get by. We can pick up water and stores in Aiotea or Apavana. We can scrounge. We can pinch if necessary. Then we can head for the Galapagos. We're nearly there then."

Willie turned to her, noticing the lines of strain on her features.

"Mama," he pointed out gravely. "We're taking one hell of a chance."

"Willie – " Rosa's flat voice suddenly seemed more cheerful and buoyed up with hope " – if we stay here, we've *no* chance. You've no chance. You know that. Let's risk it. I'm old. Joe's old. It doesn't matter what happens to us. But you and Frankie are young. If you've fallen in love, God help you, we got to do something for you. Let's go where you've got a chance together. Let's try and give you both some future."

Her shoulders were stooped and weary with thinking and Frankie put her arms round her and hugged her impulsively.

"When, Mama? When are we going?"

Rosa looked up and forced a smile. "Now. Soon as we can. I'm not fussy."

Willie studied her, then a grin spread across his face.

"OK, Captain Mama," he said. "Now!"

He swung her into his arms and planted a noisy kiss full on her lips and almost danced up the ladder with Frankie.

Joe turned to his wife as they were left alone together, shuffling towards her on weighted feet. "Rosie," he said very slowly, "you don' understand. You ain't never understand. We ain't no sails. We ain't got nothing for a trip like that. We're right in the hurricane season, and that old glass she don't look so good again. We drown."

"OK." Rosa seemed indifferent to her fate. "We stay here, we starve. We go to America, we drown. What's the difference. Let's go to America."

PART THREE

o n e

When the *Boy George* slipped out of the lagoon where she had left her stumps of mast on the white beach, she had changed her rig again. Taking the hint from the radio description of their boat, they had this time left off the mizzen mast and thought it wiser to do away with the bowsprit, so that she had regained her old squat appearance.

They were all leaner and more tired and the sun had burned them black. Like their ship, they had a poverty-stricken look about them now, for there was no longer any slack they could take in. There was no longer any possibility of replacing their needs beyond the last few pounds in Willie's money belt. Everything was desperately short and the only way they could replace their rotten canvas and frayed cordage was to resort to theft.

But suddenly there was hope in the ship again. The feeling of being harried that had grown on Rosa as they jumped from islet to islet, running westwards before the breeze, had diminished now that they had turned east and north. Ahead of them, when they had cleared the Marquesas, there was only sea and where there was only sea Rosa felt safe in spite of their poverty.

Frankie was still in a cloudy wonderland of delight full of dropped dishes and misplaced cutlery and joyous whistling over the washing-up, but Willie was inclined to be silent and uncommunicative; buoyed up by Rosa's hope but awed by the tremendous task they had set themselves.

There was a quiet determination in the way he did his work now, quite different from his early eagerness of the days of Aranga-vaa. He had chanced one night on Rosa praying before the crucifix in the cabin, silent and shapeless in her old clothes, the well-darned heel of her stocking showing where her slipper had sagged away from her foot. He had never seen anyone so still before and as he had watched he had caught his own and Frankie's name among the muttering and it had dawned on him she was praying for them. He crept away, scarlet-faced with embarrassment that he had witnessed her agony. He had seen her praying before, saying a decade of the Rosary each night without fail, and more when she was troubled by the shape of events, but it had never occurred to him that she might want to pray for *him*. It made him shrivel inside with shame that he had once considered deserting her.

Only Joe was unhappy. He knew his limitations and he was uncertain of his ability to withstand that tremendous journey from the Marquesas to the Pacific Coast of America, even provided the *Boy George* could withstand it, something he also had grave doubts about.

It was his very experience that frightened him, for while the others could see only the promise, Joe could see only the dangers, and he retired into a shell of moroseness that grew as they put more miles between them and home. There was nothing of the pioneer left in Joe and the memory of those sunny walls in Sydney, instead of diminishing with the miles, grew stronger. In his heart was a searing desire for revenge, a sweeping longing to assert himself that was born not so much of personal dislike of Willie as of homesickness and sea-weariness; of jealousy and envy and the scourgings of discomfort he had always associated with Willie's arrival on the boat. And at the back of it all was a sense of frustration and resentment. The knowledge that five hundred pounds were almost within his grasp and could not be reached left him with a feeling of anger against the others.

The atlas was frayed at the edges now with Joe's anxious fingering and the out-of-date charts were stained with grease-spots and the rings made by cups of tea. They had to rely entirely now on their fishing lines for meals, for the islands around them were too populated for safe calling. How they would replenish their canned food, Rosa had no idea, for she felt pretty certain there could be few people of any intelligence who had not heard of them by this time.

At night they watched the deck for the flying fish which had flung themselves into the sail and expired on the planking, and at dawn searched for the pattern of gulls' wings against the pale skies as they mewed over the mullet that chased the fleeing smaller fry. In the evening they sought the dark irregular patches that meant shoals to Joe and listened for a sound like the patter of a rain squall on the surface of the sea which indicated fish feeding below the weeds and spawn that stretched in a mile-wide avenue from horizon to horizon.

With salt pork on a meat hook, and a dog chain for a trace, and with Joe shrieking advice from the wheel – "Work him away from the big-a ones. It make 'em cross and they forget to be clever" – they caught a dolphin from the group that accompanied them and watched, faintly shocked at their own cruelty, as it gasped out its life on the deck, its colour changing in shimmering waves from blue-green through every colour of the rainbow and back again; and once a wolfish shark that splintered the boat hook and crushed a bucket with its leaps.

From time to time, they took the risk of putting ashore on one of the smaller islands for the daintier inhabitants of the lagoons and the crabs which they grabbed from behind while their pincers clacked away like castanets. Finding a paradise where the sky was black as nesting birds rose, they lowered the dinghy and helped themselves to eggs, and even fledglings, picking the young boobies and bosun birds from the nests with ease.

They continued to run eastwards, Joe uneasy as he watched for the signs of another storm – the too-lovely sunsets and sunrises, the haloes round the sun and the moon, the lines of cirrus radiating from a point over the horizon where the centre lay, the sultriness and the heavy swell with no wind to account for it. Several times they had to put about and waddle over the horizon as they saw the tips of an inter-island schooner's masts in the distance, and once they passed close enough to a passenger ship bound for Auckland to see the colour of the flag on her jackstaff. But the great ship was sufficiently indifferent to the tiny wooden craft to fail to investigate her, and their presence went once more undetected.

The barometer had dropped another two points and the wind was growing again when they sighted the peaks of Aiotea to the north and east of the Tuamotus and almost on the fringe of the Marquesas. There had been a slight upward flick of the glass and a wind change, then it had started to blow hard once more.

"Mama," Joe said, "she go down again. Soon she come out at the bottom. We oughta to stand near to shelter."

To his surprise, Rosa agreed to running in to Aiotea, having first reassured herself from their sparse literature that it was only thinly inhabited. What he did not realize was that her worries were growing to the point when the desire to communicate them to someone else had become intolerable, and her whole feminine soul itched to send a letter to Lucia.

Flat grey clouds like sheets of lead across the sky were closing overhead as the *Boy George* approached the island. A strong wind kept punching her over on her fat round beam as it came squalling out of the east. Lines of white spray like veins began to appear on the blackish surface of the sea, and they had to hang on to ropes and spars as they moved about.

Slanting lines of rain were blowing across the deck and the wind tugged at their clothes and beat at their faces like angry little fists. The bow rose from the troughs of the sea dripping like a dog after a swim.

"Mama," Joe said, climbing on deck to where Rosa sat with Frankie alongside Willie, who was handling the wheel. "Mama, it is down another point."

It was still raining next morning when they entered Taio Bay, the landlocked entrance to Aiotea. The spire-like peaks of the island were hidden in mist and the tall palms waved and twisted to the dictation of the wind. There was a violent current running as they sidled round the barrier reef that hid the entrance to the bay, and the *Boy George* lurched and staggered as Joe held her to the lee side of the cliff to avoid being flung by the gusty wind on the rocks at either side. Beating up the harbour was not easy work, but at last they dropped anchor off a flat beach of black coral sand that added to the gloom.

Taio was a forbidding place which seemed under the brooding influence of the hidden towers of rock that rose above the mist. Little light came into the bottle-necked lagoon and the whole place had an atmosphere of darkness and neglect and a sad stagnant silence broken only by the mourning cries of the birds. There were signs of a once-thriving community, for there was a wooden jetty and a group of native houses straggling along the beach, but most of them, with the fatalism of a dying race, had been allowed to sag into decay, palm fronds jammed into the bad patches of the silver-grey thatch.

They had dropped anchor before they became aware of another ship sheltering under the lee of the land, a trim little vessel from which at that moment a rowing boat was heading in their direction, manned by a couple of Fijians and directed by a white man who lounged in the stern.

"Name's Seagull – Harry Seagull," he said as the boat bumped alongside. He grinned up at them with a gap-toothed grin. "I'm the original deep-sea kid. I been sailing these waters since I'm a nipper. Cut me teeth on a marline-spike. I'm on me way to Nukuhiva for passengers. When my boys seen you come in they let out a squawk like a ship's siren. Ain't anybody ever comes in here but me. Howja find her?"

"Just took a chance," Willie said cautiously, leaning over the side, while the others watched nervously from behind him.

"Ain't that queer?" Seagull reached up and hauled himself on deck. "That's how I found her years ago. Just took a chance. I'm as lost as a fish in a whale's belly and I drop in here outa the blow. People here then, though. All work in Papeete now. Rather dig in the stores than dig in the earth. Eat canned salmon outa tins instead of fishing in the sea."

He glanced round him at the scarred decks and the new mast and frayed sails. "Pleased to see you nohow. Crook weather. Ain't seen weather like this since 1928. Ships in here then make it look like a regatta in Sydney Harbour. Me, I got so drunk I daren't wake up. What ship are you?" He looked hard at Joe as he spoke.

"*Boy George*, Auckland," Willie said as Joe's voice stuck in his throat. "My name's Green. Theirs is Howard. She's their daughter. They're my passengers."

"You don't look old enough to have passengers," Seagull said critically, with the contempt of the old and experienced for the very young. "You ain't got the marks of the pot off your behind."

"Just goes to show, don't it?" With Frankie half-hidden behind him, clutching at his sleeve, Willie stared back at

Seagull unsubdued. This was the kind of conversation he knew how to handle.

Captain Seagull looked them up and down, taking in their shabby clothes, Rosa's gaunt bulk and Frankie's huge eyes that seem to fill her small face. "Had a rough passage by the look of you," he commented. "Me, I don't like bad weather. I'm all for peace. Ever since I had the blue-green heeby-jeebies in 1917. Lost your mast by the look of you."

"Yeah. We ran aground. Had to stand in and rig a new one."

"Nice job you done." Seagull's sly blue eyes ran over the *Boy George* as she jerked to the tug of her anchor in the eddies of the wind. "Reckon you lost more'n your mast. You're all new topsides, ain't you? Sure was tough."

"It was a bit," Willie agreed and Frankie marvelled at his calmness. "We got to get some new canvas some time."

"I got enough canvas aboard to make a parcel of your boat and send her through the post. I got enough to make a nightshirt for the Almighty. Always carry canvas since I tore out my ass-end on the reef near Lady Musgrave Island. Had to patch her with my best suit and shirts and go ashore in Brisbane in a pareu and a screwpine hat."

"We've got to wait a bit for canvas," Willie said thoughtfully. "We're short of cash. But we want supplies. Not much. Beans. Tinned milk. Flour. Fuel for the engine."

"I can do that. You row across after me. I'll fix you up."

"Don't go, Willie," Frankie hissed. "Don't go on your own."

"Thought we'd get 'em at the store there." Willie indicated the shore, distrusting the gleam in Seagull's eyes.

"Don't go there. Rob you of your pants. Steal your eye-teeth. You leave it to me. I'll fix you up. I fix everyone up. Ten-cent store of the South Pacific they call me. Just come in from Papeete and freshly filled up. I can give you enough fuel to take you from here to the Pearly Gates."

"They got a post office here?" Rosa interrupted, clutching the grubby letter she had written to reassure Lucia in Sydney after their long silence that they were still alive, the letter which told of their severance with the old life, the letter which, if the weather were against them, might well be the last she would ever send.

"I'm the post office," Seagull lied. "I put it on the weekly trading schooner. Meet her in Nukuhiva. Goes back to Papeete. You come across to my ship and I'll give you everything you want. I got the coffee on. Come and have a cup."

They exchanged glances and, in spite of Frankie's whispered protestations, finally lowered their dinghy and followed across the dark, rain-ruffled water towards the *Teura To'oa*. Climbing aboard, they tramped noisily across the wooden decks towards the old man's cabin, where Frankie glared at the colourful and bulging nudes torn from magazines which plastered the bulkheads, her dislike mixed with a certain amount of envy.

"Blow coming up," Seagull commented. "Warnings out. You want to anchor over there in the shelter of that spit. Safer there."

"We aren't staying," Rosa said at once.

"Find it damn' difficult getting out of that bloody bottle-neck with the wind coming in like this. Blow you inside-out. Blow you into splinters. Blow you into rags."

"We aren't staying," Rosa repeated firmly. "We got to get on."

Captain Seagull pushed a bottle of gin across the table. Only Joe bothered to pour himself a drink – a quick one, which he refilled immediately.

"Where you heading?" Seagull asked, his eyes alert and suspicious.

Rosa hesitated, her mind congealed with panic. Willie looked at her quickly as she paused, and jumped into the conversation again. "Okahé," he said.

"Cargo?"

"Passengers." Willie indicated Rosa, Joe and Frankie.

Seagull didn't believe him for a minute. He knew enough of Flynn's business to have suspected immediately who they were.

"What you going there for this time of the year?" he asked.

"See their grandson." Willie interrupted again before Rosa could reply. "Ain't seen him yet. Son lives there. Engineer. Radio. They've chipped in to make this trip. Doing it on the cheap," he ended as though to explain their condition.

"You're telling me." Seagull stared at them unwinkingly. "Wasn't no radio engineer on Okahé last time I was in there."

"Musta missed him then," Willie said with a hard grin. "Been there some months now."

"Didn't even know there was enough radio to have an engineer."

"Just shows what you can miss, don't it?" Frankie chipped in. Seagull ignored her and studied Willie shrewdly. "How long you been sailing?" he asked unexpectedly.

Willie's hesitation was only momentary. "Since I stopped wearing bibs," he said. "Know it inside out."

"You weren't on the wheel when you came in."

"Just giving the old man a go."

"Coming into Taio?"

"Sure. Frightened him to death. Stopped him agitating. Been at me the last three weeks to have a go."

Rosa flashed him a look of gratitude for his quick wits and said nothing, and Captain Seagull started to rattle off to his bosun a list of their needs, apparently satisfied with the explanation, though his treacherous little eyes were shining greedily.

Joe sat licking his lips, trying to recapture the flavour of the gin on them, his eyes strangely bright, his manner tense with excitement.

He couldn't bring himself to say anything, for he had a feeling that if he opened his mouth he would condemn himself. In his closed fist thrust deep into his trouser pocket were a dozen crumpled notes from Willie's money belt. He had watched Willie take from his roll what they needed to buy their supplies and, as he and Rosa and Frankie climbed into the dinghy, Joe had dodged back on the excuse of requiring a coat and removed the rest.

He knew exactly what he was going to do with it. If Seagull had alcohol to spare, it was Joe's intention to return to the *Boy George* with some of it. All his waking hours for more than a week had been concerned with the ways and means of obtaining it. He had hit on this scheme some time before and had been waiting ever since for the opportunity to carry it out. He knew their plans were to run from Aiotea to Apavana as soon as they had picked up canned food and posted Rosa's letter and, since he knew he could smuggle the bottle back aboard in the sack he had brought for supplies, he intended to drink himself stupid as soon as they dropped anchor in the bay at Apavana. About what happened the following day Joe wasn't very bothered. It would be worth it and that day could look after itself.

It didn't take them long to choose the meagre supplies they required and stuff them into sacks, then Rosa handed her letter over to Captain Seagull.

He glanced down at the address, then he looked up again quickly, his empty mouth grinning. "You ain't the Salomios, are you?" he demanded abruptly.

There was a long silence then Willie spoke. "Who's the Salomios?" he asked.

Seagull gave him a shrewd glance and pushed back his cap with its silver-painted crown. "Coupla old Wops running off with a boat. Police want 'em. Done a murder. Carved up their grandma. Poisoned their uncle. Strangled a whole orphanage of kids. Thought you might be 'em."

"Well, we're not," Willie said as he saw the distress on Rosa's face. "I told you, didn't I? They're here to see their son on Okahé. Their name's Howard."

Seagull was still grinning at them, his peeled red face flushed with excitement. "OK, OK," he said. "Didn't say you were, did I? Just wondered when I saw the address on the letter."

"Coincidence, that's all," Frankie put in as she saw Rosa's jaw sag helplessly.

"Salomios was from Sydney. They got a daughter in Brisbane called Florentina. It's in all the papers I get sent out. This is to Brisbane."

"Just coincidence, like we said," Frankie insisted.

"Look kinda Eyetie." Seagull glanced up at them and went on maliciously. "Don't like Eyeties."

"Can't say I like little men with red whiskers," Frankie retaliated briskly.

"Can't trust the Eyeties," Seagull went on. "Fought 'em in Tobruk. Chased 'em back when they ran outa Caporetto in the first job. Tell me Sydney's lousy with 'em since the war – all coming out with the Pommies and doing our boys outa jobs – "

He caught Willie's eye and changed his tune. "Still, I ain't the one to help the police. Not me. I just left one in Papeete, mad as a mangrove fly shaping up to sting because I left him stranded. I'd like to leave all policemen stranded. I don't like policemen. Not since they clapped me in gaol for gun-running in 1913. You can rely on me, whatever you done."

Rosa began to fidget to be off. She felt she was to blame for Seagull's suspicion, but her letter had been burning a hole in her pocket for days. She climbed from the cabin and began to sort out their belongings with Frankie and Willie. In their anxiety to load their supplies, they failed to noticed that Joe wasn't with them on the rain-wet deck.

"Just one bottle," he was pleading below with Seagull.

"Ain't for sale. I don't sell booze. Not sold booze since prohibition. Then I made a fortune. Used creosote to give it kick."

"Just one bottle." Joe opened his fist and showed a bundle of notes. "I'll give you all that for a bottle."

Seagull stared at the money, his eyes bright, then he turned to the locker and returned with a square bottle of gin.

Joe thrust the money into his hand hurriedly and stuffed the bottle into the sack he carried. "OK," he said. "Good, eh?"

Seagull called to him as he turned for the companionway. "Where you bound for?" he asked.

Joe sniggered, already a little under the influence of the gin he was going to consume. He felt light-headed and foolish with delight at the thought of what was stuffed into the sack to be covered by the tins of beans, and defiance burst out of him at last. The thought of the journey in front of them suddenly unmanned him and and he was unable to hold back a spasm of anger as he saw a means of putting an end to Rosa's fantasy. "If they say we're going to Okahé," he hissed, his brows down in a dramatic scowl, "then we ain't-a going to Okahé'. You ask-a me, it's the other way to Apavana. You tell somebody that. We get-a caught. I don' care no more."

Seagull watched him waddle on deck and dump his sack carefully in the stern of the dinghy, then they pushed off and made their way back to the *Boy George*. Seagull stared at them with an expressionless face, eyeing first Willie, then Frankie, then Rosa and Joe.

"Me, I'm on your side," he called after them. "I like to be on the wrong side. I'm a rat. Nice folk won't sit down at table with me. Anything to fix the police, I'm in on it.

He was still standing on the deck of the *Teura To'oa*, his trousers whipped by the eddies from the mountain, his crew watching curiously from the lee of the deckhouse, as the *Boy George*'s patched sails heaved slowly up, flapped and filled. As she passed between the two great rocks that marked the entrance to the bay, Seagull heard the cough of the engine as Willie, taking no chances with the current and the wind, started up, then she slowly disappeared out of sight towards the west.

As the last glimpse of her disappeared, Seagull climbed below and went into his cabin where he kept the radio transmitter he used to order his supplies.

t w o

The message that crackled over the air from Captain Seagull's transmitter reached Flynn as usual through the Préfecture de Police. It had been picked up and passed on by a schooner captain on his way into Papeete, and almost when Flynn was convinced that the Salomios were not going to respond to his stratagem to bring them out of the Tuamotus and nearer to the forces he had deployed for their apprehension, a police official rang him up at his hotel and gave him Seagull's information.

He put down the telephone with care, staring at it thoughtfully. His first impulse was to hurry triumphantly to the corner of the lounge where he had left Voss and tell him the news, but instead he breathed deeply and walked slowly towards him through the palms.

Voss was sunk in a chair, half-hidden by a newspaper, and Flynn stopped behind him and rested his hands on the table alongside.

"We've got 'em, Voss," he said slowly and deliberately, "we've got 'em at last."

Voss threw down the paper and snatched off his spectacles.

"You'd never guess who's put us on their track," Flynn said and, as the other's eyebrows raised, he continued: "Seagull. He was lying in Aiotea out of the blow when they followed him in and dropped their hook alongside. You were right. They *were* going to America. They left a letter for

Lucia with Seagull and, of course, he opened it. They were headed for Apavana."

He paused, then went on thoughtfully: "With this hurricane blowing up, they're bound to stay there till it's over. That'll give us time to get near enough for them not to escape again."

Voss said nothing. He stared at the stormy clouds outside and the dancing palms. He could see people hurrying for shelter from the approaching gale, keeping to the lee side of the roads under the dripping bougainvillaea and acacias, and there was something in their bent shoulders and anxious movements that made him think of the Salomios. *Their* hurry would be twice as urgent, the glances they threw over their shoulders twice as fearful. And their pursuer wasn't just the weather – it was the rest of the civilized world, one part of it wanting to punish them, arrest them, impound their boat and insist on its debts, the other and probably the most terrifying part, that which would plague them for interviews and pictures and gape and stare and read all about it in the papers.

Flynn was sitting down now. "They've had a pretty tough time by the sound of it," he was saying. "They've rigged a new mast. They ran aground somewhere in the Tuamotus. We came darn near to losing 'em after all."

"Poor bastards!"

"They bought some stores – not much."

"I suppose they've not got much money left."

"I suppose not. And the old man – Papa Salomio – bought a bottle of gin. Paid a colossal sum for it. Keeley's money, I reckon. He blew the gaff on the way they were going."

Voss said nothing and Flynn hurried on. "A French naval launch has been into Aiotea," he said. "It'll go straight over to Apavana as soon as the weather permits. They didn't fancy dragging the navy in on a police job but they stretched a point and agreed to decide that the Salomios were taking an unnecessary risk at this time of the year and that they ought to be escorted back to Papeete. That seemed to ease consciences all round and it's good enough to hold 'em until the police can get near enough. I wish we could have picked 'em up on an island under British authority. It's bound to hold things up."

Voss nodded. "Tough luck!"

Flynn lit his pipe, finding that the other's lack of enthusiasm made telling the story difficult.

"It's all over bar the shouting," he said.

"I'm sorry."

"I gathered so." Flynn looked up quickly. "What's the matter? Sorry your story's over?"

"No, I'm not." Voss answered him angrily. "I'm sorry for the Salomios. I always have been. I must be getting too soft-hearted for this game. They tried hard but they just weren't clever enough."

Flynn frowned slightly. "I thought this would be your big moment," he said.

Voss shrugged. "Now that it's arrived, I find I don't care two bloody hoots about the story any more. I'm sick of the whole disreputable business. I'm sick of chivvying old unhappy people to make a Roman holiday for the great Australian public. To hell with the great Australian public."

He stared out of the window towards the harbour where heavy swells were rolling in from the approaching storm. The vessels lined against the sea-wall were plunging and rolling as the last of the eddies that hustled round the Diademe hit them, their masts swaying and heaving against the sky.

The rain was coming down in wavering lines across the view, blurring the pilot launch that chugged its way slowly across the harbour. Moorea, normally so close and clear, had disappeared. Then the surf on the reef became visible again as the rain lifted a little, and the phosphate ship from Ocean Island that dwarfed everything in the harbour became sharper, its colours showing through the thinning curtains of water. The rain stopped abruptly as the wind started, and twigs and branches began to shower down from the trees and litter the streets, and an empty barrel rolled along the wharf, clattering and spinning on its end.

Voss stood at the window, staring at the pools in the roadway. "Here I am," he said wonderingly. "I have it all at my fingertips. How to trot out the sob-stuff and push up the circulation. Fred J Voss, the golden boy of journalism." He dropped his cigarette end on the floor and ground it out with his foot. "And now I find it doesn't matter any more. I must be going nuts."

"Cheer up," Flynn said with a grin. "You'll get over your emotion when you get home. It won't be long now."

Voss turned from the window. "Aren't you counting your chickens before they're hatched again?"

"I don't think so," Flynn said. "Not this time. From Aiotea you can see almost into Apavana. There's only one way out – in the direction of Aiotea. Apavana has a submerged reef running south and west. They can't clear it in any direction except towards Aiotea. There'll be a constant watch kept."

"It gets dark."

"They wouldn't dare risk it."

"They've taken risks before."

There was a note of finality about Flynn's words as he replied. "No," he said. "This is it. It's all over. This time I've got Keeley – " he formed his fingers into claws " – like that. He can't get out."

three

The *Boy George* made Ania Bay in Apavana only just in time. She had taken a beating in the last few miles, rolling and plunging in the seas, sending mugs and spoons and forks hurtling to the floor from burst locker doors, tossing their few remaining stores out of the cupboard to slide backwards and forwards along the deck with the tins and boxes and mugs and plates and the old shoes and the blankets that had shot from the bunk.

The glass had dropped steadily and there was that faint queer moan in the rigging now that told of the coming hurricane. The dawn had arrived with a sickly hue and scraps of high-flying cloud. The sea was ugly and, as they staggered along, heavy sleet squalls tramped down on them, one behind the other, humming out of the gloom astern, drenching the twice-drenched sails till they were as hard as boards, while the spray, harvested from every ripple on the tortured surface of the sea, stung their faces as it was whipped smoking from the waves.

The entire horizon astern was filling with swelling black clouds like funereal galleons which trailed their sooty keels along the wave tips, and lurid streaks of light reached out from the sea.

While Frankie held the wheel, Willie and Joe unbent the biggest sails and lashed the booms and gaffs to the deck, and, bringing the anchor inboard, secured it to a ringbolt. As the evening approached, the black evil astern crept clean across the sky, smothering the last of the daylight and bringing the darkness before its time.

Rosa huddled below, tying things down whenever she could get her hands on them. Her face was green with seasickness and she had a bruise on her forehead where the lurching boat had flung her against a corner of the table.

When she went on deck, Willie and Joe had stowed all sail except the one good jib they still possessed and they drove before the weather with this, Willie struggling in the rain to batten down the hatch as they went. Joe stood by the wheel now, drenched but confident in his experience and warmed by the knowledge that below deck in the paint locker for the evening was a whole bottle of gin, safely under the spare scraps of old canvas where it could not be broken.

Fortunately for them, the tide was right when they reached Apavana with the last of the daylight, and they were swept willy-nilly through the channel round the reef, with the spray exploding in all directions, until they reached the quieter harbour. Thankfully letting the anchor splash into the water, they went below to drink the thin scalding coffee Rosa had managed to prepare as they came under the shelter of the land.

Outside, they could hear the rollers pounding against the coral and the wind howling through the palms which groped to the east like arms in supplication before it, blown inside out like old umbrellas by the growing gale.

"Thank God we made it," Joe said fervently. "Another hour and it would-a be too dark to find the channel. Then we stay all-a night outside." He shuddered at the thought and reached for a towel to wipe his face.

Frankie looked up as Willie appeared through the hatchway. "Mama, can I sleep on the floor in here tonight?" he asked. "The engine room's crawling with water. Everything's wet through. We've sprung some of the deck caulking and my bed's soaked."

Outside, the daylight was dwindling into a green-grey gloom and even in the lagoon the water was streaked with veins of white foam. Spray was whipped off the merest ripple and the *Boy George* tugged and dragged at her anchor cable like a sprightly young stallion. There was no rain now but the air had the humid atmosphere of a laundry, while overhead dark clouds tumbled along at an alarming speed.

They were all exhausted, and early in the evening Rosa lay back on the bed to rest and promptly fell asleep, a shapeless bundle under the blanket Willie had carefully placed over her. Her hair was over her face and her mouth was open, snoring gently, her heavy body moving slightly on its side every time the *Boy George* snatched at her anchor. Frankie was curled like a cat in the spare bunk, one hand still hanging over the edge, where she had placed it to be able to touch Willie until she fell asleep.

Joe sat dozing on a box in the shadows by the oil stove, his mouth dry, his arms heavy, his head throbbing with the stuffy atmosphere, watching under half-closed lids as Willie wrestled in the yellow light of the smoky oil lamp to make a spare jibsail out of two or three pieces of rotten canvas.

His eyes followed Willie's arm as it moved backwards and forwards, and several times he almost fell asleep as he watched the movements, as regular as his own breathing, the drips of water that fell to the deck from the hatchway – plunk, plunk, plunk, every second or two – impinging on his ears with the monotonous tick of a metronome. Each time his head dropped forward, he woke with a start and fought fiercely to stay awake, terrified he would waste the only opportunity he was likely to get to enjoy the gin. He knew he should have been helping, but he thought that if he feigned sleep, Willie would eventually tire and go to sleep too, and having to feign sleep made it harder than ever to stay awake as he kept losing control over his heavy eyelids.

"Think we're all right here?" Willie addressed him as he folded the canvas to use it as a mattress. "Safe, I mean." He glanced up at Frankie's thin exhausted face as he spoke.

"Sure. Sure." Joe started upright and answered drowsily. "We all-a right. Good anchor. Strong cable."

"Can't it drag?" With his growing knowledge of seafaring, Willie was anxious and uncertain.

"Why's it going to drag?"

"I dunno." Willie listened to the wind for a while. "Sounds tough up there, Joe. Isn't there something we ought to do? Maybe find a more sheltered spot, for instance."

"Nothing more sheltered than this."

Willie cocked his head again. "It just sounds to be blowing harder than anything I've heard before, that's all, and it's blowing right in the direction of the rocks." He pawed among the charts and produced one of MacGillicuddy's battered books and opened it. "It says in the *Pacific Pilot*, 'Mariners should take every precaution when anchoring in Ania Bay during a south-easterly gale –' It's a south-easter now, Joe."

Joe grunted. "That ol' book is out of date," he said, trying to discourage conversation, and Willie's face became taut and worried. "Isn't there *anything* we ought to do, Joe?" he asked.

"Mebbe. Mebbe not. I guess we OK." Joe irritably thrust the suggestion aside, wishing Willie would go to sleep. "Wind ain't too strong yet. We got a bit of shelter."

Willie glanced at the barometer. "It's dropped further," he pointed out and Joe shrugged, furious with him for his tirelessness. The thought of the gin burned his throat and made him lick his lips again and again.

Willie rubbed his aching eyes and tossed the book back to the table.

"You going to sleep?" he asked the old man.

"S'all-a right," Joe mumbled. "Comfortable. Go sleep in a minute."

Willie twitched Frankie's blanket nearer to her chin and, putting out the light, curled up under the table with Joe's overcoat. Joe sat on the box in the darkness, feeling the ship quivering under the wind, while all the time the waves chattered at the planking like hordes of small wild animals fighting to break through, and the groans of the boat came to him like the sighs of an old lady resting her aching bones.

Satisfied at last that Willie was asleep, Joe rose silently to his feet and tiptoed to the ladder that led to the deck and heaved himself up. He was surprised at the strength of the wind which almost buffeted him over the side before he had become accustomed to it. Needles of flying rain stung his skin and, as he glanced upwards, he saw the glimmer of stars in a break in the scudding clouds before they closed again and the lagoon was in darkness.

Slowly he picked his way forward to the little paint locker, clinging to the stays or the lashed boom. As he unfastened the hinged hatch, the wind snatched at it and whipped it upwards against his forehead with a resounding crack that sent him rolling on the deck.

For a moment he sat on the quivering boards, seeing stars and half-stunned, while the wind tugged at his shirt and whipped his hair, then he became aware of the hatch cover rattling against the deck like a tattoo, the catch jingling its shrill accompaniment, and he frantically scrambled to his knees and flung himself stomach-down on top of it.

His mouth open, his breath coming in gasps, the wind blowing his hair into his eyes, he listened for signs of life from below, and it was a good two minutes before he moved again, convinced that the others had not awakened. Slowly, hanging on all the time to the quivering hatch cover in case it escaped him again, he lowered himself into the blackness of the locker, thankful to be out of the beating of the wind.

Feeling with his feet, he found the deck and, closing the cover silently after him, he sank down among the empty paint tins and old rope and pulleys.

At last, his excitement, that excitement that had been growing on him all evening, took hold of him. He scrambled to his knees, heedless of the puddles that saturated his trousers. Sending an empty tin flying with his heel, he felt under the canvas for the bottle of gin and heaved a sigh of relief as his fingers found its squat shape and drew it to him.

Stretching out on the deck, his back against the quivering bulkhead, aware that on the other side Rosa lay asleep and pleasantly elated by his daring and a sense of defiance, he ripped away the silver foil from the neck of the bottle and removed the stopper.

As the alcohol ran into his stomach for the first time in weeks, the rawness of it made him cough and he went red in the face with his efforts to avoid making a noise.

"Old-a bastard," he muttered, as he thought of Captain Seagull and his sly eyes. "He make it himself."

Then the first warmth from the gin flowed through his body and he felt better immediately, willing at once to forgive. He tossed aside the silver foil in his hand with an expansive gesture and took another swig at the bottle as thoughts of Surry Hills flooded back to him. As clearly as if he were there he saw the flat-faced tenements with their cast-iron balconies and their plaster stained with damp, and he felt a nostalgic longing for home that brought tears to his eyes.

Stupefied by the gin, the stuffy locker and his own emotions, he took another swig at the bottle and felt better at once. He snuggled further down and put his knees up, wedging his back against the bulkhead.

"Sweet Mother of God," he murmured ecstatically. "This is good."

It was the sound of the wind that woke Rosa from her sleep. It had a deep hollow whine that came out of the bowels of the sea in a ghostly echoing note as it howled across the vast miles of ocean, tearing at atolls, bays and islands, ripping the sand from under the whipped palms, bringing the driving rain to wash away soil until huge pines, caught by the shrieking banshee, were flung out of the ground and smashed down in a welter of mud and water. Great rolling waves as big as houses and topped by smoking spray marched across the sea, shuddering against the immovable rocks with a force that atomized them into mist high above the bending trees, sending the spume and the spindrift scudding across the narrow islands. Houses, stores, people, animals were beaten to the earth and held there, and the rain that pounded down in the path of the wind turned the soil into a sea of mud runnelled through with torrents of water that dug away foundations and drowned in their path the chickens and the pigs.

At Apavana, the fringing reef took the worst onslaught of the waves and the encircling arms of the hills the worst of the blow. But along the skyline the young palms that had sliced the racing clouds to ribbons lay flat along the ground so that years later they would rear upwards towards the sun, permanently deformed. The surface of the sheltered lagoon was lashed into a vapour that rose and sped away across the water like thin rolling clouds, flung over the inland sea by the eddies off the mountains that stood silent and majestic against the worst the blast could bring.

The whine of the storm rose in its intensity, screeching through the bulging shrouds of the *Boy George* like a mad thing caught in the ropes and trying to tear itself free. The little vessel creaked and groaned under the stress until it seemed to shout aloud in pain, while the waves banged and thumped on the forefoot like a thousand and one lost souls trying to fight their way out of the hell of the storm.

Rosa sat up in the darkened cabin, suddenly chilled and frightened. Outside, the yell of the hurricane had risen to a shriek and the *Boy George* jolted and rolled at the end of her cable in torment, rising swiftly only to be checked and flung nose-down again into the waves with sickening lurches that burst them into flying spray, and almost flung Rosa off the bed.

"Joe," she called in alarm. "Joe!"

"What is it, Mama?" Only Willie's voice answered her, calm and reassuring.

"Where's Joe? Light the lamp."

She heard a match scratch in the darkness and saw it flare in front of Willie's face, illuminating it in uneasy lines. Frankie sat up, blinking sleep out of her eyes, her shoulders white and angular in the lamplight, the little wooden cross a dark medallion on her breast. "What's going on, Mama? What are you bawling about?" she asked.

The wick of the hurricane lamp caught and the cabin glowed a bright yellow in which grotesque shadows leapt as the lamp swung on its hook in the deckhead to the lurching of the ship.

"Where's Joe?" Rosa stared at the wooden box where her husband had been dozing when she had fallen asleep, jerked now by the vibration to the other side of the cabin. "He was here. Where's he gone?"

Her words were drowned as the wind rose to a crescendo and the *Boy George* lurched violently again so that they all braced themselves to keep upright, and the blanket slid from Frankie's bunk to the floor.

"It's sure blowing, Mama," Willie commented, turning his eyes upwards to the lamp painting its smoky whorls on the deckhead. "We'll be dragging the anchor."

"Where's Joe?" Rosa repeated in a panic, for some reason thinking of the old man as he had come courting her years before, with a white straw hat and a celluloid collar, and bearing a posy of flowers already wilting in Sydney's summer heat.

"Stop worrying, Mama," Frankie said, swathed now in a jersey that was too big for her, one hand clutching the table to keep her balance. "He's probably up top trying to do something."

"He'll be fixing the anchor," Willie said quickly. "I reckon we'd better stop yapping and go and help him. I'll bring the lamp."

"I can't hear him," Rosa said, her voice rising as she bent to heave her slippers on.

"You'd be lucky to hear anything with that row that's going on," Frankie pointed out. "I dunno how we slept through it."

As they stumbled on deck, the howling wind flattened their cheeks and plucked at their lips and ballooned the jersey on Frankie's thin body. The lagoon was in darkness with no sign of the great round moon through the closely packed clouds. They could hear the pounding of the waves against the reef and could sense rather than see the wounded surface of the water.

"Gawd," Willie yelled. "Keep your heads down or you'll be over the side."

"EEEEooooeeee!" The wind, wet and warm as a bathroom door opening, came roaring across to them, funnelling through the entrance to the bay, a monstrous crazy thing tearing at their clothes and hair, and buffeting back at them, even in its own path, as it rebounded from the mountains and circled the bay in gusts, heeling the *Boy George* over on her side as the eddies hit her on the beam. The standing rigging swung out in great arcs, humming like plucked harp strings, while the halyards rattled and slapped at the mast in a devil's tattoo.

"Jesus, Mary and Joseph!" Rosa crossed herself quickly, awed by the strength of the storm, and clutched for a handhold.

"We've moved," Willie was crouching in the bows, with his arm round the forestay, peering across the water to the dark distant shadow of the land and the solitary light they could see there. "The anchor's dragging. I said it would."

"Much?" Frankie had her arms tight round him for support, peering over his shoulder. Rosa huddled in the shelter of the mast, her fingers clawing at the wood.

"Yeah," Willie shouted. "I reckon so. If we move much more we'll pull it into deep water. The bottom shelves here. Joe showed me on the chart. If we get off that, the anchor won't touch bottom and we'll be carried across there – " Willie flung out his arm towards the other side of the lagoon " – and then we'll lose her. It's blowing straight across to the rocks. I said we oughta put out an extra anchor. She's dragging all the time and we can't wait all night. If she goes, she'll go like stinko and we shan't be able to stop her."

Rosa suddenly remembered their mission on deck. "Where's Joe?" she said again, brushing her hair out of her eyes for the hundredth time. "He must have gone overboard."

"Not he." Frankie threw back her head and shouted. "Pop! Pop! Where are you?"

Only the shriek of the wind in the rigging answered her.

"He must be somewhere," Willie said, his voice lost in the gale that seemed to rumble across the lagoon like an express train. Then the blast caught his thin shirt, tore it free from its buttons and wrenched it from his back. He was startled for a moment, then he stripped the last shreds from his arms and sent them flying after the rest of the garment.

"He went overboard," Rosa was moaning again. "The wind took him. He's drowned."

Willie was at a loss what to reply.

"Take it easy, Mama," Frankie said uncomfortably.

Rosa began to talk softly to herself swaying against the wire shroud she clung to, leaning on the wind, the clothes pressed flat against her body. "He was trying to help us and he went overboard. Mary, Mother of Mercy, protect us!"

"Listen, Mama," Frankie shrieked to her. "Pop wouldn't go over that easy. He knows the boat too well. Maybe he got locked in the engine room."

"Sure." Willie joined in on the same note of hope. "He probably went to get something and the hatch slammed shut and the catch fell. It will, if you're not careful. Maybe he's tinkering around down there. Let's look before we start panicking."

Fighting to keep his feet, he lifted the hatch cover and stuck his head below, his heart sinking as he saw there was no light.

"Joe," he shouted. "You there?"

There was no answer and he cocked a leg over to the ladder. "I'll look, Mama. Maybe he slipped and banged his head."

He swung the lamp below, calling Joe's name. "He's not here," he said uneasily above the wind.

"Let's look in the paint locker," Frankie suggested. "He might have gone in there for something."

As they moved forward, the tortured waves bubbled alongside, streaming away astern in white streamers of foam as the bow cut into the wind-driven surface of the lagoon. The *Boy George* lurched and bucked again and Willie, on his hands and knees for safety against the blast, pawed at the winch round which they had taken the turns of the anchor cable. "He's not put out another anchor, Mama," he yelled.

"He fell overboard lifting it on deck." In her sense of guilt, Rosa had the whole thing pictured clearly in her mind. She could even see Joe, his grizzled hair flattened round the bald spot on his head by the wind as he clutched the anchor to his belly and staggered about the deck. "He's not so nimble any more."

"Hold it!" Willie was bending now by the hatch of the paint locker. "This thing's unfastened and I know I battened her down."

He was answered by a rattle as the wind lifted the hatch and from below he heard the faint sound of a snore.

"Mama," he shouted. "He's in here. He's breathing heavily. He must have been knocked out or something."

Rosa handed him the lamp and they tumbled into the paint locker after him, and the thumping of the waves against the bow sounded louder than ever in the dark little cabin up in the eyes of the ship, a mere cupboard that stank of old paint and dusty rope and tallow.

Joe was still propped against the rotten canvas and the anchor cable, one foot through the handle of a paint tin.

On his face was a broad, happy smile. His dentures were hanging loosely in his mouth, and his head was nodding gently to each swing of the *Boy George*.

"He's unconscious," Rosa said. "Joe! Joe!"

With Willie kneeling alongside her, she started rubbing her husband's hands, patting his cheeks and whispering endearments. "Joe, old dear. Say you're all right."

Frankie, standing behind, sniffed and bent to pick up something from the shadows, then she nudged Rosa and held out her hand. "Mama," she said gently.

Rosa turned, glancing up at her. She saw the expression on the girl's face, and her gaze travelled down her lifted arm. From Frankie's fingers dangled the gin bottle with the remains of its contents in the bottom.

"A bottle of grog. The old bum's not hurt. He's drunk, Mama. He must have got this from that bloke in Taio Bay. I thought he was careful with that sack of beans. He put 'em down on deck like they were dynamite. He must have had this in it. He must have got at Willie's dough."

Rosa gazed at her, uncomprehending, then she pulled herself slowly upright, fighting to keep her balance in the heaving little cabin. Vaguely ashamed of her panic, she stared at her husband, shocked that she should have been so weak as to weep for him.

She gave Joe a shove so that he rolled over on his side and finally sprawled on his belly. Smiling, he tucked one hand under his chin and snored comfortably.

"Drunk," she said. "You damned old stiff. You dirty, double-crossing, thieving old fool. Pinching our money. Getting drunk when we need your help. I wish you *had* gone overboard."

Willie watched her storming for a while, then he took the bottle from Frankie and tossed it on to the canvas and straightened up. The wind's shriek seemed louder and now, in the bow of the ship where they could feel every kick and lurch of the boat, the movement of the *Boy George* seemed particularly violent. "Mama," he said anxiously. "I reckon we ought to do something about that anchor before it's too late."

"Can we do it on our own – without him?" Frankie indicated Joe sprawling at their feet in the shadows cast by the lamp.

Willie turned towards her, swaying on his feet. "Looks like we got to, kid," he said. "Do you know what to do?" He held the lamp higher to look at her face.

She stared back at him, frightened and unsure of herself and her skill. "I think so, Willie. Maybe I do. We can fix something."

"Willie – " Rosa had forgotten Joe in her anxiety for the boat " – what should we do? Do you know?"

"Not too rightly, Mama. I can only think of things Joe's told me and things I've read. We ought to put out another anchor. I know that. Load it in the dinghy with the cable and row up forrard and toss it overboard."

"It's too late for that, Willie," Frankie said quickly. "We can't do that. The wind's too strong. We'd never be able to pull the dinghy. We ought to use the engine. Go ahead on it and put out the other anchor when we got the first one abeam. Then let her fall back. That's the only safe way. We can keep the engine running slow ahead all night, in fact, to hold her up to the anchor. Have we got enough fuel?"

"I reckon so." Willie nodded and grinned, relieved. "We'll get the other anchor out first, though, just for safety."

Rosa turned to Joe and kicked him in his fat ribs. "You drunken old fool, you," she stormed. "Just when we needed you."

Willie pushed her to the ladder. "Look, Mama," he said. "Leave him till later. We got to get a wriggle on. We haven't got much time and I'm getting scared."

four

The wind seemed to be rising still as they struggled to heave the heavy anchor out of the locker. Its noisy lament as it whined across the lagoon had grown more powerful and its buffets several times threatened to topple them into the water as they worked.

The *Boy George* was digging her nose deeper into the water now, so that great gouts of spray were flung upwards to whip across the deck in low stinging arcs that rattled like shot against the ventilators and the cabin top. The deck was greasy with moving water and lurching to every snatch of the anchor chain, so that they stumbled as they moved about, bent double against the wind and falling over ringbolts and equipment in the darkness.

They dragged out the lengths of greasy chain cable and flaked it along the deck, Willie thrusting it upwards from the locker, taking most of the weight as he passed it to Frankie, while Rosa, one hand always on the rigging for safety, stumbled forward dragging it behind her through the waist of the ship where the water was coming in green through the scuppers and sloshing backwards and forwards round her feet. They had pushed Joe to one side so that he lay in the shadows with only the lamp to keep him company, rolling inertly against Willie's feet as the ship moved.

"If only he'd been sober," Rosa panted as she fought her way along the deck, her skin beaten raw by the hammering of the iron-fisted wind. "If only he'd been sober."

"Now, listen, Frankie," Willie panted when they had shackled the chain to the anchor. "I've talked to Joe. I've read things. I've learned a lot. If we shackle something heavy half-way down the cable, it'll keep it from snatching. If we don't do that, this wind could break the chain or lift the anchor. Ain't that right?"

Frankie nodded and Willie went on, looking up at her as she crouched with the lamp alongside him in the meagre shelter the winch provided. "What we got that's heavy?"

Frankie thought for a moment, while the wind beat her hair into her eyes with blinding force. The rain had started again now and sheeted down on them in squally gusts that plastered the clothes to their bodies. From the entrance to the lagoon they could hear the mountainous, monotonous waves smashing against the rocks and bursting through the pass in a welter of foam and flying scud.

"We got some coal weights," she shouted. "They were in the bilges aft when we took her over. They'd taken an auxiliary engine out or something and they put 'em there to make up the weight. The screw didn't bite."

"OK, kid, I'll get 'em up."

Laboriously, they got two of the weights forward to the plunging bow, where they were almost thrown to the deck by the sudden thudding jolts as the anchor cable checked the ship's lift on the crests of the seas. Drenched by the water that came over the forepeak, Willie shackled one of them to the chain of the anchor that was already out. Then he fastened one end of a rope to the weight and the other to the deck and, as the *Boy George* rode forward between gusts, managed to slip the shackle over the fairlead and ease the weight into the water down the chain.

"OK," he shouted. "Now we'll do the same again."

They finished shackling the second weight to the chain of the new anchor, then they stumbled aft to the engine room and fell thankfully below deck out of the blast of the wind, their feet scattering the tools that had been jolted from the racks. Around them the planks and ribs of the *Boy George* creaked – not now with the regular protests of a ship in a swell, but with the tortured squeaks of agonized wood as each gust flung her against the chain. Willie glanced at Frankie's pale face and bent to the starting handle.

"Now for it, kid," he said with a grin. "Soon be safe. We're all right for juice and she'll ride all night the way we fixed her."

He swung the handle, but the engine was like a lump of dead metal.

"Oh, Christ," he said bitterly, his smile dying immediately. "Don't say she's going to let us down *now!*"

He dragged at the handle again, but once more there was no sign of life and he looked up at Frankie, his face drawn with sudden alarm, before he bent to the engine again.

"Y'old bastard," he muttered in an agony of disappointment. "Come on. Give."

He swung on the starting handle, his shadow huge against the bulkhead, heaving until his hands were raw and blistered, then, while he regained his breath, Frankie put her meagre weight against it and Willie worked the choke.

"Willie," she panted in despairing tones, looking at him with scared, white-edged eyes. "What we going to do?"

Willie shoved his head out of the hatch and glanced at the sky. "God," he muttered, tumbling back again. "We can't wait all night for this bastard. It's getting worse and we've moved again."

He bent again to work, depressed by a feeling of utter helplessness that they had no power to fight against the wind. Knowing nothing about engines, Rosa stood miserably in the background, holding the lamp for them while they worked, her eyes fearful as she saw Frankie's fingers fumbling with tiredness.

Willie tried the handle again with no result, then he seized a spanner and started wrenching at the couplings of the fuel feeds.

"Try the other end, Frankie," he said. "And put a jerk on. We've got to look slippy."

They worked feverishly, tearing their skin and flesh on the sharp edges of metal in the poor light, cursing bitterly when they dropped a spanner in their haste or a nut proved difficult, the engine room silent except for the creaks and the bubbling water beyond the planks.

Half an hour later Rosa was in tears and Willie stared over the engine at Frankie's weary little face.

"She's had it, kid," he said despairingly. "We can't do it. There's only one thing for it now. We got to use the dinghy."

"Willie." Frankie's cry was a pitiful exhausted bleat. "It's too dangerous!"

"Frankie, if we don't do it, the lot of us have had it. You know that as well as me. We're still moving. We're moving all the time. There's a light out there. Shove your head out. It's a church or a store or something. When I last looked it was over here." Willie's arm swung towards the bow. "It's over there now. If she goes careering all over the lagoon in this lot, she'll hit the reef or a niggerhead somewhere and that'll be the end of the lot of us. Frankie, don't you understand it's a matter of life or death? We've *got* to get out an extra anchor. We ain't got an engine to help us any more."

They stumbled amidships, Frankie staggering and grey-faced with fatigue as the gale beat them to the deck, and struggled to lower the dinghy. It was a murderous job, for the wind kept getting between it and the *Boy George* and swinging it out so that it thumped sickeningly against the side of the ship, threatening hands and fingers.

"God, we shoulda done this hours ago," Willie panted. "When I was agitatin' about it. While we'd still got time."

When they had the boat in the water forward, Willie jumped into it through the spray that shot upwards like shellbursts and lashed it fore and aft. In the light of the lamp, Rosa could see his face was strained and taut with weariness.

"All we got to do now, kid," he panted to Frankie as he scrambled back aboard," is get the anchor in her."

They lowered the cable into the tossing boat, Willie lying down for safety to work, the water sloshing along his legs, catching the rays of the lamp and glittering with a murderous green beauty. Laboriously, he flaked the cable on the bottom boards so that it would run free, then they lowered the heavy anchor across the stern, having to heave it up again and again as the dinghy rode away from them with the wind. When they had finally made it fast with a lashing to the thwarts, ready for the push that would send it to the bottom, Willie climbed aboard the *Boy George* again.

"All we got to do when we've got rid of her is shove the other weight over and adjust the cables so they both take the strain," he panted. "Then she should be good and safe."

He was gasping in the humid air as they made a final anxious inspection of all the shackles and the turns round the winch, wishing Joe were sober enough to check what they were doing, wishing their experience was great enough to give them confidence.

Satisfying himself that everything was secure, Willie turned to Frankie as she huddled behind him. "OK, kid," he shouted. "Here I go."

"I'm coming too." Frankie moved forward immediately.

"No, Frankie, you're not. Too easy to go over the side and you're only a kid. I'll handle this."

"I'm not a kid. I can row."

Willie pushed them both below deck where they could talk without having to shout against the roaring of the wind, down in the cabin where the floorboards were strewn with broken crockery that had been jerked out of the lockers again, and the blankets that had slipped off the bed and now slid about in the quivering puddle of warm water which had leaked below and slowly spread. He turned to face Frankie, his back against the moist bulkhead, his hand on the top of the once-polished table that was blurred to mistiness by the damp air, while Rosa, her arm hooked for safety round the ladder, watched them like a spectator at a theatre, the panic in Frankie's eyes tearing at her heart.

"Listen, Frankie," Willie was saying, his features haggard in the lamplight. "You can't come. You aren't strong enough to row. Honest, you're not. Not in this wind."

"I can hold the dinghy steady for you," Frankie insisted, her eyes full of tears. "It isn't safe for one man in the dark."

"Frankie, you stay here with your ma and keep that lamp alight," Willie said fiercely. "It's going to look good while I'm out there."

"I'll lash it to the mast. Mama can look after it."

"Frankie," he persisted over the crashing of the storm, "this is a man's job."

"I want to come, Willie." Frankie's voice was shrill with fear. She stumbled against him as the *Boy George* butted a wave and lurched, and she flung her arms round him, holding him tightly, love and fear all mixed up together inside her.

"Willie," she begged. "I don't care what happens. I just want to be with you."

Willie's arms were round her now and he was speaking over the top of her head. "Sure you do, kid," he was saying quietly. "And I'd like you to be but I want to know you'll be here when I come back. If you go overboard what'll I do?"

Rosa was blinded with tears as she watched them.

"Now, listen." Willie's strong hands on her quietened Frankie at last. "Just leave this to me. Suppose the light goes out? Suppose we get blown away when we let go the anchor?"

"I don't care," she moaned, shaking her head. "I'll be with you. That's all that matters."

"Suppose we don't know which way to row? I'll do this on my own. If anything happened to you, who'd look after Joe and Mama and the others?" Willie paused, while the spray that came across the bow rattled down on the cabin top over their heads like bursts of heavy rain. "Listen, kid, I'll tell you what: let's have one last go at that engine. It might work now. How's that? If it doesn't, we'll do the job together."

Frankie nodded speechlessly, thankfully, her eyes full of blessed relief and tears, and Willie kissed her quickly.

"OK, then. You get along and keep your head down. I'll be with you. There's a wrench somewhere in here I want."

She tried to smile and hurried to the ladder. They heard the momentary shout of the wind as she opened the hatch, then it died again as the hatch dropped back and they heard her making her stumbling way aft.

Willie made no attempt to look for the wrench and Rosa knew he had never intended to.

"Willie," she said, her voice quavering. "There must be an easier way than this."

"Maybe there is, Mama," Willie's face was set, as though the flesh were drawn tight over the bones. "But if there is, I don't know it."

He reached across the table and rattled the curling chart in the puddles of water and spilled tea. "Look, Mama, we're here. There's a ledge that drops into deep water." His hand swept across the paper. "If we drag the anchor off that, we've had it." He paused, staring at his hand for what seemed ages, as though fascinated by its movement, then he raised his eyes to Rosa's. "Mama, do you reckon we've done it right? The anchor, I mean."

The moving lamp threw shadows across his face so that his expression seemed to be constantly changing, but Rosa could see he was torn by doubt and oppressed by his inexperience. "It looked all right to me, Willie," she said, clinging to the ladder and swinging about it as the boat moved. "I don't know any other way."

Willie sighed. "Maybe Joe could think of one. I can't. I've got to chance it."

"Willie," Rosa begged. "Can't we risk it till daylight at least?"

"No, Mama. We're moving all the time. We can't wait. Any time now she'll take off. If we don't do something, we've had it. The lot of us. You've had it. Joe's had it – " he paused before he completed the sentence " – Frankie's had it."

"I'll speak for the lot of them, Willie," Rosa said earnestly. "We'll chance it together."

Willie looked up and smiled faintly. "No, Mama," he pointed out. "*I'm* speaking for Frankie now. And *I* say she's *not* chancing it. I've got to look after her now, see?"

As Rosa looked at him, she realized the old aggressive youthful Willie had gone and in his place was a man, mature and responsible.

He paused, then he reached upwards for the hatch. "I'm going now, Mama," he said abruptly. "Look after Frankie."

And before Rosa had the sense to realize what he was doing, he had scrambled to the deck. A gust of wind smashed him to his knees immediately, but he dragged himself up again, heaving on the rigging. Snatching the axe from its hook as he passed, he hurried aft and, slamming the hatch of the engine room shut, slipped the catch.

"Willie – " His face went hard as he heard Frankie's despairing shriek and heard her fists thumping on the wood, then he slipped over the side into the dinghy.

While Rosa was still heaving herself out of the cabin, he hacked the stern rope free and severed the bow rope with one blow, then he grabbed for the oars as the dinghy started to drift backwards. Within a few seconds, he was out of sight, blown out from the beam of the ship, straining his muscles hopelessly against the wind, watching the anchor cable slide over the stern as he went.

Rosa saw the boat vanish into the darkness, the tears on her cheeks blown away by the wind. Heedless of the screams and hammerings of Frankie in the engine room, she crouched against the blast, waiting and muttering and praying.

"Hail Mary, full of grace, the Lord is with thee; blessed art thou among women and blessed is the fruit of thy womb – "

five

The tempest blew through that night and the whole of the next day.

Rosa and Frankie were still on the foredeck saying Hail Marys, crouching by the winch, stiff with cold and hungry, wet through and exhausted by the weather, when the dawn came, a cheerless grey dawn like a thread of pale light that showed only the white-veined water and the slanting spears of drizzle that drove in from the sea.

When Rosa had released Frankie from the engine room, she had leapt on deck like a wild animal, frantic as she saw no sign of Willie, and for a while Rosa had thought she would fling herself into the bubbling water alongside.

When she had finally managed to control herself they had fought together against the elements for half the night. At one point, when the first anchor had been finally wrenched free, the *Boy George* had been flung backwards stern-first until the second chain had dragged taut and the anchor had bitten and held long enough for the first anchor to grip again and make the *Boy George* secure. Their minds numbed by the noise, their fingers bruised and split by the snatching chains, they had managed to get the second weight over the side as Willie had instructed, Frankie working with a stumbling weary fanaticism that broke Rosa's heart.

"Willie said to do that," she had repeated mechanically again and again as they stumbled about the deck in the darkness. "Willie said to do that."

Joe appeared on deck during the afternoon. By this time, the storm was clearly abating, though the rollers were still exploding into the entrance to the lagoon so that the passage was a turmoil of white foam, while ashore the palms still bent to the smashing of the wind. The light, grey-green and murky, continued to be feeble and, astern of the *Boy George*, the lagoon stretched away into a mist which was still more spray than rain – blank, empty and grey.

Joe stumbled forward, noticing the empty dinghy davits, the ropes streaming astern, and the teeth that had snapped off the winch, the bent links of the anchor cable. One anchor streamed to starboard of the bow and the other to the port, while the *Boy George* lay back unevenly between them. As usual, Willie's work, while inexpert, was secure.

He stared at them a little longer, then he clattered into the cabin, his eyes red, his tongue and throat dry. As he licked his lips, he felt the rough stubble that made his face bluish against his pallor.

"Christ Jesus our Saviour," he muttered to himself fighting to throw off the nausea and the blinding headache he was suffering from.

Unable to say anything, Rosa looked up at him as he poured himself luke-warm tea from the pot she had made when they had first stumbled below. Frankie crouched on the bunk, her eyes wide and accusing as they stared at him, her face pinched with misery.

Joe looked from one to the other of them and opened the conversation warily. "Where's the boy?" he asked. "Where he get-a to?"

"I dunno – " Rosa said heavily.

"Who put out the other anchor?" Joe looked boldly at his wife, trying to brazen out his conduct, trying to hide his shame. "I would have done that too. Only I feel-a ill. I have to go and sleep it off."

"I know," Rosa said. "You were drunk."

Joe glanced at Frankie, who stared through him unseeingly, then he studied Rosa cautiously again, wondering why she didn't throw the teapot at him.

"No, Mama," he said carefully, feeling his way towards an excuse. "Not-a drunk. Not Joe."

"You were drunk," Rosa said more loudly, her voice metallic and flat, like the ring of a cracked coin. "You were drunk just when we needed you."

Joe put down the cup, uneasy at her quietness. Calmness of this kind was usually the prelude to fireworks, but somehow this time it was different. The fireworks seemed to have gone out of Rosa.

"Did *you* put out the anchor?" he asked.

"No. Willie did. We helped. That's all."

"Where's he went then?"

"He's not come back. He put the anchor out but he never came back. I reckon he let the wind take him. He'd never try to row back against this. He'll be on the beach now, waiting for it to die, or sheltering in somebody's hut."

Joe rubbed his stubbly chin slowly, looking at his wife, bent and old, his belly sticking through his worn vest like dough.

"He use the dinghy?" he asked eventually. "In this-a lot? On his own?"

"What else could he do?" Rosa turned her empty mug round slowly in her hands: "The engine wouldn't go. You weren't around to help him. He did what he thought was right."

She paused and sighed. "I guess he tried hard. He stopped us moving, that's for sure."

By the following morning, the wind had died altogether. The clouds had dispersed and they could see the big palms along the ridge upright once more, their tufted tops motionless against the clear sky.

Neither Rosa nor Joe said anything about their thoughts but they were both thinking of Willie. Throughout the previous day, Frankie had prowled restlessly in the wind, watching the shore, impatient for Willie's return, her eyes sweeping the bare expanse of the lagoon, searching the ship as though she expected to find him there, dependable and solidly reassuring as always.

Rosa had watched her miserably, unable to offer anything in the way of comfort beyond the same reiterated sentence – "He'll be ashore waiting for the wind to drop" – and in the evening, Frankie had crouched silently in her bunk, staring into nothingness, unspeaking, uninterested in food. Rosa and Joe had sat in the cabin beneath the dim lamp whose glass was blurred by smoke from an uneven wick, drinking tea without talking, until eventually Frankie had turned her back on them, and without saying a word, they had gone to the old iron bed and lay in the darkness, still occupied with their thoughts.

None of them slept much and the following morning as soon as it was light Rosa and Joe went thankfully on deck, glad to be out of the silent, stuffy cabin.

The sun was out as they climbed through the hatch, and a group of island pirogues were approaching them across the lagoon from the distant decaying houses that huddled against the slopes of the mountains, the crews of Polynesian mixed blood and wearing screwpine hats and trousers marked with the American army stamp. None of them spoke English and as they drew alongside, they began to point astern of them.

"They've got the dinghy!" Rosa turned as she saw Frankie had followed them on deck and was now staring at the pirogues excitedly, her dark-ringed eyes hopefully bright again.

"I don't see no Willie, though," Joe said heavily.

Frankie ignored him. "He'll be ashore, Pop," she said. "Perhaps he's hurt. Maybe he wants me to look after him. Maybe he broke a leg. What are they shouting, Pop? What are they shouting?"

Joe turned his sad spaniel eyes on her. "They want us to go with 'em," he said. "They want us to go ashore."

The beach was littered by the sea-wrack of the storm, broken palm fronds like shattered scimitars, a tree shorn of its roots and branches so that it was naked-looking and indecent, a few small sharks and dead jellyfish; scraps of driftwood and broken shells, one of their own oars, saturated and black with water, a door from a house, boxes, a wrecked canoe, its outriggers splintered. The land crabs stalked their way through the debris, following the water down the beach as the tide receded, sidling unheeded among the mynah birds and the flocks of scarlet finches that picked among the rubbish.

The untrodden sand was cool after the rain, and the lagoon was shot through with colours like a butterfly's wing. The bush beyond the beach was soaked and silent, steaming slightly as the sun rose higher, the leaves drooping in the heat.

One or two islanders laboured over shattered houses that the hurricane had destroyed and flung against each other, sagging, their silver-grey thatch torn away and spread in great swathes along the ground, their poles bare like gaunt ribs in the sunshine. Under the weight of a great fallen tree, the village store leaned in a tangle of woodwork through which they could see kerosene lamps and buckets and tins of food scattered about in pathetic heaps.

A village pig was rooting among the long morning shadows that draped the rocks and a blue heron trod daintily in the shallow water where a piece of sennit rope and the remains of a bamboo fish trap washed backwards and forwards with a couple of rotting coconuts. The air was crystal clear and still.

They found Willie when they least expected to, just above the high water mark, surrounded by the litter of the typhoon. The islanders had pulled him out of the sea and covered him with palm fronds and they could see his hand protruding from beneath the greenery as they approached, covered with wet sand and starred by the sodden flowers that had showered from the trees. Rosa crossed herself quickly as Frankie stopped dead, the colour draining from her face, shocked into rigidity, and all the others stopped dead with her, waiting for her to go on.

She stood straight up, slender and stiff in the sagging jersey and the ragged pants that clung to her legs and hips. Her eyes were wide, a look of stricken disbelief in them. Her hands were straight down at her sides, her fingers twitching. For a moment, Rosa thought she was going to fling herself down on top of Willie but she just stood there silently, her lips moving, her eyes staring in that anguished way that was agony to Rosa.

Joe looked at his wife, undecided, wondering what to do.

"We ought to bury him," he said.

"No. We'll take him back aboard."

Rosa was quite calm, devoid of feeling. Her eyes were dry and all the emotion seemed to be drained out of her in the need to care for Frankie.

"Bring him along to the dinghy, Joe," she said in a voice so hard it didn't seem like her own. "I'm going back with Frankie."

Joe stood on the sand, old and bent and fat, then he watched Rosa and his daughter face the sea, and he turned and signed to the islanders to help him.

When the islanders arrived with Joe, they stretched Willie on the cabin table and covered him with the best blanket they had left.

Frankie was sitting on the bow, staring at the land, her fingers fiddling with the cross Willie had given her. She had not turned her head as the canoe had bumped alongside, had completely ignored the silent shuffling as they carried him below, and Rosa was anxious to be finished with the heart-breaking business before the feeling came back into her and her senses began to function again.

"I'm going to lay him out proper," she said. "Make him look decent."

"You want me to help, Rosie?" Joe faltered, still uncertain of her reactions.

"No. You keep Frankie outa here. I'll do it on me own. I'll say something over him. I'll do it nice." She held up her hand as he began to speak. "Don't say anything or I'll bust out squawking."

She took a basin of water and washed Willie's face and combed the sand from his hair. Then she crossed his hands and put near him a flower she had begged from one of the islanders who had worn it in his hair. Slowly she took out a scrap of candle and lit it.

"It isn't a holy one, Lord," she pointed out, lifting her eyes humbly. "But it's all we got."

Then she slowly and painfully lowered herself to her knees.

When she had finished praying, she stood up, her eyes burning but still holding back the tears, and Joe gave the islanders one of Willie's notes as payment for their help. From the deck, he watched the canoes disappearing again across the lagoon. Frankie was still on the bow, still heedless of what was happening, and Joe glanced at her for a second before he lowered himself slowly into the cabin.

Rosa was sitting on a box alongside the table with its shrouded shape, her hands pressed tightly together, wishing Joe could give her strength and courage when all the time she knew he couldn't. Oh, Lord, she was saying, repeating it with fierce persistence, make it come right. Don't let me give in to it. Make me keep going to look after Frankie and the others.

I should have known, she kept upbraiding herself. I should have known it was the certainty of death in him that sobered him and made him old before his time.

She had vivid frightening pictures in her mind of Willie sinking down into the dark fathoms, rolled backwards and forwards by the eddies of the tide, and she prayed that Frankie wasn't seeing them too. Make it come right for her, too, Lord, she begged. Make it easy for her. Frankie was far too young for grief such as only the old should have to bear.

She looked up questioningly as Joe stood beside her, eyeing the blanket uneasily.

"What are we going to do, Mama?" he asked.

Rosa raised her eyes slowly to his. She knew that Joe and Joe alone was responsible for Willie's death. Tired, doing the job the wrong way, the hopeless way, there would have been no hope for him. She looked again at her husband and knew she would never face him with his guilt. It was too late now, and Joe was too weak and too old to be held responsible. They were both too old. They had always been too old for the thing they had undertaken. They had never had a chance of succeeding.

"I reckon we ought to take him to Papeete," she said. "Then folks will know what happened to him. There's his mama and the other boy's mama too. She'll sleep easier then."

She looked gaunt and older than Joe had ever seen her, and he resolved on the instant to behave himself in the future, knowing all the time it was a promise he couldn't hope to keep.

"It was my fault, Rosie," he said humbly.

"No, it wasn't your fault."

She saw him again as a plump young man with a collar that was too tight for him and the limp posy of flowers and, oddly, at that moment he was nearer to her than he had been for years.

He eyed the blanket again.

"Mama," he said thoughtfully, "when they see the way you fix him, they mebbe think we like him a little bit. Then we get into trouble."

"I laid him out decent," Rosa said stiffly. "If the Devil was dead aboard of here, I'd do it for him too. They won't think things like that. It doesn't matter if they do now, anyway," she pointed out. 'We got nothing to lose. It's all over and done. We've nothing left. We'll lose the boat and we've spent all our money."

Joe looked up, remembering the notes he had taken from Willie's clothes, the dwindled roll he had rifled at Aiotea to pay for the gin which had been the indirect cause of Willie's death, and it suddenly felt hot in his pocket and poisonous. He fished it out and spread it slowly on the table alongside Willie.

"There's a few quid here, Mama," he said. "That's all that's left but it'll help. You'd better have that too." He shoved it at Rosa, trying to get rid of it before he began to regret what he was doing.

"He was just like a son," Rosa said, staring ahead of her.

"Yes, Mama. I guess so."

"We had two sons, kind of. Now we got none at all. But I reckon it's the best way. They'd have got him in the end and then what would he have to look forward to? What could Frankie have looked forward to?"

"I had everything in the world to look forward to!" Frankie had come silently into the cabin while they were talking and they turned to face her, flushing slightly as she spoke.

"There was nothing I was scared of with Willie," she went on. "Police. Gossip. Doing without. Nothing. I'd have gone on running and doing without – and starving, too – if Willie'd been with me."

Rosa watched her daughter. This was a new Frankie, no longer the old harum-scarum Frankie who had sped barefoot along deserted miles of beach after crabs. This was a woman, adult and mature and facing life. The wonderment that had been in her eyes had disappeared and it saddened Rosa to think it had gone so soon.

"I'd have gone on for ever," Frankie continued. "Willie showed me what it was like to love someone. He was kind and gentle. I had nothing to be ashamed of in loving him, whatever he'd done."

As she stared at them, her face crumpled and, with a sob, she flung herself into Rosa's arms.

"Oh, Mama," she cried. "I feel so lonely."

Rosa held her close, heavy and tired in her shabby clothes. "Come on, Joe," she said slowly. "Let's be off. We got a long way to go."

"They'll impound the boat, Mama."

"Yes, I know."

"That means we don't be able to dodge-a no more."

Rosa shrugged. "Ain't any point no more," she said.

Joe studied for a moment, staring at his feet, trying to put his feeling for their grief into words. "Mama," he said after a while. "He growed into a man with us. We oughta to see him off proper. We oughta to have a flag and fly it at half-a-mast."

"He won't mind either way." Rosa spoke without looking at him, her head held high.

"Allasame," Joe pointed out. "I guess he'd be proud. We got a old red blouse of yours. I could tie that up."

"OK," Rosa said. "Go ahead. At least, it'll make 'em realize we're coming in of our own accord and not because we've been caught. We wouldn't ever have been caught," she ended defiantly, "if he hadn't gone and died. Willie'd have thought of something. That's for sure."

six

Fred Voss started up in bed at the thunderous knocking that quivered his door.

"Who's that? What the hell goes on?" he snapped.

"Oh, it's you," he said, as Flynn burst in, and sinking back on the pillows, he reached for a cigarette. "What's happened? Have we missed 'em again?"

Flynn's face was white and for a few minutes he didn't speak. "He dodged me in the end," he said at last, keeping his anger back with difficulty. "He's dead."

"Dead?" Voss sat up sharply. "Who's dead? Keeley?"

"Yes."

"How do you know?"

Flynn gestured. "The Salomios – they're coming in."

"Coming in? You mean, they've given up?"

"Yes. The launch that went over to Aiotea set off for Apavana this morning when the weather subsided and met them coming out. They went alongside to put a party on board but the old woman wouldn't let them. They want to bring her into Papeete on their own. They'd only accept the help of a couple of sailors to work the boat. That's all."

"Good for Mama Salomio. Go on."

"They had Keeley's body on board."

"What happened?"

"I don't know." Flynn seemed calmer now. "I suppose it happened during the hurricane. It's all a bit garbled by this time. The doctor on the launch took photos and identified

232

him and they buried him at sea. There's no doubt about it being Keeley."

"God, what a story!" In spite of his words, Voss looked serious and devoid of enthusiasm. "How's Mama Salomio?"

"Why?"

"Oh, nothing. I thought she might be a bit cut up."

"They're all right." Flynn suddenly seemed indifferent now that Willie was dead. "Tired as hell, I understand, and pretty thin, but they're fit and well. Your story's reaching its grand finale." He looked up at Voss under his eyebrows. "You can cable home and tell 'em to get out the band and tune up the trumpets."

"I've a suspicion the Salomios aren't going to enjoy trumpets and bands." Voss scowled. "I got a cable this morning. The readers' poll is finished. I've got the pleasure of telling them what every nosy bastard in Australia thinks they ought to do with their lives. There's a move on foot to make the boat into a museum and put them in charge of it. That'll be fine if they don't want a museum. I only hope they'll feel what they did was all worth while."

"Does it matter?" Flynn asked.

"I don't know. They'll have enough money now to buy a new boat anyway. Two if they want 'em." He stopped and his eyes opened wide, as an idea occurred to him. "By God," he said, "I'm going to take on an unpaid job of fending off all the bloody sharks who want to sell 'em something, all the pompous bastards who want to be condescending. I'll make it easier for them and see they get what there is for themselves. Perhaps it'll make up for the readers' poll."

He looked at Flynn, feeling better. "When will they be here?" he asked. "I've got to prepare myself for the role of protector of the poor and lowly, the friend in need and the friend indeed."

"I don't know." Flynn seemed to have lost all interest in the chase. "It's a long way. We might as well wait here.

Keeley's already identified and buried. We can't do anything and they're in safe hands – unless you want to go half-way and meet 'em."

"God, no! Let's leave 'em alone. There'll be plenty of ghouls deployed about the place without us." Voss looked up at Flynn. "Who gets the reward?"

Flynn hesitated. "I don't know. Seagull's after it naturally. He's coming into Papeete with the naval launch and the Salomios – determined to get his share of the kudos and the money. He's been on the radio. I've been holding him off."

"Why?"

"I thought the Salomios might qualify more."

Voss' face wore a gentle expression. "Flynn, you soft-hearted old cluck. That makes two of us now."

The day they set off for the waterfront the whole of Papeete seemed to be on the move with them, Tahitians laughing and joking as though it were a holiday, solemn-looking Chinese shuffling among the crowds, young Frenchmen on motor scooters, a negro on a bicycle, Polynesians, Tongans, Indians, Tonkinese, Europeans in taxis, American tourists by the dozen loaded with cameras.

"Looks like a gala welcome," Voss commented as they hurried through the crowd.

"The word's certainly got around," Flynn agreed.

The waterfront, where the heavy smell of copra and vanilla hung in the air, was crowded and children were clinging to the rigging of moored schooners. Canoes and launches and dinghies crowded the bright water where the tropic fish darted in fright among the stones. Some of the vessels were even dressed with flags and one or two launches were making their way out filled with sightseers. People were leaving the business houses across the road and the sheds where the copra was stacked in pyramids, and the stores and the tourist hotels and the government offices were empty, while the Chinese traders closed their market stalls and stopped their bargaining over hogs with the schooner captains from Raiatea.

Girls decked with flowers and young men in military uniforms rubbed shoulders with the weighty Tuamotan women who had come in on the inter-island schooners.

A native boy was offering leis for sale, accompanied by a barking chorus of dogs.

Voss and Flynn found the little group of police, naval men and harbour authorities and joined them. The other newspapermen were there too and eyed Voss with envy. Below them, a launch waited to take them out to the *Salomios* as soon as they dropped anchor.

"Thank God old Seagull's not around," Voss said. "I don't think I could have stood his remarks just now."

They had been waiting some time when they heard a distinct rustle among the crowd that indicated that some watcher outside the harbour had signalled the arrival of the *Boy George*, and immediately several launches put to sea to welcome her in.

It was some time before anything further happened beyond a considerable amount of pushing and shoving among the crowd that toppled a small apricot-coloured boy into the water, and numerous minor agitations among the island boats as various small ships appeared round the head. Every time anything appeared, a murmur went up, only to die again as the crowd realized it did not contain the fabulous *Salomios*. Ice cream and fruit drink sellers were moving about, doing a great business, and it was obvious the welcome was developing into a public holiday.

"I don't know that I'm enjoying this," Voss muttered to Flynn after a while as he watched the excited and jovial French authorities and port officials. "I keep thinking of Mama Salomio." He was unusually quiet. "I'll bet she doesn't feel very much like cheering. Still –" he shrugged

" – the crowd thinks they're pretty hot stuff to outsmart the police and catch a murderer into the bargain, so who the hell am I to tell 'em?"

"They'll be all right," Flynn pointed out, "if they play their cards right."

Voss frowned. "I doubt if they knew they were playing cards," he said.

As he stopped speaking, another murmur ran through the crowd and this time it did not die away but swelled to a tumultuous roar, rippling across the moving heads towards them.

"This must be them," Flynn said.

A pilot launch, fussy and important, glided into view round Venus Point where Cook first set foot in Tahiti. It was followed by a police launch and the *Teura To'oa* with Captain Seagull posturing on the stern, indifferent in his desire for glory to the plight of the passengers on Nukuhiva who were still waiting for his ship.

"He's put some fresh silver paint on his cap," Voss said, "and damned if he isn't wearing a suit."

"Hold it!" Flynn caught his arm. "Here come the Salomios."

Surrounded by a bevy of small craft all flying flags and followed by the larger naval launch, the *Boy George* hove into sight, tiny beneath the towering peaks behind Papeete.

She headed slowly towards the harbour, matronly, shabby and elderly, like some old lady arrested for shoplifting who was maintaining a dignified defiance to the end. A piece of red material, little more than a rag, fluttered half-way down her halyards.

"They've got a flag at half-mast," Voss said uneasily. "I told you I wasn't going to like this."

As the *Boy George* entered the harbour, the crowd started to cheer, a spontaneous warm-hearted gesture that indicated their admiration. The crew of a cutter from the Tuamotus, discharging mother-of-pearl and copra, started the yell and the passengers crowding one of the inter-island schooners took up the cry, hanging over the rails with their possessions, the bananas they had brought to eat, the chickens and the eggs and the children and the baskets of fruit and coconuts. Boats' hooters and the siren of a tourist ship started to add to the clamour, then the foghorn of the phosphate ship from Ocean Island spat steam and a second later its deep-throated boom vibrated across the water.

On the bow of the *Boy George*, one of the Tahitian sailors, wearing the pom-pom of the French navy, was standing by the anchor. Another one lounged by the sail awaiting instructions. Rosa was with Joe at the wheel and Frankie sat alone on the stern, her mind questing all the time after the happiness she had had with Willie. But she could remember so little of love, for there had been so little to remember before she had come abruptly to the point where a curtain had slammed down in front of her, leaving her only a moment of heart-breaking exhilaration as a memory. Unable to cry any more, her eyes stared dark-ringed out of a pale face that was desolate and rebellious, the bitterness in it changing abruptly to bewilderment as she thought of Willie. Everywhere she looked she saw him. He was waiting with the sailor by the mast and standing by the wheel with Joe. He was below in the engine room tinkering with the tired old engine that had let them down at the last desperate moment. He was in every nook and cranny of the ship, and she tried desperately to believe he was flesh and blood and not just her own imaginings.

"I never thought we'd get a welcome like this," Rosa said, trying to keep her from too much thinking. "With all these people waiting – and flags and everything."

Frankie didn't turn her head. "It doesn't make much difference now, Mama," she said slowly. "It doesn't make any difference one way or the other. Everything's over." She paused, making an effort to speak normally. "We'll be seeing Lucia and Tommy soon."

Rosa nodded, anxious to keep her talking. "I guess Tina'll be there too with all the boys. It sounds as though there's going to be a party or something when we get back, with reporters and flashlight pictures and all that."

As the shouting increased from the shore, she turned her head towards the splash of colour along the waterfront, pathetically trying to show some enthusiasm to stir Frankie from her silence.

"They're cheering," she said. "They must be pleased about something."

"They caught us, didn't they?" Frankie said. "They ought to be pleased."

"It's not that," Rosa went on, forcing joy into her voice. "You can hear them shouting our name. Think it's us they're cheering, Joe?"

"Maybe," Joe said. He was feeling better now that his sense of guilt was wearing a little thin, for the praise that had been showered on him had made him feel as clever as he had always thought he was. His pockets were full of French cigarettes and he was mellow with the wine that had been thrust aboard the *Boy George*. Swallowing it, one eye on Rosa, he had felt a twinge of conscience as he remembered what had happened on the last occasion he had lifted a bottle to his lips, but even that memory was slowly fading now.

Rosa moved towards her daughter and stood behind her, her hands on her shoulders. For a while, Frankie stared ahead, unheeding, then she turned and looked up at Rosa.

"Mama, it's nice to know we haven't to go on running all the time any more," she said.

"Yeah. Sure." Rosa found that she too could feel only relief in her heart that they hadn't to face any more problems of food, of weather, of their failing old boat. The realization that she would not have to fight any longer came on her abruptly, and she sat down alongside Frankie, suddenly aware how tired she was, how sick of struggling.

The din was terrific by this time, then, perhaps because of some signal from one of the French sailors or because someone caught the significance of the scrap of bunting half-way down the mast, the hooters began to stop, first one, then another, until finally the siren of the phosphate ship went on booming alone for some time after the others in solitary groans.

The mood spread to the passengers in the boats and the cheering died and the tricolour flags stopped waving and eventually even the noise of the crowd on shore died away to silence. The chattering of the French officials alongside Voss and Flynn stopped and the *Boy George* glided into Papeete's lagoon in silence.

There wasn't a sound as she swung round behind the pilot boat and the shout of the pilot could be heard distinctly across the water. Then the sail slatted down and they heard the splash of the anchor and the rattle of the chain running out. The crowd watched without speaking and over the silence, the bark of a dog echoed down one of the streets and the sudden honk of a horn turned a few heads.

"That's better," Voss murmured.

The *Boy George* swung slowly round her anchor and one of the Tahitian sailors tossed a line ashore. Half-a-dozen people, eager to be concerned with the triumph, grabbed at it and fought for a moment for the privilege of turning it round a bollard, and the old boat became stationary, stern-on to the quay.

The crowd began to surge closer but there was still no noise, no cheering. Even the high-spirited Tahitians seemed to be subdued and Captain Seagull, on the stern of the *Teura To'oa*, wore a puzzled look as he was ignored.

Rosa waited calmly for the arrival of the authorities, who obviously didn't intend to hurry them ashore just yet in the hope that the crowd would disperse a little. Boats still clustered round the *Boy George*, their passengers gaping but silent, staring up at Rosa who stood slightly apart, dignified and matriarchal, holding her shabby cardigan together over her faded frock.

Then a launch bumped alongside and the deck was suddenly swarming with officials, tight-waisted Frenchmen in uniform, who chattered noisily and waved their arms; and two other men who had the familiar look of Australians – one big and bulky and neat who looked like a policeman, the other, a lean man with shaggy hair and a rumpled suit, clutching a bundle of newspapers across the top of which she could see her own name in square black letters.

"Mrs Salomio?"

As they spoke to her, she turned to the cabin hatch and indicated it with a sweep of her hand.

"Maybe you'd better come and sit down," she said. "It's quieter below and we can have a cup of tea while we talk."

Her head was up as she followed them. There was plenty to tell them – and nothing she need be ashamed of. She was thinking of Willie and though the pain in her was dying a little now, she knew she would never forget him or the things they had achieved together – she and Willie and Frankie and Joe.

Flynn and Voss were sitting down when she got below, eyeing with curiosity the shabby little cabin where the tremendous adventure had been planned and lived. Frankie stood by the stove, her eyes down, pretending to be engrossed in making it work, and Joe waited in a corner, nervously smoking a cigarette they had given him.

As Rosa appeared they stood up. Neither of them spoke as she pulled a box forward, then as she settled herself and looked up, brushing the hair out of her eyes, they leaned forward eagerly and Flynn spoke for them both.

"Right, Mrs Salomio," he said. "How about telling us all about it?"

JOHN HARRIS

CHINA SEAS

In this action-packed adventure, Willie Sarth becomes a
survivor. Forced to fight pirates on the East China Seas,
wrestle for his life on the South China Seas and cross the Sea
of Japan ravaged by typhus, Sarth is determined to come out
alive. Dealing with human tragedy, war and revolution,
Harris presents a novel which packs an awesome punch.

A FUNNY PLACE TO HOLD A WAR

Ginger Donnelly is on the trail of Nazi saboteurs in Sierra
Leone. Whilst taking a midnight paddle in a canoe cajoled
from a local fisherman along with a willing woman, Donnelly
sees an enormous seaplane thunder across the sky only to
crash in a ball of brilliant flame. It seems like an accident...
at least until a second plane explodes in a blistering shower
along the same flight path.

JOHN HARRIS

LIVE FREE OR DIE!

Charles Walter Scully, cut off from his unit and running on empty, is trapped. It's 1944 and, though the Allied invasion of France has finally begun, for Scully the war isn't going well. That is, until he meets a French boy trying to get home to Paris and so what begins is an incredible hair-raising journey into the heart of the French liberation and one of the most monumental events of the war. Harris portrays wartime France in a vividly overwhelming panorama of scenes intended to enthral and entertain the reader.

THE OLD TRADE OF KILLING

Set against the backdrop of the Western Desert and scene of the Eighth Army battles, Harris presents an exciting adventure where the men who fought together in the Second World War return twenty years later in search of treasure. But twenty years may change a man. Young ideals have been replaced by greed. Comradeship has vanished along with innocence. And treachery and murder make for a breathtaking read.

JOHN HARRIS

THE SEA SHALL NOT HAVE THEM

This is John Harris' classic war novel of espionage in the most extreme of situations. An essential flight from France leaves the crew of RAF *Hudson* missing, and somewhere in the North Sea four men cling to a dinghy, praying for rescue before exposure kills them or the enemy finds them. One man is critically injured; another (a rocket expert) is carrying a briefcase stuffed with vital secrets. As time begins to run out each man yearns to evade capture. This story charts the daring and courage of these men, and the men who rescued them in a breathtaking mission with the most awesome of consequences.

TAKE OR DESTROY!

Lieutenant-Colonel George Hockold must destroy Rommel's vast fuel reserves stored at the port of Qaba if the Eighth Army is to succeed in the Alamein offensive. Time is desperately running out, resources are scant and the commando unit Hockold must lead is a ragtag band of misfits scraped from the dregs of the British Army. They must attack Qaba. The orders...take or destroy.

'One of the finest war novels of the year'
– *Evening News*

TITLES BY JOHN HARRIS AVAILABLE DIRECT
FROM HOUSE OF STRATUS

Quantity		£	$(US)	$(CAN)	€
	Army of Shadows	6.99	11.50	15.99	11.50
	China Seas	6.99	11.50	15.99	11.50
	The Claws of Mercy	6.99	11.50	15.99	11.50
	Corporal Cotton's Little War	6.99	11.50	15.99	11.50
	The Cross of Lazzaro	6.99	11.50	15.99	11.50
	Flawed Banner	6.99	11.50	15.99	11.50
	The Fox from his Lair	6.99	11.50	15.99	11.50
	A Funny Place to Hold a War	6.99	11.50	15.99	11.50
	Harkaway's Sixth Column	6.99	11.50	15.99	11.50
	A Kind of Courage	6.99	11.50	15.99	11.50
	Live Free or Die!	6.99	11.50	15.99	11.50
	The Lonely Voyage	6.99	11.50	15.99	11.50
	The Mercenaries	6.99	11.50	15.99	11.50
	North Strike	6.99	11.50	15.99	11.50
	The Old Trade of Killing	6.99	11.50	15.99	11.50

ALL HOUSE OF STRATUS BOOKS ARE AVAILABLE FROM GOOD BOOKSHOPS
OR DIRECT FROM THE PUBLISHER:

Internet: www.houseofstratus.com including author interviews, reviews, features.

Email: sales@houseofstratus.com please quote author, title and credit card details.

TITLES BY JOHN HARRIS AVAILABLE DIRECT
FROM HOUSE OF STRATUS

Quantity		£	$(US)	$(CAN)	€
	PICTURE OF DEFEAT	6.99	11.50	15.99	11.50
	THE QUICK BOAT MEN	6.99	11.50	15.99	11.50
	RIDE OUT THE STORM	6.99	11.50	15.99	11.50
	RIGHT OF REPLY	6.99	11.50	15.99	11.50
	ROAD TO THE COAST	6.99	11.50	15.99	11.50
	THE SEA SHALL NOT HAVE THEM	6.99	11.50	15.99	11.50
	THE SLEEPING MOUNTAIN	6.99	11.50	15.99	11.50
	SMILING WILLIE AND THE TIGER	6.99	11.50	15.99	11.50
	SO FAR FROM GOD	6.99	11.50	15.99	11.50
	THE SPRING OF MALICE	6.99	11.50	15.99	11.50
	SUNSET AT SHEBA	6.99	11.50	15.99	11.50
	SWORDPOINT	6.99	11.50	15.99	11.50
	TAKE OR DESTROY!	6.99	11.50	15.99	11.50
	THE THIRTY DAYS' WAR	6.99	11.50	15.99	11.50
	THE UNFORGIVING WIND	6.99	11.50	15.99	11.50
	UP FOR GRABS	6.99	11.50	15.99	11.50
	VARDY	6.99	11.50	15.99	11.50

ALL HOUSE OF STRATUS BOOKS ARE AVAILABLE FROM GOOD BOOKSHOPS
OR DIRECT FROM THE PUBLISHER:

Hotline: UK ONLY: 0800 169 1780, please quote author, title and credit card
details.
INTERNATIONAL: +44 (0) 20 7494 6400, please quote author, title,
and credit card details.

Send to: House of Stratus Sales Department
24c Old Burlington Street
London
W1X 1RL
UK

Please allow for postage costs charged per order plus an amount per book as set out in the tables below:

	£(Sterling)	$(US)	$(CAN)	€(Euros)
Cost per order				
UK	2.00	3.00	4.50	3.30
Europe	3.00	4.50	6.75	5.00
North America	3.00	4.50	6.75	5.00
Rest of World	3.00	4.50	6.75	5.00
Additional cost per book				
UK	0.50	0.75	1.15	0.85
Europe	1.00	1.50	2.30	1.70
North America	2.00	3.00	4.60	3.40
Rest of World	2.50	3.75	5.75	4.25

PLEASE SEND CHEQUE, POSTAL ORDER (STERLING ONLY), EUROCHEQUE, OR INTERNATIONAL MONEY ORDER (PLEASE CIRCLE METHOD OF PAYMENT YOU WISH TO USE)
MAKE PAYABLE TO: STRATUS HOLDINGS plc

Cost of book(s): —————————— Example: 3 x books at £6.99 each: £20.97

Cost of order: —————————— Example: £2.00 (Delivery to UK address)

Additional cost per book: ————— Example: 3 x £0.50: £1.50

Order total including postage: ———— Example: £24.47

Please tick currency you wish to use and add total amount of order:

☐ £ (Sterling)   ☐ $ (US)   ☐ $ (CAN)   ☐ € (EUROS)

VISA, MASTERCARD, SWITCH, AMEX, SOLO, JCB:

☐ ☐ ☐ ☐ ☐ ☐ ☐ ☐ ☐ ☐ ☐ ☐ ☐ ☐ ☐ ☐ ☐ ☐ ☐

Issue number (Switch only):

☐ ☐ ☐

Start Date: **Expiry Date:**

☐☐ / ☐☐   ☐☐ / ☐☐

Signature: ————————————————

NAME: ————————————————————

ADDRESS: ——————————————————

——————————————————

POSTCODE: ——————————

Please allow 28 days for delivery.

Prices subject to change without notice.
Please tick box if you do not wish to receive any additional information. ☐

House of Stratus publishes many other titles in this genre; please check our website (**www.houseofstratus.com**) for more details.